The Last of the Silver Wings

The Last of the Silver Wings

KIM VERMAAK

Yakhal Publishing

Title: The Last of the Silver Wings
Series Name: Book One | The Chronicles of Nadine

Author: Kim Vermaak
Cover Design: Ilze & Jayden Brand
Typesetting: Books by Bella
Illustrations: Kim Vermaak
Author Photo: Hush Naidoo
Edited by Judy Ward
Published by: Yakhal Publishing
First Edition: 2019

ISBN: 978-1-990937-40-8
Text Copyright: Kim Vermaak 2019 ©
Cover Concept: Ilze Brand
Cover Image: www.Freepiks.com
Cover Layout: SHAHRUKH HUSSNAIN
https://www.fiverr.com/shahrukhshah000

Website: www.kimvermaak.com
Facebook: https://www.facebook.com/thechroniclesofnadine
Instagram: https://www.instagram.com/kimvermaakauthor/
Linkedin: https://www.linkedin.com/in/kim-vermaak-a4682b1/

To my CCBSA friends
I have finished what I started.
Kim Vermaak

To my precious parents
Denzil and Belinda
who were my first heroes.
You are in every page of my story.

My Heavenly Father,
the very first creator,
thank you for the blessing of creativity.

I have fought the good fight, I have finished the race,
I have kept the faith.
2Timothy 4:7

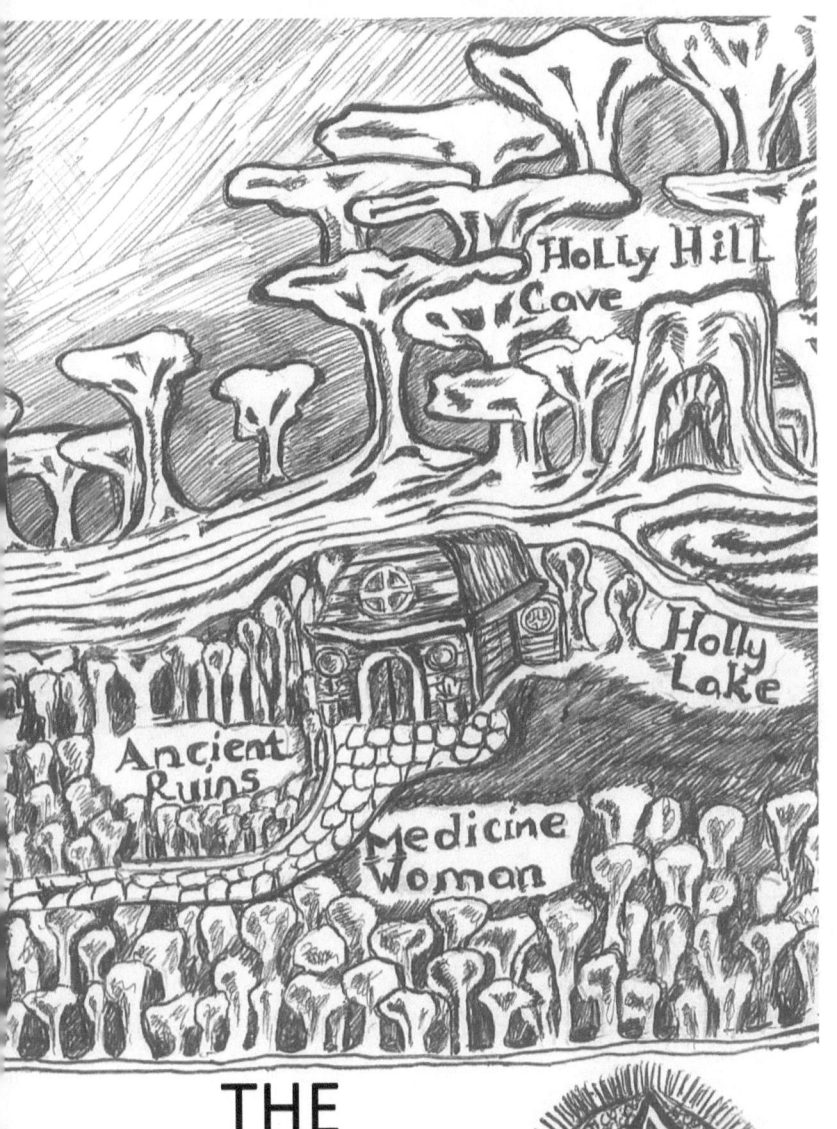

THE
NORTHERN
KINGDOM

CONTENTS

PROLOGUE

Ruin Mountains, 700AD

Below the village lay the secret passages. Passages forged by fire and sweat. The allies of the dragons had found a way to protect these great beasts of the sky.

But in the end, only a handful of them remained, scattered over the earth. The once majestic canopy of trees over which the dragons soared, lay scorched on the ground where the dying moans of the dragons echoed in Muquin's memory.

Her Dragon Whisperer had imprinted the map and instructions into her mind with his dying breath. "Go Muquin. Flee this place. Find the oak near Forever Gone Lake. Hide in the tunnels. You will be safe."

Gravely injured, she summoned the last of her strength to carry her to the ancient oak. Risking the daylight entry, she placed her claw into the lever. The ledge opened for her to enter. Her torn wing ached, but she survived.

Φ

The last of the Silver Wings.

Their betrayal had come from one of their species, a Copper Fire Dragon. Born to be a master of fire who forged dragon villages, his heart was now under the command of a warlord. His massive form had darkened the skies. And Muquin saw that the legends were true. Mankind had darkened a dragon.

The sun could not dance on the coppery scales of his body. His life force light had evaporated. His once brilliant orange eyes had dimmed to a smoky charcoal, devoid of joy. He flew in mechanical circles, destroying all before him. His copper luster turned to the colour of the soil which lay scorched below them.

The land that both humans and dragons lived off, burned. Mothers on all sides cried out at their loss, their hatchling nests incinerated. The suffering of war did not discriminate. All mothers suffered. All fathers despaired at the loss of their young.

The warlords' desire for power had reduced human suffering to mere collateral.

Darkness knew no compassion. It held no fear. There was no hesitation. A darkened dragon would fight without conscience. No Dragon Whisperer could ever reach it.

The Warlord Commander sat erect on the back of the Copper

Fire Dragon. Strength surged through his hardened form. The warlord's eyes were dead to emotion as his dragon destroyed both dragons and men in his insatiable lust for power.

There would be no more alliances with mankind. Man would tell every child of this day. They would learn that it was a dragon who burned against mankind. Tales of the dying screams of mothers and children would incite fear and loathing. They would write tragedies of the day fire consumed entire villages. The day the dragons destroyed them.

Would they hear it was one of their own kind who carved this plan? That it was one of them who had stolen a hatchling? It was their own act of cruelty that had destroyed the mother and forced the hatchling to become their weapon. Not even the Dragon Whisperers were shown mercy. Those who were able to bear witness to the carnage would be silenced. The dragon's only advocates lay dying with them.

Φ

Muquin moaned. Her heart ached with the loss of her mate, Megadeus.

How they had soared together through the trees, bursting from the forest with their bodies swirling and dancing in the moonlight. She felt the strength of his body even now, as if he was still with her, ever gentle with her as he made the forehead greeting. The sky had been their playground.

The magnificent cave that he created, would have been their nest, close to a lake where they could fish and hunt, their wings dipping into the water, as they glided over the clear surface. She could never return to that cave. Dragons mated for life. Megadeus was gone.

There would be no other.

Megadeus had sacrificed himself for her, intercepting the Dragon spear intended for Muquin. His roar of pain had pierced her heart and his dying breaths tore at her soul.

She was alone.

Φ

The villagers here knew nothing of the war. Here she would be undetected. While they fished the fearsome Forever Gone Lake and carried on with the trivial parts of life, she would live in quiet solitude below their village.

But to what end? Her mate was gone. The only human she ever trusted lay in an incinerated pile of corpses.

In her grief she could have flown again into the danger. She sometimes wished she had. She was the one who should have died that day. Yet he had died so that she might live. To squander his gift would dishonour him. But she did not know how to live without him. The cold nights in the stone tunnels dragged on. Her loneliness grew thick and impenetrable.

Sometimes she heard laughter. The sounds of the village children's games vibrated through the tunnels. Human mothers waited for nine full moons to hear the first wail of their young. But a dragon waited 100 years for a hatchling.

She and Megadeus had seen many full moons. She had lost count. But she felt the stirrings. A chink formed in her grief over her lost mate. Could it be?

Hope teased her mind. She dared not believe. In the horror of war, they had comforted each other. But any thoughts of a hatchling lay buried under the flames and death that had surrounded them.

But perhaps, Megadeus's seed had really brought new life to their kind. She could feel the egg as it formed within her. She was sure. "Oh, Megadeus! My love. The new life we made is upon us now."

She had flown as high as she dared to the stars to share her news.

When he died, his life force had surged through his body, exploding it into a million silvery pieces. For a moment they floated about above the battle - a cloud of brilliance illuminating the destruction below. Then without warning, the heavens welcomed him into his new realm. A place where new star formations were created. Here his wisdom would lie in wait for those who sought it. It was the way of the Silver Wings.

She could see his formation every night. But his new voice had not yet formed. It would be decades before she would hear him.

How he would have soared with joy at the news of a hatchling, his powerful body tumbling through the air. He would have shot great fiery bolts at the sun and come splashing down into the lake. His laughter would have echoed in her ears as she shook off the water from the splash. She would have scolded him for wakening the forest. He would have responded by shaking all the water off his wings onto her after she had already dried.

No enemy could ever stand against him. But he had never lost this special blend of hatchling-like mischief. Their love was bold and playful. They had taken the sacred vow that bonded them for all eternity. Then Mankind had cruelly ripped eternity from their grasp, as Megadeus had given his life for hers.

Each day, the bond between Muquin and life in the egg had grown. When the shell had hardened, she had passed it. She dared not pass the egg in an open cave. It lay hidden, buried in the darkened tunnels. It would never feel the breeze or the sun's warmth. The egg had to be kept safe.

Without her mate, she had no choice but to hunt alone, leaving her egg unattended. Without the hunt, they would both perish. In the past, other Silver Wings would have helped. Their colonies had once been filled with the chirp of many hatchlings, tussling and wrestling as they built their skills. Exasperated elders had flicked off swarms of hatchlings whose tiny sharp talons were too rough in play. Except for the occasional roar to keep a naughty hatchling in check, their colonies were peaceful.

But now she was the only one left.

For the sake of all the Silver Wings before them, she would do whatever it took to ensure that the hatchling lived.

But soon, mankind would find a way to rip everything she held dear away from her once again.

ONE

The Wall of Fire

The awakening was brutal. The chaos of the village tore Nadine from sleep. Her heart thundered through her body like a wild stallion fleeing from a pack of wolves.

The ground vibrated with a soul-wrenching roar that appeared to engulf the entire world. Nadine's wild eyes searched their clay hut for the rest of her family. She saw no one. Danger screamed in the air.

Her body betrayed her. Dread gripped her arms, weaving around them in a snake-like crushing embrace. Her stomach knotted into a cold ball of fear. "Think Nadine. Calm your mind," she ordered herself.

There was something moving outside the hut. Massive. She forced herself to slow her breathing. "Anchor your thoughts," she commanded herself.

"Tiber," she called. Her kitten was still in bed with her. Its frightened, rigid body pushed up against her. She picked up the small tortoiseshell cat and held her close. They had adopted the abandoned creature into their home even though cats were not allowed into human dwellings. Nadine was her champion.

Today was a day that even champions might tremble. But cowering was not an option.

Nadine pushed Tiber into a bag and raced towards the danger. A wall of heat slammed into her. Ferocious orange flames clawed at her. Tiber squirmed and clawed her way out of the bag. Nadine grabbed the terrified kitten and held her tight to keep her from bolting. Choking black smoke clouded the early morning sky.

All around the confused sounds of terror pierced her core. So many screams. So much chaos. People ran in all directions. It was hard to recognise anyone with the huge and glaring flames and smoke as the thatched huts were caught up in the blaze.

Nadine screamed for her parents, her older sister, and her baby brother. Just then she heard them calling to her, in a panicked stretched out "Nadeeen!!!"

It was a desperate cry from the other side of the burning wall. "Get away Nadine!" she heard her family call. They had combined their voices in an unusual act of unity to drown out the roar of the flames to reach Nadine.

Nadine, a natural climber, saw the rope that her father had knotted along the side of the wall, which she often used to test her climbing skills. With a running start, she hauled herself up. She gained her first footing with a great gasp, but the shock of the smoke and heat penetrating her eyes and lungs caused an involuntary spasm of choking coughs.

She slumped down. "Think Nadine, Think. Shallow breaths. Protect your lungs." This is what her father would say. She tore off the bottom of her sleeping tunic to make a covering for her nose and mouth. Steeling herself, she tried again. This time using slower, more deliberate movements helped fight against the screaming panic in her mind.

Nadine saw that the villagers were trapped. With no escape, they were huddled into a group for protection. The fire held no pity for them. The sweet smell of scorched flesh clung to the air.

Tiny sparks flew up, like fireflies, lighting up the sky as they searched for more thatch to dance on. Nadine tried to take it all in, she had only one goal and that was how to reach her family in the midst of all this chaos and danger.

Overhead the piercing sound Nadine had heard earlier wrenched her from her thoughts. She looked up. An enormous fire-breathing dragon swooped towards them.

It was Muquin. The dragon's crystal blue slanted eyes held the fiery reflection of the flames as her anger burned against the inhabitants.

Her rows of large jagged teeth terrified them, as blast upon blast of fire from her gaping mouth added to the surrounding flames. She had magnificent silver and slate coloured wings that ended with a large gripping talon at each tip. Nadine could see the pearly white scales of the underside of her belly, as she flew in closer and closer towards the circle of fire in which the villagers huddled. Nadine was almost deafened by the cacophony of angry shouts, terrified screams and wails that came from the men, women, and children captured within the ring of flames.

Muquin had lived a life undetected beyond the immediate borders of humans. But this transgression brought her from her hidden tunnel, and she would have no mercy for this cruel act of humankind. Her hatchling was gone. She would extract her justice.

Muquin's eyes scanned the group. She circled repeatedly. But she could not find what she searched for. These people held what she was looking for, she was sure of it. She had tracked its scent to this place.

No more would she cloak herself. She would show them just how terrifying a dragon could be. In her search she would burn down every dwelling if need be. She would not stop until they obeyed her will.

Why did they not yield? Only a fool would not give up the prize when a village burned. Did they care so little for their own offspring that they would resist her?

They were a pathetic species. Devoid of honour or courage. Let them burn then. For what she had lost, she could never forgive mankind. Never.

Nadine gasped at the sight of the great beast. Tiber hissed and her hair stood up on end. The dragon tilted her head towards the sound. "Shhhh Tiber!" hissed Nadine. She gritted her teeth and crouched behind the chimney, panting with panic. Maybe if she closed her eyes, she thought, she might become invisible. She bundled her body into a tight ball hunched over the kitten. Sounds and visions flashed through Nadine's mind. "Stop it, stop it!" she despaired". Had the heat and shock been too much for her?

She took a deep breath and decided. Hiding would do nothing for her family. She had to find the courage to look.

She curled herself around the chimney to peek at the horror on the other side. Before Nadine's petrified eyes, the earth sucked her family down through the blaze into a gaping hole. Darkness enveloped their screaming bodies. Then they were gone.

TWO

The Dragon Thief

All things die.

What Nabal had done would invite death. He had turned away from the light and all his lessons as a child. He was now lost to the truth of who he was. His actions would destroy the fragile peace that his ancestors had given their lives to preserve. Nabal was a man without honour.

The stirrings had called to him. The life force that Muquin had waited for over 100 years had begun. But on that night, he had ripped her hope from her.

Φ

The deep silver of the moon signalled the time was near. The inky blackness of the midnight sky so stark against the moonlight had paid homage to a new Silver Winged Dragon.

Muquin had taken flight. She had to hunt.

Nabal had laid in wait. From his hiding place, he had seen the egg, shimmering with life.

Then he had felt it. The Surge. A tiny talon had pierced the shell. He knew what he must do.

Muquin's rage had torn at the edges of his mind. He fought to keep her out. He had wiped the fluid off the dragon hatchling. She was coming. Rushing through the sky, back for the hatchling. Her panicked roar signalled her arrival, and he knew he had only minutes, perhaps only seconds.

For several weeks he lived in the inn at the village. Close enough to sense the power created by the hatching. But beyond the greatest surges, he was too feeble to penetrate Muquin's thoughts.

He thrust the hatchling into his bag and ran.

In his haste, he forgot to shut the secret passageway that led him to the outside. He had a moment of hesitation, but it was too late to return. His mind was churning with panic. Why did he think he could do this? He should have let the Northern King kill him a long time ago.

Muquin's roars penetrated his thoughts like a blade.

Nabal did not have the mental strength of his grandfather to help him ward off fear. His arms burned. It was more than fear. The acidic bile rose to his throat. He was terrified.

He hurtled through the tunnels under the village, exiting just behind the stables. Still clutching the hatchling tightly, he mounted his horse and pushed it hard. The thundering hooves of the stallion split the silence of the night air as Nabal made his escape. His lungs burned. Cramps from the run gripped his legs. But he was not yet free.

The king had provided coin for lodgings and the fastest horse that the royal breeders could offer. For the first time, Nabal lived beyond the life of a pauper. But it was all for the King's gain.

Many times, he had wanted to run away. But the memory of what happened in the dungeon tormented his dreams. The King read people's weakness. Nabal himself had had no beatings or tortures. Instead, he had been chained to the dungeon walls. He witnessed many, many tortures. If he tried to turn away, a guard would hold his head tightly and force him to watch.

He could not betray the king. The king's cruelty had reached legendary status. No one would dare cross him. He left in his wake a wave of brutal lessons for those who defied him. Nabal was very aware that at a time of political struggle for power, he was but a pawn in the King's plan for the ultimate domination.

Had he turned back, Nabal would have seen the village in flames. He would have known that he was the cause of so much human suffering. He would have heard the terrified cries of women and children. But he thought only of his own preservation.

A combination of stress and lack of oxygen due his hurried, shallow panting like a man who has forgotten how to breathe, now caused him to vomit over the side of the horse. The stallion reared, but Nabal managed to pull it back down with the reins using only one hand. His other arm still clung to the bag where the tiny hatchling was bundled in his cloak.

He dug in his thighs to steady the horse and it surged forward. At the crossing, there was a fresh horse waiting. There was a saddlebag with wine and food. Nabal tore at the bread and gulped down the wine, grateful that it was strong enough to ease the jagged edges of his fear. There was a fresh tunic, for which he was grateful, as his was drenched with sweat. He was careful to place the discarded tunic in his bag. If Muquin were to find it, she could easily track him and find him.

Even though his muscles burned in protest and cramps crept through his legs, making him cry out in pain, he knew that he must not stop. He dared not stop and sleep. Between the threat of torture and the thought of being burned alive by an outraged mother dragon, there was no choice. He had to keep going.

Just as he felt he was about to collapse; the final change over came into sight. There was once again a fresh horse, with more wine, some dried meat and another fresh tunic. The wine tasted bitter. But he downed it yet again. The bitterness meant it had been infused with herbs from the court healer. Herbs that could keep a man from collapsing from exhaustion.

Now as if in a trance, he kept going. Inside the bag, the hatching grew weak. But Nabal did not even think of feeding the hatchling. It was dehydrated, the precious life-sustaining fluid from the egg so thoughtlessly removed. Its life force ebbed away. Weak and still blind, it felt only the jarring of the horse's strides. In its weakened mind, it called out for a mother unable to trace the fading connection between them.

As the first rays of the sun kissed the earth, the outline of the castle came into sight. Knowing that the villagers would now emerge from their homes, he pushed harder for the final stretch.

At the gates, he dismounted, pulled out the King's signet ring and showed it to the guard. The guard opened the gate and let him into the outer court.

Nabal pulled the small bell from his bag and rang it three times.

At the sharp tone of the bell, a man dressed in a black, embroidered cloak and a heavy iron mask appeared from the darkened edge of the courtyard. Nabal sensed something in the man, something he could not discern. But the iron rod of silence across the front of the mask was a sign that the man could not speak. Yet Nabal's mind felt the man calling to him. There was an unspoken truth. A cold warning lay in the masked man's eyes. Nabal shuddered.

The silent man whisked the hatchling out of Nabal's hands and left as suddenly as he had arrived.

As Nabal turned, another guard took him by the upper arm and thrust him through the King's secret doorway on the far side of the courtyard, muttering gruffly, "The King is waiting for you."

THREE

Prisoners

Mikael wailed in terror for his mother. "Mami! Mami!" But his voice did not reach his parents. He searched the hut with frantic eyes. As Nadine's younger brother, Mikael had some of his sister's independence, although he still needed the warmth of his mother.

Mikael and Nadine shared startling blue eyes framed with the kind of dark lashes that many of the Nobel women desired. Now fear had replaced his usual twinkle. The roaring flames and the screams reached a place deep in his heart.

Maireid rushed to him. As firstborn, she cared for her siblings.

"I am here Mikael, I am here." Maireid's soothing voice belied the panic she felt inside. Maireid clung to him, trying to keep him calm while suppressing her own instinct to run away. Her parents had run outside. She had heard her mother shout, "Take care of the little ones."

Mikael needed the comfort of food, often growing agitated if he did not eat early enough each day. She hoped to calm him a little with normal things. If he stopped crying, he would not wake Nadine. She was still asleep with her arm around Tiber on the sleeping mat. She slept so deeply, the family always told how she had slept right through Mikael's arrival in the world, despite the agony of the birthing room.

"Let's get you something to eat," Maireid told Mikael. "Look, here is father's secret stash of dried meat." She smiled at him. Her father always hid some provisions from his two scavenging younger children. They seemed to have insatiable appetites, which made storing for winter a considerable challenge. She also found oatmeal and apple cookies. Just then, she heard her mother, Dorothea, scream and call her name, "Maireid, come and help me. I need you right now!"

Maireid tossed both bags of food into her pack and ran outside. She saw immediately the pain in her father's eyes. He clawed at a burning beam that had come down on his leg, trapping him beneath its scorching weight. The flames blistered his hands.

Her mother was trying to pull the beam away at the end that was not in flames. But the sheer weight of it was too much for her. "Maireid, help me! Take that side." With a grunt Maireid put all her strength into heaving the beam alongside her mother.

She did not see Mikael follow her out, bringing the little red wooden toy cart that his father had carved for him. Mikael stood frozen at the sight of his father trapped beneath the beam. Power surged through Dorothea. She would not let the boy witness their father burn to death.

"Cover your face," she yelled at the father of her children. Dorothea and Maireid heaved the beam off his leg and upward. Nicolous pulled his injured leg aside and pushed himself up and away from the flames.

As the beam came crashing down once, the dragon flew around again, spewing more fire and separating them from their home.

The intense heat was suffocating. Villagers clung to each other as the flames pushed them back. Mikael stood, frozen with terror. They heard Nadine calling from the house. "Get away Nadeeen," they called out together.

The ground gave way, drawing them down into a pit. The great volumes of soil and grass formed some cushioning for the fall, as it slid down into a tunnel below, like a wave carrying them to an unknown destination.

Soon they were on hard rock, in a vast tunnel that stretched on into the dark. People scrambled around. They tried to gain a footing and get out of the way. Surges of villagers fell over one another.

"Mikael!" called Nicolous. "Come on, boy! Get on my shoulders." The pain in his burnt hand was searing but he did not hesitate as Dorothea helped to pull the boy up to his father's shoulders. At over six foot in height, he could keep Mikael safe from being trampled by the panicked villagers.

Flames lit up the tunnel as they stumbled forward. The burns on Nicolous' leg triggered surges of pain with each step. His every movement was an act of will.

A woman started screaming in a hysterical frenzy of panic. Her cries grated at everyone's nerves. Soon the people will turn on her," he thought to himself. "Keeping the family calm is a matter of survival," he muttered to his wife.

Dorothea told Mikael about the big adventure they were going on. "We are going on a magical journey. They will reward only the brave. You are a brave boy. We need you to be our lookout boy. You are sitting high on Father's shoulders. Tell us what you see."

A small child's fear was difficult to manage.

"We will stay close to the wall, Mikael," the boy's father told him. He needed to keep his family away from the terrified bulk of the people, whose panic made them push and shove with a power that could trample a child quite easily.

"I can see the end of the passage," said Mikael. It appeared to be a dead end, and everyone crumpled down in exhausted piles. Some were coughing from the smoke they had inhaled. Others were in a daze. Several women were sobbing.

Nicolous settled with his family at a spot along the side wall of the shaft. No longer the lookout, Mikael complained. "I'm hungry!" Maireid remembered that she had the dried food with her, and that she had yet to give her brother something to eat.

In times of trouble, Maireid and her parents would speak in a secret language they used when they did not want the younger children to understand. "What shall we do? We don't know how long we will be here. How should we ration this food?"

Dorothea looked at her husband with a desperation she tried to hide from her son.

"If these people see us with the food, they will kill us. We do not have enough for long. We will have to share some of it." Nicolous told his family.

He had served as a knight and been in many battles. His experience with rationing and survival skills would serve his family well. He guided them with a simple plan of how they should manage the rations.

Their eyes adjusted to the darkness. There was a faint glow in the walls. Dorothea saw an enormous eggshell, lying among the stones. It gleamed with faint silver and blue light and she realized this must have been where the dragon's baby had hatched. A dragon only produced one offspring every 100 years. An egg was a rare find.

Some people believed that these eggs had magical powers, but the blue light came from a phosphorous filling that protected and nourished the growing hatchling. Yet she saw no baby dragon. Dragons, like birds, were born without flight. It would take months of care before the hatchling was mobile. That meant the mother would have to leave her baby in the cave unattended while she hunted for food. Dorothea strained her senses to see if she could see a little dragon. Nothing stirred.

Someone must have taken it, she decided. She wondered if the missing hatchling was related to the Dragon attack. Despite her own fear of what may happen to her family, she felt a surge of compassion for the dragon. As a mother of three children, Dorothea could imagine the anguish of losing a precious part of herself.

A woman of great independence and fierceness of spirit herself, she understood that few people had the wisdom to deal with an angry or grieved mother. But she had heard the ancient stories of the great Dragon Whisperers who communicated with dragons and calmed them. From her conversations with their local healers, she knew that there was still a Dragon Whisperer alive, in Holly Hill Cave. A groan from her husband interrupted her musing.

"You know that Nadine will come for us," Dorothea told Nicolous. His eyes glazed with pain, but he nodded. Nothing ever stopped Nadine when she had set her mind to a task.

Dorothea realized that she had to plan to communicate with Nadine. It was then she thought of the ledge she had seen when they had entered the tunnel. It was low enough for Nadine to reach without climbing, low enough to reach without alerting the dragon with too much noise or movement.

She took the parchment from her garment pocket and scribbled a quick note. Then she whispered to Mikael, who she knew was a generous and caring boy. Mikael grinned at the secret plan and gave up his carved wooden cart.

Φ

Muquin entered the smooth stone tunnel, through the secret Dragon entrance. With her head held high, and her wings tucked in close to her body, she sniffed the air trying to distinguish between the odour of mankind and her hatchling. But she did not detect it in this group. Her inch-thick talons made a tapping sound on the rock, as she herded the terrified survivors to the end of the tunnel.

The villagers all crept into the pockets of rock at the end of the tunnel. The tunnel walls were smooth enough to appear to be man-made. Trapped between the small pockets of the cavern the villagers tried to settle. The dragon positioned herself between the eggshell and her prisoners. Except for the faint glow on the walls, which cast few shadows, everything was dark.

"Sit around me, so that people cannot see me," Nicolous told his family. With sheer determination and gritting his teeth with every movement of his burned hands, he made small parcels of the dried meat and instructed Maireid to hand these out to families who had children with them.

He was still concerned that with time the hungry villagers might turn on each other for food.

"Maireid, please let Mikael eat facing away from the others. They must not see him eat," he whispered. It would have been cruel to let the others see him eating. There was not enough to sustain everyone. While Nicolous had compassion for all the villagers, he knew that he had to keep the bulk of the provisions for his family.

The villagers were simple people. They had not known the horrors of battle and there was a deep sense of fear in the group. Nicolous sat watching them.

Two men had captured his attention. These men had guided their families to safety without fear. He pushed himself upright with his elbow, and slowly approached the tanner.

"These people are too fearful," he whispered. "I have seen courage and calmness in you. I will need men to help keep the people at ease and prevent infighting. If any of them panic, it will be disastrous for all of us. Can I count on you to help manage the group?"

"I am ready," replied the man.

"Good," nodded Nicolous, "We must also keep an eye on the dragon. It is volatile and will react if the people panic. I will take the first watch. Can you do the second?"

When the tanner agreed, Nicolous dropped a second ration of meat into the man's tunic pocket.

The other man he had picked out was a blacksmith. He agreed to keep the third watch and was rewarded with an additional ration.

Now that Nicolous had level-headed men to help him, his jaw relaxed a little, as he eased back down beside his family. He would have liked some of the strong honeyed wine they had prepared over winter to help ease the pain.

Nicolous had chosen men of great strength and patience. Each of these professions required physical work and honing skills. They had the patience to follow through until a finished product could be displayed. Men, who required patience to complete their work, would not make hasty rash decisions. He needed their help to keep the people calm.

Judas, the tax collector of the village, was watching Nicolous closely. He could see that Nicolous was forming a plan. He was yet again organising, planning, calculating and preserving his family. Just like he did at tax collecting time, thus preventing the tax collector from seizing too much. His eyes narrowed and he exhaled through his teeth with a snakelike hiss. His thoughts were angry.

"No one is above the tax collector. I have the power to have a man's lands seized and his children turned into indentured slaves. But here - Nicolous is recruiting a tanner and a blacksmith instead of me. A tanner! What kind of leadership could a tanner have?"

The tanner's dwellings always reeked of urine. They kept jars of it to help rot the fur off the skins they treated.

How he wished that he could send these stinking tanners to

debtors' prisons. But the tanner produced such quality work, that he was never short of coin for taxes. Judas could not conceal his impotent rage against men like this. They always complied with tax laws. Every compliant villager was a way for Judas to line his own pockets, with the cut that he always took. For self-preservation, he could not afford to sabotage his own earnings with a personal vendetta.

In Judas's mind tanners were akin to the waste collectors. Yet, here was Nicolous choosing a tanner. Over a man as important as Judas. To add insult to injury, he even gave the tanner and blacksmith rations. They thought he did not see the pouches slipped to these men. But Judas' ever-shifting eyes saw everything. He could find a hidden coin in the most cluttered homes.

Why bother to give provisions to people who had children. Most of them would die before they were five years old. What a foolish waste of resources. He sat marinating in his hate and jealousy, thinking of ways to undermine this trio of worthless men.

As if feeling the heat of the glare on his skin, Nicolous glanced up toward Judas. He caught the briefest flicker of venom in the tax collector's eyes before Judas turned away. He then looked at the blacksmith. He had seen it. Nicolous threw a small pebble at the feet of the tanner. The blacksmith glanced up. Nicolous made a V sign using his index and middle and pointed to the tax collector.

The three men rearranged their positions to create a web around Judas. Just one impulsive man could cost them their lives.

Φ

Maireid was loved by the villagers. She helped many an overwhelmed new mother with a baby or a boisterous toddler. She was of great comfort to the frightened children and mothers who struggled between managing their own fear and the fear of their children. Maireid moved from family to family, to hold a child's hand, smile at an anxious mother and kiss the forehead of a baby.

As Nicolous had taken the first watch, Dorothea felt more secure in her plan to communicate with Nadine. When all the children had fallen asleep, the dragon slept. Dorothea removed her boots. She put the note in the wooden toy cart and crept past Muquin. She placed the little cart on the ledge she had seen on the way in. Dorothea prayed that her daughter would see it and that God would protect Nadine on her quest.

FOUR

What Lies Beneath

"Nooo" screamed Nadine. Hot stinging tears pooled in her blue-green eyes. "Mami, Daddy, Maireid, Mikael, come back!" She clung to Tiber, sobbing until her body ached with the tension and effort.

Nadine held onto the cat a little too tightly and Tiber squealed again in terror. Muquin looked in Nadine's direction. Nadine ducked out of sight and prayed. "Look away, look away, please, look away." She almost sobbed with relief when Muquin hovered for a moment and then flew off in the opposite direction.

She crept down off the roof. While many of the neighbours'

thatched huts roared and crackled in the flames, by God's grace, theirs was still untouched. The silence of the house was a welcome reprieve from the chaos outside.

Simple town life had always been too tame for Nadine. Her games with the village children were full of adventure and battles. She loved to listen in to her father's nightly whispers of the political rumblings in the Northern Kingdom, hushed talk of a King's plan that usually never left the castle walls. Her father spoke of rows of heads on spikes for those who dared cross the King. At night, he whispered of needing to ready themselves. Spies who had thought they could reveal the king's secrets now fed the Ravens. They said that flocks of them nested near the castle... a sure sign that death was freely available for enemies.

Though Nicolous taught his children ways to defend themselves and ways to disappear into the woods, the actual danger for which they were preparing never revealed itself.

But her father had been agitated in the preceding months. He had never been so restless. Her mother had stared ahead into the distance.

Nadine imagined herself a brave warrior. A leader of the children's games. Nothing could have prepared her for the horror of the day. It was now brutally carved into her mind.

She felt hunger clawing at her. She and Tiber had to eat. Food was normal. It was soothing. She had to find comfort. Trembling, Nadine found some leftover pigeon from their meal the night before in a bowl on the table.

Clutching the bowl, she retreated with Tiber to her parent's room for the meal. She wolfed it down. But in her mind, she relived the sights and sounds, and her random thoughts struggled to find a resting spot.

Images of something she knew she had not seen flashed with jagged edges in her vision. She felt a rising panic. She told herself that it was just the shock of what she had witnessed. But no. This was something else. Things she knew she had never watched, yet there they lay in her mind, like memories stolen from someone else.

"Daddy, I do not know what to do." she softly cried. The impressions came all at once. War, fire, death. She desperately pressed her palms to her eyes. Trying to block them. Was she going mad? At the edge of her parent's bed, Nadine rocked backwards and forwards, her arms tightly clutched around her slim body.

"Be still Nadine." She leapt up, scanning the room. Who was that? Was there someone else in the room with her? Were there other survivors?

"My mind is playing tricks. It is nobody." But her heart confessed otherwise.

Now was not the time to unravel. She had to plan.

"Think," she ordered herself out loud.

The familiar note of her own speech filled her with relief. She laughed. "You are okay, Nadine." Yes, the sound of her voice told her she was sane. Just a little shaken. Nothing that the meal settling in her belly could not cure.

She revisited the memory of the sinkhole into which the residents had faded. The sand had flowed smoothly, like a slide when they had gone down. She replayed the scene in her mind.

Outside, she heard Muquin's circular flight. Nadine did not know how, but she felt that the dragon was searching. But for what?

The diminishing vibration of the dragon's flight told Nadine that it had flown off, and Nadine realized that for at least a while, she was safe from its wrath.

Where had this beast come from? Why was she here? Nadine's impotent mind would not unlock these secrets.

In the distance, thunder rolled overhead. The boom was a welcome promise of rescue for the village. Thick sheets of water descended. The charred skeletons of the trees reached up to accept the mercy of the rain.

"Tiber, we have to get them back, girl. We have to find them." She said to the cat, as she sifted through their belongings.

No one in the village knew Nadine's father had once been a knight. After witnessing the brutality of war, he had lived the life of a simple farmer and hunter. But he had trained her with basic survival skills. She went through the house, making a pack with provisions for herself and Tiber. Once Nadine had decided to do something, no one could ever persuade her otherwise.

Nicolous was trained in reading and the art of chivalry. He and Nadine's mother had ensured that all their children could read and write. Their family did things differently from the rest of the village. In a world where few children survived past five years old, Nadine's parents had observed many of the ways people became ill. They had arranged their lives to give their children the best chances of surviving.

Nadine grabbed a pinch of the mixture of fat and salt infused with fragrant oil and mixed it with the bowl of water her mother kept. She washed away the soot from her hands and face. This and only drinking rainwater that they harvested helped to keep the family free of many of the ailments that the villagers suffered from.

Nadine stared at the cleanly swept floor, wondering what to do next. "I will go down that sinkhole," she told Tiber. Her father's workshed provided the equipment she needed for her trip. She found a coil of rope and pulled out one of the grappling hooks, a ground peg and a hammer to secure her rope. These she packed into the leather satchel, with the rest of her provisions.

Nadine grabbed one of the oiled skins and covered her head, and she and Tiber made their way through the maze of smoldering rubble and went to inspect the sinkhole.

Thankfully the rainstorm had only lasted a short while, so Nadine did not have to work in the rain. The ground was slick with mud and Nadine had to search for a firm part of the ground to hammer the peg into.

"Come on Tiber, we have to get down to the bottom. But you are going to have to be very quiet!" With the rope wrapped around her, she eased her way down into the sinkhole. The rain had washed away much of the sand, which now lay in muddy puddles, but here and there she could see exposed rock underneath.

The inky blackness of the tunnel overcame her. She had not brought a torch. The utter stupidity of her lack of foresight infuriated her. Nadine climbed up again and went back to the house. She snatched up the fat her parents used to make candles, some cloth and her father's tinderbox.

Nadine's parents had long ago given up trying to stop her doing things they thought may be too dangerous for her. By the time Nadine was three years old, her independence had been so fierce that her parents were forced to teach her things that many older children did not know.

They simply knew that she was going to try to do things she saw her parents and other adults do herself in any case, so they felt it better that they teach her the correct way of doing those things. Now Nadine had the skills uncommon for a young woman of her age and a quick mind to come up with a workable plan.

By any means, she must reach her family. But deeper than that, there was something else. A sense of purpose that ran alongside her quest, something ancient and powerful. A silent scream for help. Nadine felt it brewing. But could not discern it.

FIVE

The Crying Dragon

Nadine landed with a gentle thud on the sand where the villagers had slid into the tunnel. As she entered the tunnel for the second time, she could better take in her surroundings. This time she lit a torch to see where she was going. Nadine froze, dead still. In front of her was the crumpled body of the waste harvester's son. She clamped her hand over her mouth to stop from crying out. "Oh no, Toby," she whispered.

With his eyes staring ahead and his skull oozing over the ground, he made a grotesque find. Knowing the boy by name made it worse. What about her brother? Was he even alive? Overcome with horror, Nadine pulled herself away and stumbled forward.

There was a sweet stench in the tunnel, mingling with the charred smell of roasted meat. Like the smell when her father prepared a meal from a hunt on the fire. But this was different. It was nauseatingly sweet. She shook her head. Just ahead she could see a shape. Nadine bent down and stared at the charred body of another villager. A girl. The fire had burned away part of her hair. Her charred skull gleamed pink under the burn. The remaining strands of hair formed a halo around her face which was streaked with scorch marks. The girl's lifeless arms stretched out as if welcoming the angel of death. Nadine knew her, too. She was a former playmate. A once beautiful girl. Her father had just accepted a marriage proposal on her behalf. Now she was just another one of the hideous corpses that littered the tunnel entrance. Nadine's stomach churned.

You could not live in a village and not know death. But the death Nadine knew was from old age or stillborn babies that her eyes never saw. This was not the quiet cycles-of-life kind of death. Here was a violent, horrible death that no girl should ever have to witness.

Despair enveloped Nadine as she moved through the dead searching for her family. The villagers had trampled some of their own neighbours. Others died on impact and many from the burns.

"Please, Lord, my family - let them be alive," she moaned through her tears.

The mourner's words, so familiar from village events, popped into her head. "Mourn not the passing of a life well-lived. Celebrate the times your souls smiled together."

No! She shook her head again. Nadine could not celebrate. Many of the dead were children. Children who were crushed by adults in their panic to escape. Her heart ached for the mothers who had to leave their dead behind.

She pulled Tiber closer, remembering the day her sister had picked up the little orphaned kitten to bring it into the house and care for it. She stroked Tiber's head softly and was comforted.

Stopping to compose herself, Nadine stared ahead. The tunnel seemed to stretch on forever. The rocky walls were not jagged, as she would have expected them to be. Nadine wondered if human hands made them because they were so smooth.

She had visited many caves whose exposure to the wind and rain had weathered them smooth like this. Those kinds of caves had a smoother look than buried caves. But this tunnel had not been exposed to nature. Nadine wondered how it had gotten its smooth appearance.

She saw a small carving about the size of her fist on the wall. Nadine traced her fingers over the grooves of the etching. A dragon wing in painstaking detail marked the stone. The artist must have laboured many hours to achieve the lifelike muscle tones that supported the wide stretched out wings. As delicate as a butterfly, but as forceful as a crashing wave of the ocean. What secrets did this tunnel hold?

The tunnels were ancient of that she was sure. Why had no one ever spoken of this place? What secrets lay in its depths? She had lived her whole life above these tunnels, and never known they were there. In a different time, Nadine would have dragged the village children into this mysterious place to find adventure and games of glory. Now she found only the crushed bodies and shattered dreams of children who would never again join in her adventures.

The walls of the tunnel glistened. She did not know what it was. The only sound was her fur-lined boots padding softly over the rocky surface.

"Let's keep moving, Tiber," she whispered. "What would the villagers say if they heard me talking to a cat?" she smiled at the thought. "I think you should breed lots of pretty kittens, for all the widows in the village. Maybe that would give them something else to talk about instead of grumbling and gossiping all the time."

Nadine padded through the tunnels, careful to not make any sudden or loud movements.

She heard a sound in the distance. It was a low and deep rumbling, almost like an enormous cat purring. Nadine extinguished the torch and crouched next to the wall of the tunnel. She allowed her eyes to adjust to the darkness. Then stilled her beating heart and allowed her senses to take in her surroundings.

In the darkness, a shape in the shadows began to form. Nadine could just make out the outline of a large dragon lying with its forearms wrapped around an object she could not make out. Something glistened on the face of the dragon, catching the light. A single large tear rolled down and with an audible splash, dropped into a puddle forming near the dragon's talons. Nadine stretched her neck to peer around the corner of the rock. As the dragon moved her body, Nadine could see that the dragon was cradling a large broken egg. It was empty. The outer shell was a smooth silvery hue with slate coloured speckles and the inside a luminescent crystal blue. The glow of the inner egg illuminated the dragon's stricken face.

Nadine narrowed her eyes in thought. She began to piece together the events that had happened. This enormous and ferocious fire-breathing dragon, who had burned up a substantial portion of her village and caused the disappearance of almost everything she held dear, was crying.

Nadine sensed that she and the dragon were kindred spirits. Nadine had an intense personality. A combination of personal power, intelligence and stubbornness. It was the torment of her family. But she was fiercely possessive and protective of her little cat. Her intensity may not always be understood, but she would do anything she could to protect those that she loved.

Nadine felt that the disappearance of this baby dragon had something to do with what had happened to her family and the rest of the villagers. But what was the connection and how could she get them back?

Knowing that she could not get past the dragon until it moved or slept, Nadine had no choice but to wait. With each passing minute, Nadine grew sleepier. The events of the day had drained her strength. Unable to stay awake, she slumped into dreams that pulled her into a world unknown to her.

In her dreams, two silver winged dragons swirled and danced in the moonlight. Their soaring bodies glowed under the stars. Nadine had a feeling of utter joy and freedom. Then a flash of light pierced one dragon and it fell from the sky. Two roars filled the air. One of despair and one of death. A burst of light came as the fallen dragon's body evaporated and filled the sky. Nadine awoke and pulled her thoughts away from the scene that lingered on the fringes of sleep. She looked around, there was nothing but the solitude of the tunnels. And the empty loneliness of being left behind.

As she lifted her head, something caught her eye. Something that seemed familiar... After squinting her eyes and focusing just below the glint in the wall, she saw that it was the little red cart her father had carved for her brother at Christmas. The realisation brought a surge of joy that evaporated her fear. It was a message. Someone in her family had left a message.

"Oh, thank you, thank you, thank you, Lord." Tears stung her eyes. She sobbed in her relief.

The cart was positioned on a low-lying ledge of the tunnel. Something was sticking out of it. Nadine knew that she had to retrieve the cart, but that would mean getting past the dragon.

She settled down onto the rocky bottom of the tunnel. Time passed slowly while she was waiting for the dragon to either move or fall asleep.

She shifted - the hard rock was making her lose circulation. But there seemed to be no comfortable way to sit. She knew that if she stayed in one position too long, moving would cause an intense prickling in her limbs that would make it difficult to move at all. She kept on adjusting her position every few minutes.

Nadine waited for what seemed like an eternity, and then, at last, the dragon put her head down, closed her eyes and fell asleep. Nadine crept as quickly as she could to where the little cart was resting on the shelf. She did not want to take the cart, in case the dragon realised that something was missing, but she slid the scroll out the cart and then made her way back to the opening of the tunnel.

Nadine yanked on the rope to test if it would hold true. When she felt that it was secure, she began to hoist her body up through the tunnel. Climbing up the rope required her to use only the power of her arms to pull the full weight of her body up.

As she neared the opening, she saw it again; the stone ledge. But this time she saw that there were carvings on the underside of it. She swung her body closer to the ledge and as she did her foot pressed against one carving. Without warning the ledge started to move with a grinding sound towards her.

Nadine could see the opening get narrower and narrower. She pulled harder and faster on the rope. She was panting for air. As they reached the top, the rope caught in the sliding stone and snapped. Nadine slipped and only just managed to grab the approaching ledge. With a final burst of effort, she used all the strength she had left to haul herself on top of the ledge.

She stood up unsteadily and jumped. She hit the ground just before the opening snapped shut.

Nadine stood staring at the slab of stone. On this side, there were none of the carvings that she had seen on the underside. "What is this?" Nadine mused, while she stared at the stone

She wondered what to do. The tunnel had been concealed for many years. Should she leave it this way, or should she hide it again?

In time, the corpses below would rot. She knew that she did not have the strength or time to haul each body out of the tunnels to bury them. The smell would become overbearing. But her father had said that nature has a way of cleansing the earth of its dead. Perhaps by the time she returned that would be true for the souls below who lay without ceremony or prayer.

"What secrets do you hold?" Nadine asked the rock. "Why

are you here?" Nadine wondered what would happen if someone who was not trustworthy were to find this rock. Would they rescue her family? Or would they slaughter them? If she perished on her journey, would concealing the entrance just create a tomb for the villagers? She had to make a judgment call and do it fast.

Using a shovel, Nadine scattered sand over the slab. She arranged clumps of grass over the whole area and flattened the grass into the sand with the back of the shovel, to cover up any irregularities. "May you be protected until I return," she prayed.

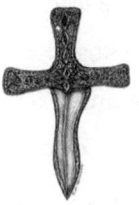

SIX

A Time to Plan

Back in the village, Nadine sat alone in the middle of her parent's bed. The room filled with the kind of silence that forms when someone is alone and trying not to think or feel or do anything to ignite the sorrow of losing their entire family in one go. It was the kind of silence some people call 'deafening.' That had never made sense to Nadine, but now the real meaning filled her awareness. She longed for the sounds of household activity. A scraping of a stool in the dining area, the sound of the vegetable peeler at work, even her parents scolding... anything would have been welcome now.

Tiber was her only real connection with her family and she felt somewhat comforted by the little cat asleep next to her. Nadine willed herself to fight back the tears as she unrolled the tiny scroll. As she recognised her mother's handwriting, she felt the hot stinging tears roll down her cheeks blurring her vision. She angrily brushed them away. The betrayal of her emotions lost her precious seconds to put together the pieces of the puzzle she needed to help find her family.

The words were scrawled with a piece of charcoal she knew her mother always carried. It was unusual to see so few words - her mother always seemed to overflow with words.

But Nadine could sense the hurried panic that her mother must have had when writing them. They simply said "All Alive. Dragon Whisperer! Holly Hill Cave! Go quickly!"

Nadine held the note to her cheek and thought of her mother. Of the stories that her mother told her at night and the special tangle story, her mother once made up when brushing her hair. Her heart ached for her family. But she could not let sorrow take her captive. Her mother had trusted her with this note and the belief in her came as both a comfort and a burden. Could one girl do anything that could help a whole village? She had to shake off the self-doubt. Fear and doubt would not serve her now. She just needed to start.

Holly Hill Cave meant a trip across Forever Gone Lake. Nadine had received many punishments for going anywhere near Forever Gone Lake, so named because so many people had vanished beneath its depths.

The locals believed that there was a magical monster that

devoured the souls of all who crossed this lake. In fact, some of the travelling friars who were mockingly called the 'fire and brimstone' clergy had tried to make the villagers believe that the lake was a punishment from God for disobedience and evil. No one dared speak out against this belief for fear of being labelled heretics or even having their village excommunicated.

Excommunication from the church was a great fear for many people. Not being able to take sacrament was not just a sign that their souls would perish, but also it would remove a sense of hope of a better afterlife than the life they were now living.

It was not just for their souls that they feared, but once word spread that a King, Lord or village was excommunicated, no one would ever be willing to trade with them again. Kings were said to have received their authority from God. Excommunication would mean that their authority could be challenged. This would bring war. No one ever openly questioned this view of Forever Gone Lake.

Nadine's mother was not prone to superstition and she had always taught her children practical and honest lessons. Dorothea had explained that the lake was full of a water plant that grew so densely and so intertwined, that if anyone fell into the water, they could become entangled. The combination of the currents caused by the constant wind over the lake and the entangled tentacles of the plants would pull the victim down, causing them to drown. It was ignorance and lack of skills that killed people when they fell into the lake.

Dorothea had taught her children there were many people who tried to control people through fear. Nadine had learned not to live her life based on other people's opinions. Her knowledge of

God, as taught to her by her parents, was that He had designed her with a purpose. She wondered now if her mother's teachings were in some part preparing her for this day. Nadine's own blend of characteristics was now being called to a purpose higher than herself. Of this she was sure.

There were few opportunities for villagers to learn how to swim, but Nadine had taught herself to hold her breath for a long time, by holding her head down in the wash trough outside their home. She hoped that this skill would prove useful should she be faced with the prospect of falling into the lake. Nadine's activities were about endurance and independence. She allowed no one to hold her back. No amount of horror stories about a soul-sucking lake would stop her from making this journey as quickly as possible.

To make it across the lake would require more than a two day journey and would mean sleeping in the boat, out in the open. Nadine knew that fishermen fished the edges of the lake but had never heard of anyone going to the center of the lake, let alone all the way across. Villagers had told her that the waters in the middle of the lake were an inky black, that reflected no light. Nadine had always wondered, "How would they know what the center looked like if no one ever crossed the lake?" She saw the eerie-looking mist that arose from the lake at night. Was it really the souls of the departed reaching up for new victims? Her mother did not believe these stories. But now alone, she wondered if the stories had a ring of truth to them.

Nadine thought she might travel around the lake via land. However, a land trip held other dangers. It would mean an entire week's journey instead of two days. This would cost her precious time. And time was one thing she did not have the luxury of. She had no way of knowing how long her entire journey would be. The prospect of adding two weeks to a journey that could take just two days was absurd.

As a girl travelling alone over land, there were other dangers. She had heard of a group of terrible traders who traded in humans. Many a family had experienced the trauma of having their female children stolen from them. Once a girl had escaped the human traders, but she was never the same again. She had a haunted look and trembled every time there was any sudden or loud noise.

Nadine had also overheard the adults speak of some terrible 'shame' that girls who had ventured too close the road alone had endured. Although she did not know what this 'shame' was, she was not willing to risk it.

Once across the lake, she would have to enter the forest that had been the home of the Ancients. They had been a mystical people who few others understood. Her mother had told her that the Ancients had taught many of the best healers their craft. But the unknown always brought superstition and fear. A group of bandits who feared no one had driven the Ancients out. These bandits were unconcerned with clergy, armies or threats of curses.

Ancients had been scholars, healers and teachers of the law. Many considered them wise, but also to be conjurers of curses and magic. Some believed the magic. Many believed that the spirits of the Ancients still lived in the woods.

There were some advantages to this route. Except for the bandits, almost no one was foolish or brave enough to travel along that way. The rumours of magic left by the Ancients made the average ignorant person extremely afraid to venture into this area. This meant that human traders would not use this route. The other advantage was that there were a vast number of trees in the area. Many of the ancient trees had branches that had grown in such a way that the branches had grown into one another. Being an excellent climber, Nadine thought that she could perhaps use the trees to her advantage.

She made up her provisions from her family's vegetable garden, some meat from the drying hut and some handfuls of the crushed wheat from the family stores. After packing a container for watered wine, she hastily added a small fishing net for fresh food, some oilskins for protection from the rain and some furs to keep warm. She was now ready for the trip across the lake.

When she tried to carry everything, Nadine realized that she had too much. She got the small sled her brother used to play in the snow. She could drag her equipment behind her.

She knew that the uneven ground would cause the provisions to wobble and possibly fall off, so she secured the parcels to the sled with rope. The provisions were not in truth very heavy. They were simply too much to carry.

But dragging the sled with the provisions was a far harder task than she had imagined. Her only experience of the sled had been in snow. The softness of the snow made it far easier to drag a sled than the coarseness of the pre-winter ground. The sled frequently caught on rocks and twigs along the ground. Nadine was growing increasingly frustrated at the lack of progress but gritted her teeth and trudged on. The constant abrupt stops to bend down and clear the path were exhausting and infuriating.

Was the entire journey going to be like this? Why could things not just be simple? She tried to visualise her reunion with her family. The laughter of her brother. Her father playing 'tickle monster' with her. Her big sister braiding a special hairstyle for her. She could see them at the dinner table together saying what they were grateful for that day. The vision of her family all together again, gave her renewed strength.

SEVEN

The Hatchling

Galdolf, the Prison Master, opened the King's secret entrance into the stronghold immediately he heard the set pattern of knocks. Before him stood a masked man, holding a bundle and a scroll sealed with the King's ring.

The masked man silently handed the Prison Master the bundle and turned away. Galdolf bolted the door and opened the bundle. The weakened form of a dragon hatchling lay in his hands. He knew the legend that a dragon hatchling was only born every 100 years, and he stared in amazement. He opened the scroll and read the King's instructions to rear this dragon within the confines of the prison.

The preparations he had noticed within the stronghold over the last few months became clear. The cage under construction would be able to contain a fully-grown dragon.

But would this hatchling live to fulfil its purpose? It was clearly dehydrated and had not yet had its first meal. The Prison Master looked frantically around, his mind racing as to how to resurrect the hatchling. A recognisable squeak provided the solution.

Taking his crossbow in one hand he fired at a rat running across the floor. Then grabbing the still squealing rodent, he squeezed its life juices onto the closed mouth of the tiny hatchling. Rats were indeed the scum of the food chain for animal hunters, but at this point, the Prison Master had no choice.

This is what a mother dragon would do for a hatchling. She would hunt, but only partially complete the kill. It allowed the hatchling's instinct to come to the fore.

"I'm not much of a match for your mother, little one," he said while rubbing the juice onto the hatchling's closed mouth. Gradually, the hatchling began to stir and then its tiny tongue made its way out of its mouth and licked at the juice.

Galdolf wondered what kind of ignorant fool had brought this hatchling to the castle. He had no doubt that the King had heard of the might of dragons and the destruction of the Dragon Wars.

Galdolf knew that this path would prove to be a double-edged sword. Yet the King's orders would have to be obeyed. Moreover, he had his own family to be concerned about. They were the only reason he remained here to do the King's bidding. He knew that defiance would come at the price of a man's kin.

"How do I care for you in this miserable place?" asked Galdolf.

He wracked his brains to find the hidden memories of the tales passed on by his ancestors. Inside those legends, the knowledge was hidden.

Φ

Muquin's rage had turned inward. In her desperation to find the hatchling, she had tracked the human's scent right into the village. But as her anger burned against the unknown human thief, all traces of her hatchling's scent had been destroyed in the intense heat. She had not been present at the birth of the hatchling, so she had not yet formed her bond with it.

She was now without two essential things she needed to get the hatchling back. She had lost the scent of the thief and she had failed to bond with the hatchling. The bond would have given her a telepathic connection to the hatchling. It would have allowed her to track it. But her own foolish and impulsive anger had caused a devastating loss.

Once her initial anger had burned away and she knew that the villagers were trapped, she circled the surrounding area in search of the hatchling. Its life force was so low, that she could not even tell if it was alive.

A mother dragon, even when she has not bonded, could feel the life force of a hatchling. But because the thief had not cared for the hatchling in the first hours of its life, the life force was far too low for her to sense. Now in despair, she had to think of what to do with the villagers. Incinerating all of them would be but a small act of revenge for their denying her the hatchling she had waited over 100 years to create.

Φ

Far away, at the King's prison, the hatchling's body began to absorb the life fluids of the rat and its life force began to flicker. The hatchling felt the force begin to rise, like dying flame, fanned back to life.

Muquin instantly felt that flicker burst forth in her giant heart, like the second beat. Two heartbeats side by side in her body. There was a new path in her heart that carried the rhythm of this precious heartbeat. "Ah..." she murmured to this new presence, "these pathetic villagers may hold the key to getting you back." She paused, following the rhythm she had waited for so long. While she knew that the thief was not among these people, she could keep them captive. Someone might search for them, and through that champion, she would find a way to get her hatchling back.

She began to sense the desire of the hatchling to bond begin to shift.

Galdolf knew that a dragon's life force was not only linked to nourishment and its mother, but that its life force was also strengthened by its name. In the Dragon Wars, there had been some orphaned hatchlings. But their naming ceremonies were only ever conducted when the mother's death had been confirmed. Galdolf held an impossible choice in his hands.

The weakened hatchling desperately needed its life force kindled. But this would cause a further break in bond with its mother. By breaking the bond, the hatchling would be easier to bend to the King's will.

In the care of a King whose only love was for power, the fragile mind of a new hatchling could easily be molded to the will of the King.

"Will you not eat?" Galdolf asked in desperation. He pulled his cloak out, laid it down on the ground and gently placed the hatchling on it. Then he carved up the rat into tiny portions. Using the handle of the dagger, he pounded the rat flesh on the ground.

The Prison Master pried the hatchling's mouth open a little way and dropped tiny clumps of the pounded rodent flesh onto the hatchling's tongue. He gently closed his hand around the tiny mouth. The hatchling swallowed. After a few more mouthfuls, the hatchling slowly opened its eyes and stared straight into Galdolf's eyes.

Φ

Muquin felt rising despair in her heart; the first bond for the hatchling had been formed. She could still feel the life force, but it was flowing in a different direction. She also knew that the next step for life force had to be taken. By rights, she should do the naming ceremony. But the naming ceremony had to be done. She knew that the hatchling was not with a Dragon Whisperer. That kind of energy was impossible to miss. But what ordinary human could ever know how to do a naming ceremony?

The hatchling's crystal blue eyes searched Galdolf's face. It somehow knew that there was a next step to be taken, and it arched it's neck in anticipation, without knowing what it was.

"What shall I name you?" asked the Prison Master. "Is there no scroll of instructions?" he despaired. The name was an instinctive name that the mother formed inside her upon laying the egg. The bond was the event that solidified the choice of name. A name was also more than that. It was a destiny that the hatchling would grow into. He would need to find a name and quickly. Galdolf closed his eyes, held the hatchling a little closer and ran through his memory the names he had heard as a child, sitting upon his grandfather's knee.

"Yakhal" he finally said.

When Galdolf was a child his grandfather would affectionately call him this. From an early age, Galdolf had displayed a way with sick animals, as he now did with the hatchling. His patient touch and gentle care, whether it was a sick horse or a milking cow who had fallen ill, always brought hope to the family that the animal would live and continue to fulfil its purpose. Yakhal was an old word of the Hebrews in biblical times that meant hope; not just a blind hope of some distant future, but the kind of patient hope where people who endure trials believing that something better is truly coming.

It had been a long time since Galdolf had genuinely believed that something better would come.

For too long he had worked in this place of despair. His grandfather had told him of the time when the King's parents had ruled. A time of wisdom and kindness. But the death of the Queen by the hands of those who hated the light had changed things.

Power did not corrupt. It only magnified the hearts of those who had power. Galdolf knew that hearts could turn. But he wondered if the King could ever turn. The light that the queen mother had brought to the land, seemed forever snuffed out.

The Prison Master lived in a place of darkness and cruelty. What was there to hope for? What chance did this hatchling have?

He understood that to keep this hatchling alive, they would both need the kind of hope this name held. By using this name, perhaps their destinies would merge together and through their bond thwart the plans of the King. Perhaps there could be hope for mankind.

"We have to try, little one," said Galdolf.

Placing his fingers in some wine, he rubbed a patch of the dragon's leathery forehead and then touched his own forehead. He repeated the name three times and finally placed his forehead against the hatchling's forehead, sealing the bond.

With a flash of light, the hatchling's body began to glow. It arched its back. Yakhal spread his fragile wings. The surge stretched the young dragon. The ceremony had released the power for the hatchling to double in size.

Galdolf's heart filled with joy. Perhaps there really was something to hope for.

Muquin felt the life force created by the naming ceremony. "Oh, Megadeus. Our hatchling lives."

The shifting of the bond began to tear at her heart. No dragon mother could endure the pain of separation. The muscle in her heart began to split in two to create as a separate heart in which the hatchling's bond would lie. She roared in pain. The force of it caused her to stumble as she tried to steady her body.

The wrenching feeling was too much for her. There was no one to comfort or heal her. If only she could hear Megadeus.

Silver Wings were the carriers of wisdom. Their purpose was to pass on the wisdom of their ancestors. But she was alone. Not even Megadeus' star formation spoke to her.

The force had pushed her beyond her endurance. She slipped silently into the abyss of sleep.

EIGHT

The Game of Kings

King Radolf's eyes surveyed the men at his war council. He tried to control the rage that he felt when he looked at the bishop. The Bishop Rawlin's gluttonous belly strained at the seams of his robe. While he saw the benefits of the travelling Friars and the Monks who dedicated themselves to knowledge, he despised the Bishops. They aimed to rule, but not through their strength, but by manipulating the minds of the ignorant.

There sat the Bishop stuffing his face with his greasy fingers with the rind of the pig fat that the cook had roasted to form a crackling golden outer crust. At the same time, people in the villages struggled under two sets of taxes.

Taxes were necessary to create an ordered society where trade could thrive. But overtaxed starving peasants would eventually seek a leader from their own ranks to rise and bring anarchy to a Kingdom. A King's best strategy was to keep them just comfortable enough to not question his rule.

Were it not for the threat of excommunication, King Radolf would never allow Bishop Rawlin, this despicable leech of society, anywhere near his Kingdom, let alone his table. Allowing the Bishop to partake at the war council was a necessary evil. He knew that the common assumption that God placed leaders in authority, was one that these Bishops used to their advantage. An excommunicated King would lose not only his right to have the sacrament in his Kingdom, but also the people's respect for him as a ruler. Life in the villages was harsh. Without the promise of paradise, who would want to bother at all? Life would be pointless. Let them have their hope of an afterlife, that way they could breed strong sons for the King's army.

King Radolf's own mother had taught him about the teachings of the Christ, and it did not ring true to the way the Bishops manipulated people's minds. Their practice of selling indulgences nauseated the King. The indulgences were a way that villagers could buy their way out of punishment for sins. But only the wealthy could afford indulgences. The Christ had been a carpenter. A simple man, working with his hands. He had a true love for people. No carpenter would have been a weak, pot-bellied manipulator of people, like this bishop.

While he did not live his life according to the Christ's teachings, he knew that the simple-minded drew strength from these teachings and that they gave strong people some sense of hope for the afterlife. Either way, they certainly served to make the people more able workers.

He thought of the creature in his stronghold. A dragon! His time would come. The creature would grow to be strong and fearsome. Then with this powerful weapon by his side, he could rule without the need for the clergy he so despised.

But he needed to make his move before the Pope could name his successor. After suffering a prolonged bout of illness, the Pope was weak. Leaders, whether spiritual or political, need a show of power and strength. Any weakness could prove to be a chink in their armour that would be capitalised on by the enemy. If the Pope named a successor, then the lines of leadership would be solidified, and structured leadership would fortify their control of the people.

In King Radolf's plan for domination, he had realized that his own Kingdom's lack of a queen would cost him. A campaign of such an epic nature would require that he make a show of his own physical power. Which would mean leaving the castle. To do that he needed a strong queen to rule in his absence. The first queen had inconveniently died of a fever after delivering a stillborn heir.

So far, his search for a new Queen had not produced a woman of enough substance to rule alongside him. He needed a queen who was made of the same steely stuff as he was. But someone who was not so power hungry that she would seek him quietly murdered in his bed and take over his Kingdom for herself.

None had seemed worthy. He needed a Queen like Jezebel. But then she was a Queen to a weakened King whose decisions were dominated by her. He could not show himself to be a weak king.

"Tell me Bishop Rawlin, what does the Pope require of us this time?" asked the King.

"A mere trifle," replied Bishop Rawlin, noisily sucking the grease from his fingers. "There is an uprising of heretics in the South and they are spreading teachings that are of a great evil. One that will surely destroy the people," continued the Bishop, snapping his fingers at a peasant to bring his own personal finger bowl.

He thought this ridiculously lean King only kept enough treasures to show strength to other Kings, but not enough to show true power. He refused the Bishop the honour he deserved. He did not even keep jewel-encrusted gold finger bowls. Why be a king if you behaved like a commoner? But, no matter, the Bishop brought his own treasures with him, and no one would deny this sign of opulence - not if they valued their throne or soul.

"I fail to see what this has to do with us. Surely the Pope's army is capable of snuffing out this uprising or are the peasant offerings waning?" tested King Radolf as far as he dared. Bishop Rawlin's eyes narrowed for the briefest moment as he absorbed the King's trace of sarcasm. He added his best diplomatic smile before answering.

"Of course, this campaign is well within the Church's resources. Yet one must always think of the future. A prudent man and all that sort of thing. As you know a full-bellied warrior will fight for longer. We would not want the enemy to reach your Kingdom and then find the Pope reluctant to send his weary army to assist you in your battles."

King Radolf picked up his most prized dagger, with a fine steel blade and elaborate dragon forged out of silver and steel. It was said to have been designed by two craftsmen. It was a blend of the best of art and the deathly precision of an assassin. He had plucked it from the dying hand of a noble who dared to defy him. He kept few treasures. But he had a passion for daggers.

Daggers were personal defense tools, a sort of last resort of personal protection. By the time you had broken down the defenses of a castle and reached the inner chambers of a noble or King, or even one of their women, victory was within your sights. This is where the true test of strength was. A one-on-one battle, where only the strength of your body and the steel of your mind would win.

His display of daggers was a show of personal power, and a reminder to those who managed to enter his inner circle of what could become of anyone who defied him. He would love to use it on this worm of leadership. But why waste a blade on someone so far beneath his dignity.

Instead, he used it to slice off the head of the suckling pig that lay before them. Then he made slices into the face and finally removed the eyeball, plunged the dagger into the center, which sent a splattering of some of the inner juices directly into the Bishop's face. King Radolf ate the eyeball slowly, all the while staring at the Bishop.

King Radolf purposefully cleaned the blade, while watching the Bishop with amused, cold eyes. "Of course, you shall have your special tax Bishop Rawlin. I shall send my collectors to announce to the people that the Pope's army needs our assistance."

Bishop Rawlin shuddered involuntarily, as he wiped some of the eye juice from his robes. He was aware of the King's collection of daggers and very aware that this was a display of unspoken power. "It is God's army that your people will be helping," retorted the Bishop.

At this King Radolf could feel the bile rising in his throat. His one shred of humanity lay in his connection to his mother, whose life had been cut short through the lies spread about good and evil. The God she had served would not condemn innocent people to death through self-serving lies.

"Bishop Rawlin, the decree will go out as the Pope's army or not at all. When your great Paul, whose letters you so readily recite, had his encounter with your Christ, he stopped persecuting. When the Christ comes to tell me that He wants me to finance the Pope's army, then my decree will say 'God's army,' but until then, you will have my money, but not my words." King Radolf spat, showing a thread of the contempt he had for the Bishop.

He snapped his fingers at his scribe. "Scribe make out the decree for Bishop Rawlin. But know this, should it deviate from the words that I, your King have spoken, not one of your relatives will live to tell the tale. Your children's heads will adorn the spikes outside this Kingdom with your own, and their entrails will feed the birds."

He threw two bags of gold at the Bishop's plate. "My dear Bishop, here is your customary travel gift. You may tell the Pope that our "*offering*" to his interpretation of God's work will be ready by the next full moon.

King Radolf retired to his personal chambers. He removed a small gold key from his neck and opened the secret compartment in the chest. In the bottom was a small leather-bound book no bigger than the palm of his hand. On the first page was a portrait of his mother. The second page had been torn out by the King's own young hand. The pages had read, "for God so loved the world." He stared at his mother's face. She had tried to spread these words of love to her people. But in the end, this 'love' had been the weakness that cost her, her life. The Friars had tried to protect her and scurried her away to the monasteries, where the monks had also tried to protect her. But one of the Bishop's spies had found her. To retain his Kingdom, King Radolf's father was forced to denounce his wife and her teachings. This had come after not only the threat of excommunication, but also at the hand of a holy torturer. In the remaining years, the emotionally defeated King had become a shadow of a man, filled with impotent regret.

The young prince had learned to despise his father's weakness; despise the Bishop's ruthless rule. And he turned against the 'love' that did nothing to protect his beautiful mother.

It had hardened and blackened his heart.

He did not see that perseverance in the face of persecution is an act of sacrifice. He only knew that he was abandoned, that she had left him with a weak father, who spent no time with the young Prince.

The sight of the young Prince had only fueled his father's regret. The Prince was left to mourn his mother alone, with his only companions, indifferent tutors.

"I am sorry mother," said Prince Radolf. "I cannot follow your ways. But I will exact my revenge. I will make them pay for what they did to you. I will show them that strength is the only way to rule. I will be the King that my father never was."

NINE

Yakhal

No, No!" The terrified screams echoed through the stone walls of the stronghold. "Please, tell the King that I will do better next time. No, don't let them take me there."

Yakhal had heard screams before. The stronghold was a place of despair.

Yet, he knew no fear in this place. Galdolf had always kept him safe. But this time it was different. Yakhal felt afraid. He did not know what the feeling was, only that he knew he needed to get away from something. And quickly.

His talons gripped the cage bars. He stared at the small window at the top. It called to him.

Guards roughly pushed the man down the stairs. The inmate tumbled, crying out with fright.

"I will take him from here," said Galdolf. One of the guards scoffed. "The merciful Galdolf. I have no idea why the King has such a weakling in this position." Not easily baited, Galdolf's fingered his own ear.

"It seems that you need another lesson in hearing."

The guard's eyes widened, and his hand grabbed hold of his ear, where a small section of the lobe had been torn away. A training exercise had left its mark. A reminder that Galdolf's quick cunning in battle could teach a man a lesson without the need for unnecessary brutality.

Humiliated, the guard snorted.

"Enjoy your spoils. There will come another day," he warned. "Perhaps then, I will get a chance to play with your new toy," he said sneering at Yahkal.

Galdolf took a step towards the young dragon, his hand already on the hilt of his sword. "Need I remind you that King Radolf wants this hatchling to reach fully grown status. Do you think that the King will take only your ear? I think the Ravens may find that you add some extra spice to their daily meals." He narrowed his eyes. "I hear they favour the eyes first. It is the juiciest and easiest part to pluck."

The guard's hand disobeyed his mind. He rubbed at his eye, a sure sign that Galdolf's threat had hit its mark. Just yesterday another head had adorned the row of spikes outside the castle. The ravens grew fat with a steady supply of delicacies.

The guard kicked the prisoner in retaliation. "Bah. You and

your games," he shot a parting comment at Galdolf.

"Come on" called the other guard. "Enough with your duelling. Our shift is about the end. And there is ale and that pretty waitress waiting for me at the tavern. You can wash away the bruised pride there."

The new inmate lay clutching his side. He groaned.

Galdolf reached down. Pressing he could feel no broken ribs.

"There is nothing to heal. Just the start of a broken spirit," he soothed. The prisoner shot a vengeful glance at Galdolf, then quickly looked away. Galdolf looked again at the man. This inmate had been through these gates before. He was sure of it. Leaving the prison usually heralded death. But here lay a survivor. "Why?" Galdolf was silent in his pondering.

He lifted the inmate to his feet. "Welcome back. The King must have something special planned for you. Here are your new chambers. I hope that you will find them to your liking." he smirked.

Again, came the poisonous glare. "Really?"

"Is that the way it is going to be? You will find that your stay here will be vastly improved if you find a little humour in life," he instructed.

Yakhal grew agitated. He chirped a warning. Inmates came and went. But today was different. Yakhal quickly jumped from bar to bar in the cage. His talons noisily chattering on the metal bars.

Galdolf was puzzled. He had never seen Yakhal climb. He remembered racing home to find his own boy taking his first uncertain steps.

He quickly pressed the inmate into the cell. Fumbling for the keys, he locked the gate and hurried towards Yakhal. A glow of pride spread over his face as he watched his ward jump from bar to bar until he reached the window.

An inky black sky speckled with stars greeted the effort. Yakhal chirped and craned his neck to see more.

A wave of sadness washed away Galdolf's pride. He looked away lest Yakhal should see it. A hatchling needed the sky. But as Prison Master, he was powerless to give it to him.

The dragon chirped again, calling to Galdolf. Yahkal wanted to show off. "Ah, the stars. They speak to you," smiled Galdolf. The scales on Yakhal's body glowed. A shimmer of silver. Yakhal's little wings spread out, in the way a man spreads his arms does when he feels the first rays of summer sunshine on his back.

It was a life force moment. The Silver Wing grew, his body arching to give free rein to the surge. Galdolf saw the full joy permeate his body. Even the stars in the sky seemed to dance.

From deep in the tunnels, Muquin felt the surge. It had called her from her sleep. The hatchling. She could feel it. Where was it? She sensed the pride of a father. But it was not Megadaeus. It was the pride of her hatchling's bond. For the briefest moment, she felt peace. Then the relentless sadness came.

The new inmate rattled at the cell, breaking the spell of the moment. Yakhal and Galdolf were roughly returned to the gloominess of the prison. Muquin felt them withdraw. She felt numb.

Somewhere in the distance, Nadine felt a sense of joy surge through her, but then a sense of melancholy hurriedly swept it away.

In the East, a falling star lit up the sky like a single glistening teardrop.

TEN

Forever Gone Lake

The wispy outstretched fingers of the Lake beckoned to Nadine. For a moment she stood mesmerized by its sinister milky embrace.

She pulled her gaze back to the shore and looked around for a boat. She could vaguely make out the form of two boats in the mist. Choosing the smaller of the two, she tried to push it towards the water's edge. She may as well have tried to uproot an oak by hand. The boat stubbornly resisted her efforts.

"Cursed boat!" she shouted. Then gritting her teeth, she pushed from deep within her soul as she willed the boat forward. Her muscles screamed with the effort. Sweat stung her eyes. But she remained steadfast, fueled by the burning desire to see her family. She would not fail.

The boat lurched forward. The sudden movement threw her off balance. The gravelly shoreline stung her palms, and the impact grazed her knee. But Nadine threw herself back at the boat and pushed forward once more. Finding the moist sand of the water's edge, the boat now slid silently into the lake.

Grabbing an oar, she pushed the boat deeper into the water. She washed off the grit peppered with drops of blood from her hands and steadied her mind. She tore off a piece of the hem of her tunic and wrapped up her palms to protect the broken skin from the splintery oars.

The mist seemed to creep up the side of the boat, calling her to join the souls in the inky depths below. Nadine shook her head. This was not the time to let superstitious tales wrap a blanket of fear around her mind. She picked up the oars and rowed towards the unseen center of the lake. She had underestimated the sheer weight of the boat and strained to find a rhythm. But gradually the waters began to release their iron grip on the boat, and she found to her relief that she was moving.

The mist jealously guarded any view of the sun. Nadine began to feel the teasing fingers of despair coaxing her to give in to their embrace. She had never travelled beyond the borders of the village. She had no way of marrying time and distance.

Doubts began to dance in her mind. They craftily shone a light on the ache of her upper arms, which burned from heaving the oars. The weight of the responsibility she bore seemed to add to the burning pain in her neck and shoulders.

Tiber's tiny body stretched the sleep from her joints, as Nadine silently fought her demons. Playfully awake now, she plunged her needle-like claws into Nadine's leg. The sharp pain yanked Nadine from her brooding. "Tiber!" she yelled, rubbing the sting from her shins. "How many times have I told you, I am not a scratching post." Tiber's gentle green eyes stared at Nadine as if innocent of any wrongdoing. She butted her head on Nadine's outstretched hand. Despite the gloomy surroundings, Nadine laughed. "Thank you, Tiber," she said, rewarding the little cat's rescue with a tasty treat.

Nadine built a rhythm by counting her strokes. The counting allowed her to focus on the task at hand and did not leave room for other thoughts.

After every hundred strokes, she would stop, rest and eat something small. As the day stretched on, the sun banished the mist and Nadine began the feel a renewed glimmer of hope.

Tiber reached up to the edge of the boat and with her paws dangling over the edge, watched the swirling ripples as the oars pushed the murky water back. "Get back here, girl. The water is not safe." Tiber's pretty face stared at Nadine as if to say, "Why do you always have to spoil my fun?"

Soon fatigue began to leave telltale signs of the hours of physical work. The oars frequently slipped, and Nadine started to lose count of her strokes. She could feel the chill begin to envelop them as the sun set. "Time for bed, Tiber," Nadine told the little cat, stroking her silky fur. She picked her up and rubbed her cheek against the softness of Tiber's body, cuddling her for a moment. The soft warmth relaxed Nadine and she happily chatted while they ate their meat and cookies together.

She untied her pack and pulled a warm fur over them both. Nadine's body soon welcomed sleep's embrace.

Φ

The great bird's piercing yellow eyes searched for movement. His magnificent black wings welcomed the freedom that the rush of air sliding under his powerful body provided. King of the sky, the eagle's razor-sharp talons were primed to pierce the flesh of any victim. The pointed tip of his beak demanded the sacrifice of a fresh kill. He would tear the flesh of his prey. His lust for blood was the fuel that would preserve his fearsome reputation of the deadliest hunter of the skies.

Far below, Tiber's white paws beckoned to the eagle. Focusing his eyes, the eagle circled, then with a piercing screech the great bird dropped out of the sky and sped towards the kitten.

The bird's cry as it reached for the kitten snatched Nadine from sleep. Its enormous wings beat past her face, and it angled its feet ready to grasp the kitten in its talons. Tiber's tiny feline form narrowly missed being impaled. Instead, the eagle's enormous talons encircled her torso. Nadine's blood rang in her ears. She screamed. Grabbing the dagger from its sheath in her boot, Nadine lunged forward, propelling her body into the air.

The blade sank into the flesh of the eagle, and it released its grip on the kitten's body, plunging Tiber into the icy depths of Forever Gone Lake. Nadine leapt into the frigid water, watching as Tiber flayed helplessly just out of reach.

The icy water forced the air out of Nadine's lungs with a gasp of shock. Panic gripped her. Nadine kicked frantically but her foot hooked on one of the predatory lake plants waiting below. Its snake-like tentacles began to creep around her leg, sucking her down. Nadine screamed – a primal scream of terror that echoed over the lake's surface. She was trapped. The lake sought to claim her.

Seeing Tiber's wild and frightened eyes, Nadine fought and kicked again, which served only to tighten the plant's grip. "Be still and know that I am God." The words echoed in her mind. A passage read to her by her father.

"Be still Nadine," she told herself. A calm clarity of thought filled her. Reaching for the knife in the sheath on her arm, Nadine held her breath and dived under the surface. She couldn't see anything in the darkness, but she felt for the stems capturing her leg and sawed through them. Finally, they released their grip and the plants fell silently back to the depths. Nadine's lungs were screaming for air as she burst to the surface. She gasped and gulped to get her breath back and turned to search for Tiber.

The little cat was struggling and beginning to sink. Nadine grabbed a handful of sodden fur and lifted Tiber's face out of the water. Flattening her body, she swam towards the boat and tossed the cat to safety. Then she clawed her way over the side and heaved her own sodden body into the boat.

Nadine fell back. She stared at Tiber's lifeless form for no more than a moment. Pushing at the little cat's body, Nadine began to massage and squeeze. Tiber sputtered and then vomited the remaining water out. She was going to be alright!

Overhead, the injured eagle screeched and plummeted one last time to the water below. Nadine stretched out the oar and claimed the fallen eagle as her spoils of war. She rubbed Tiber's shivering body with their sleeping fur, then wrapping it around herself she pulled off her tunic and placed it on the seat to dry. Then she pulled the cat close to her body to keep them both warm in the chilly morning air.

The day began to warm, and with no one in sight, Nadine dropped the blanket and covered the early blossom of womanhood with her tunic, which had dried quickly in the sun.

The massive eagle's body almost filled the boat. Nadine plucked some of the feathers from the breast of the giant bird. She sawed through the muscle and finding the liver, cut it out for Tiber. "There you go young lady," she gallantly presented the meat to the cat. "I think it's fitting that you claim the first portion."

The ancients had a practice of devouring the liver of their victims which was said to infuse the warriors with their power. The little cat's terror from the morning's attack was still evident. Nadine sought to ignite Tiber's instincts by claiming the eagle as her prize. Watching the little cat eat, Nadine felt a change come over her.

The shock of the attack had drawn something out of Nadine that she hadn't felt before - a primal thirst for survival. Except for the odd stinging bug, Nadine had never killed anything. Now, as she watched the cat, she felt powerful. For the first time, she felt as if she could succeed. Before, the urgency she felt came from the thought that she must not fail. But now as her power grew, she could almost trace the emerging form of victory in her mind.

She recalled the old passage her father had read to her from the Psalms: "When the wicked came against me to eat up my flesh, my enemies, my foes, they stumbled and fell." She felt exhilarated. What a tale she would share when she saw her father again.

Sleep came happily to Nadine that night. She would spend this last night on the lake filled with hope. In the distance, she saw the island of the Ancients; a man-made island of oak and rock. As the boat glided past its shore, she could see the tools hanging just below the water's surface. Legend told that the Ancients believed that heaven lay below the depths of land and water. They had constructed this island linked by underwater poles and suspended tools for the dead to use in the afterlife.

Thinking about the ancient's bodies that were said to be buried there sent a chill up her spine. She shook off the feeling and counted her strokes out loud to fill her ears with the sound of an earthly voice.

By midmorning, the boat bumped noisily onto the edge of the shoreline. Climbing out of the boat, Nadine stretched to ease the stiffness of her joints. She managed to drag the boat onto the beach and gratefully secured it to a stump. A nearby bush provided shelter for some of her excess equipment.

She made a small fire on the shore and prepared a smoking circle. With some loose leaves and sticks she fanned the smoke to preserve some of the meat from the bird.

She was as careful to keep the feathers of the eagle. They would fetch a good price from the quill maker. Smiling to herself, she also put aside one of the larger feathers for Tiber. They would have a fine game later.

Nadine reorganised their provisions. She picked up Tiber and stepped through the clearing of the trees, ready to make her way to Holly Hill Cave.

ELEVEN

Dissent

The villagers had been trapped in the tunnel for days. The gnawing hunger in Judas' belly consumed his mind. He had watched how mothers had daily fed their loathsome children tiny slithers of the dried meat that that girl had divided amongst them.

He swallowed hard to fight against his rising nausea. If he could just find something to eat... How much longer would they be in this miserable hole for?

The children of the three so-called leaders of this pathetic pack seemed none the worse for wear, to his mind. The fact that all the men suffered, did not even occur to him.

His naturally nervous nature was amplified by his hunger, as his body began to turn on itself, first harvesting what fat he had in his body and then beginning to eat at his muscles.

He had taken to picking at a scab on his ankle, from a cut that occurred when they had first fallen into the pit. The wound, although small to start with, had begun to fester due to his constant nervous picking. He watched with disgust as the villagers had squatted in their allocated waste spot. He had tried to relieve himself only when the rest of the villagers were asleep. But always one of those three were watching.

"If I could but create a small chink in their armour, then I could find a way to overthrow them," he muttered under his breath. His deceitful eyes narrowed as he looked for a way. Then he spotted the wine merchant. Known for drinking away the profits, the wine merchant was always short of coin for his taxes. He had only managed to escape the debtor's prison by offering the tax collector a constant supply of free wine.

The wine merchant had suffered first, as his supply of wine had suddenly been cut off. His body had been wracked by the shudders of a man who was wrestling with demons.

Judas began to sow little seeds of discontent into the wine merchant's already tormented mind.

"Brother," Judas said slyly as he settled down next to the wine merchant. He used the Christian greeting, reserved for those who wished to spread the teachings of a loving Christ. "You and I suffer together," he said in a fake soothing voice. "Was it not I who saved you from the debtor's prison?"

The wine merchant moved his pounding head to face Judas. Pressing his hands against his throbbing temples, he nodded slowly, as if every movement caused unbearable pain.

"Yet, these men, these three, what have they done for us?" he asked. "One of them is already weakened by his leg wound. But does his suffering make him feel for us? No, if anything, it makes him more self-preserving," he sneered.

"They even presume to tell us where to squat. Now, we must live in this rotting stink-hole." He spat out the last words to demonstrate his disgust. Although at night when the dragon had been out hunting, he had witnessed either the tanner or the blacksmith looking out for ways to escape their stone prison, he did not share this knowledge with the wine merchant. In his paranoia, he did not realize that these men returned to their prison to report that there was no visible way out. If they had found a way out and did not have the villagers' best interests at heart, they would not have returned.

The dragon obviously knew the way out.

But she had never left a trace of her exit route. So, try as they may, they could not find it. Yet still night after night the search continued.

It was true that Nicolous was succumbing to his injuries. The pain had intensified and now only his single-mindedness in keeping his family safe was the driving force that kept him hanging on. His wife and daughter had prayed for him each day and did what best they could to comfort him, but without healing herbs and nourishment to fuel his body to fight the infection, his strength was being drained day by day. But paradise would have to wait. While on this earth, he would be their shepherd, just as the Lord was his.

The trio had watched Judas since their arrival. Although he had not yet made a direct move against them, they all knew that it was a matter of time until he snapped. Each day he had unravelled a little more and his nervous tension was like a festering boil that needed to be lanced. But now the infection of his discord had spread to others through his lies. One or two of the starving villagers began to share glances.

Φ

Muquin had gone out for her nightly hunt. It was now time to care for the villagers. As Maireid moved around the small children, trying to comfort them even in her own weakened state, her ankle accidentally brushed against Judas. She paused for a moment to work out who she had touched when suddenly he pounced on her. He grabbed her by the neck and unravelling a woven cord, he wrapped it around her neck and began to back away into the tunnels.

Nicolous forced himself up, but the pain sent him tumbling back down to the ground. "Get back, or I will snap the girl's neck" screamed Judas. The tanner and the blacksmith steadily and slowly got up.

"Do not be a fool Judas," said the blacksmith. "Let the girl go. No good can come of this."

"What do you know of good? The three of you sit merrily there while the rest of us suffer." Judas felt his world closing in around him. His eyes darted back and forth, watching as the men inched step by step toward him.

Using his wife's support, Nicolous was able to ease himself up into standing position. "Maireid," he called in a steady and calm voice. Her eyes, wild with fear, found the source of her father's voice.

Nicolous' steady warm brown eyes calmed her. For a moment, he held her gaze. He willed her to keep her eyes fixed on him. A calmness came over her as she slowed her breathing. Her father rolled his one shoulder and turned his head slightly. It was a deliberate movement which she immediately understood.

Ignoring the pressure against her neck, she turned in towards her attacker's body, which released the airway on one side of her neck. Then she bit down hard on his arm.

Judas screamed in pain. He grabbed wildly at Maireid. But she was already running towards her father.

Suddenly the tanner, finding a clear gap, threw a dagger directly at Judas, piercing his heart. Judas slumped to the ground, yet another casualty of their captivity.

Maireid fell sobbing into her mother's arms. Her father, still holding onto his wife for balance, encircled his daughter with his free arm and kissed her gently on the top of her head. They had survived another day in the tunnels.

But would they survive long enough for Nadine to find help? There were many dangers on the path to Holly Hill Cave. Few dared to travel the path alone. Dorothea pushed back her fear for Nadine's safety to comfort Maireid. But her thoughts returned to her younger daughter. It was so great a burden for Nadine. She knew her daughter had a determined spirit. But would it be enough to save them?

TWELVE

Nathan

S unlight streamed through the canopy of leaves as Nadine entered the ancient forest. Her breath danced in white wisps in the late autumn air. Ahead she heard men talking. She drew Tiber closer in the bag beneath her cloak.

Nadine pulled herself up to the safety of the branches of a tall ancient oak. She could see a group of men, two of them heaving under the weight of a fallen tree on the path. An embroidered banner signalled that a high-ranking Lord was in the group.

From between the trees, three warriors appeared like silent ghosts. An arrow whistled through the air striking a horse's flank.

The burning pain of the arrow tearing through its flesh caused the frightened beast to rear. Its rider's bone-crushing decent echoed through the trees, the agony of the jolt vibrating through his body.

"Bandits!" bellowed the Lord. Spinning around, the men at the trunk grabbed their swords. They roared towards the intruders. Swords danced before Nadine's eyes with the ringing sound of clashing metal in close combat. The echo of the blades rang in Nadine's ears. She was innocent in the ways of war, and she felt a cold ball of fear in her stomach.

Using defensive moves, the intruders sought to stop, but not kill, the travellers. With a circular formation, they used their shields to drive the men back. More roughly dressed bandits poured into the clearing. Outnumbered, the travellers retreated.

Nadine saw that the Lord had found himself isolated. From behind another tree a scarred man appeared and grabbed the back of the Lord's neck. He thrust a blade at the Lord's throat, stopping just short of its mark. Nadine could tell that he was their leader. Two more bandits reinforced their leader's position. The Lord was trapped.

"Lay down your weapons," the leader roared. The travellers obeyed. A tense silence formed around the group.

"We mean you no harm. But if you provoke us, you will die." he roared. He signalled to one of his fellow bandits. "Get the banner." he ordered. Raising the crumpled banner from the ground, the bandit revealed the identity of the Lord. The bandit leader caressed the blade on the Lord's face as he smiled. "Well Lord Logan, we shall soon see how well you are loved by your people."

"Now ride," he ordered his man who held the banner." The

man attempted to claim the stallion, but it reared, throwing the man into the sandy path.

The other bandits roared with laughter. "Too much mead last night?" jested the leader. More humiliated than injured, the offended bandit mounted a tamer mare and raced off with the banner.

"Now Lord Logan, if you please, we invite you all to be our guests until your ransom arrives." Over his shoulder, he called, "Bring the horses."

One man tried to subdue the stallion. But the beast would not be calmed. "Leave it!" called the chief. "It will only be a hindrance."

Outnumbered, Lord Logan and his men submitted and began the journey on foot to the bandit's lair. A scrambling sound alerted the party. They paused, cocking their heads to listen for another sound. From her vantage point, Nadine could see a boy on the brink of manhood making his way through the trees.

Nadine almost gasped out loud. Twisting around Lord Logan held up his hand and then dropped it again. At the signal, the boy dropped out of sight.

"What was that?" demanded the chief. "I seek to calm the stallion," replied Lord Logan.

As if on cue the stallion reared again. His eyes darting around, the chief scanned the area and then turned, leading his men through the trees. The forest swallowed the defeated travellers, as they trudged towards an uncertain fate.

Nadine clung to the tree trunk trying to steady herself, her heart thundering in her chest. For what seemed like an eternity the boy remained hidden. When all was quiet again, he emerged. The movement disturbed the distressed stallion, who reared once more.

Although he was tall and looked strong enough, Nadine sensed that he could not calm the horse. Nadine climbed down and approached cautiously.

The boy lunged for a discarded sword. He spun around with the sword extended. The tip greeted Nadine's face. Her brilliant blue-green eyes transformed his defiant look into a dumbfounded stare. Nadine's mouth curved into a faint grin and a mischievous glint appeared in her eyes.

"Are you in need of assistance with this horse?" she asked. Dropping his sword hand and eyeing her, he asked: "Who are you and where do you come from?"

"I am Nadine. I come from across Forever Gone Lake and I am travelling to Holly Hill Cave to find help for my captured family. I see that you have had some adventures of your own. May I ask your name?"

"I am Nathan. I was travelling with my Lord Logan, when the party was ambushed," he told her, with slumped shoulders.

"Yes, I saw the whole thing," she replied.

"May I?" she asked gesturing at the horse.

"He cannot be subdued," Nathan told her.

"Is that so?" replied Nadine with slight annoyance. Nadine's grandfather had a way with horses. He had instructed her. The magnificent stallion was a true noble's horse. Its finely chiseled face, long arching neck and deep muscular chest, showed it to be a distinctive breed.

Nadine gently removed Tiber from her pouch. She kissed the little cat and hand fed her a slither of dried meat. Eager for more,

Tiber searched Nadine's outstretched hand. Gently lowering the cat, Nadine dropped a few slithers on the ground and let Tiber enjoy her feast as she moved towards the horse.

Nathan strained to hear as Nadine approached the horse speaking in hushed tones. The stallion eyed her nervously, ready to bolt at the slightest sound. Nadine let her hand linger as she touched the powerful body. She slid the palm of her hand over its quaking muscular form, all the while soothing and coaxing it into a calmer state. The horse relaxed. It snorted softly, and the once panicked bursts of his breathing slowed to an even rhythm. The back leg was twitching, so she slowly moved her way down, never changing her pace and pressure. Nadine rhythmically rocked her body in time to the horse's breathing. Like a mother rocking her baby to sleep.

She slid her hand down, caressing the stallion's leg. Finally, she felt the source of its discomfort. There was a large thorn lodged in the horse's leg. Slightly increasing the pressure, she swiftly grabbed the thorn and forcefully yanked it out, tossing it behind her. "There, there, now you can be free again. Keeping the same pace, she slowly ran her hand back up the horse's body. Then untying the reins, she eased them forward and led him to the food parcel that was secured at another tree.

"Where did you learn to do that?" Nathan asked in awe.

"I am a girl of great mystery." she toyed. "Now let us speak of important matters," she said, her mood changed. "Who are you and why were you and your companions on this road?"

"I am a groom for the House of Logan. We were travelling towards the Town of Moores to find a medicine woman to help my master find a cure for his wife. She has an illness that no one can help. I was getting water when we were attacked.

"Look," said Nadine, "I think that we may be able to help each other" I am going to Holly Hill Cave to see the Dragon Whisperer. Along this same road is the Town of Moores. If we travel together, we can stop there to find medicine. Then if we go to Holly Hill Cave and meet the Dragon Whisperer, perhaps he will also be able to help."

"How will a Dragon Whisperer be able to help me to get my master back?" asked Nathan.

"Dragon Whisperers are said to be able to see through the eyes of dragons and call out memories of things that Dragons have seen," replied Nadine. "If the Dragon Whisperer can get in touch with a Dragon who roams these parts, perhaps he can plot out a map of how to reach your master."

"Honestly I will find it difficult to travel this great distance by myself and so having a horse will help greatly. I have enough provisions to keep us both fed until we get to the Town of Moores," she continued.

Nathan thought about how easily Nadine had soothed the horse and could see how working together might well be to their advantage. This was what his master would have called a win-win situation.

"The horse will suffer if we ride today. Although it was just a thorn, our weight will cause pain. We must set up camp, to allow it to rest," said Nadine.

"Agreed. But let's travel by foot a short distance. I don't want to set up camp here," suggested Nathan

Nadine said a silent prayer of thanks for getting this far and for the gift of the horse. She thought of her mother, who always told her that grateful people were always happier people. As Nadine calculated that this was her third day since her family was captured, she wondered how her mother would find a way to be grateful at this time.

They selected a place to camp away from the road, which helped soothe their nerves. Seated by a fire, Nathan began to feel the shock of the attack. "I do not know where they have taken him," he lamented.

"I expect to the Ancient's ruins" replied Nadine.

"What is that?" he asked.

"A wise ancient people lived there, close to nature. They were scholars, healers and keepers of the law. But they are all gone now," Nadine explained.

"Gone? But to where?" asked Nathan

"My mother says that people who are misunderstood are often feared. She says that many healers were trained there. But because they healed so well, some of the other healers grew jealous. They said that it was impossible for diseases to be cured so quickly without witchcraft. The lies they spread made people even more fearful. Soon campaigns started to drive them away. Some were killed. But some fled their homes. Eventually, none were left."

"But why would the bandits take my lord there?" Nathan asked.

"Do you go to places that you are afraid of?" asked Nadine?

"Not usually," he replied

"Well, there is your answer. Fear. People are afraid of the ruins. They believe that the spirits of the ancients are still there, waiting to cast spells of vengeance."

"Do you believe that?" asked Nathan

"No. Not really. I think that they are just stories to frighten children from coming to visit this place. They never wrote things down like the Christian monks. They passed on what they knew by stories. There is no way to see if what is being said rings true with any written down stories. But people say that inside the stone walls are carvings."

"What kinds of carvings?" asked Nathan intrigued.

"How should I know? I have never been into any of them?" snapped Nadine.

Embarrassed by her over-reaction, Nadine quickly continued. "But these trees, these ancient oaks were especially important to them. And the ruins were built to show the setting sun for as long as possible."

"If you have not been in there, how you know all this?" Nathan challenged her.

"My grandmother knew one of the ancients. She spoke of it to my mother."

Nadine and Nathan spoke about their adventures so far.

Nathan had been orphaned in the sickness that had swept across the country a few years earlier but had been taken in by the local clergy, who had found him employment with his master. Nathan spoke of the horror of the plague and how entire villages had been wiped out. The very young and very old had died first and then the disease had lingered with the remaining adults until all of them had been taken. Nathan had been the only survivor. He had never gotten ill and the monks had believed that he had immunity to the disease.

"I used to wish that I had died in that plague. The horror of the oozing pus that came from the sores still sometimes haunts my dreams. It had a foul stench. One that would make your stomach lurch. Their faces became hollow, making their eyes look enormous. And their throats would begin to close, making it difficult to breathe. They could no longer swallow, which meant that they also began to starve. They turned into rasping, clawing wrecks of people. Many people fled from their own families when the sickness came. Only the bravest stayed to care for the sick until they too succumbed to the plague."

Nathan stared out into the distance in silence for a moment. His eyes filled with tears at the memories that now rushed back. Nathan had a sorrow that never seemed to leave him. It lingered just below the surface of his mind. His dreams for many months had been of his skeleton-like mother choking out her last gasps of air, while her nails dug into his arm in her final moments of life. Her once beautiful hair hung in sparse oily clumps from her head. He felt robbed of her and angry at his inability to help.

Nathan sniffed, exhaled and steadied himself. He looked at Nadine and could see that she felt his pain. He wondered if she thought that he was weak because he had cried. But he saw no condemnation. He only saw compassion. She too sniffed, wiped her eyes and gave him a soft smile. To connect with another human being was a special thing. Nadine could sense that by talking about his ordeal, Nathan had taken another step towards healing.

Thankfully, working for Lord Logan had kept Nathan's mind more occupied and allowed less time for dwelling on loss and sorrow. He had seen even great men lose their drive and will to succeed by focusing on loss and the past. The depression was as devastating to the soul as the plague had been to the body. He instinctively knew that being connected to others and doing tasks every day would be his best defense against the cold blackness that had captured the hearts of so many after the devastation of the plague.

Nathan told Nadine of Lord Logan and Lady Christine. Lord Logan was a kind master and treated Nathan as well as a father would. In fact, Nathan knew that a great many men did not treat even their own sons kindly at all. In a time where fathers could administer severe beatings to children who defied them, many a boy could be seen to bear evidence of this form of discipline. He was he therefore grateful that he had a master of this calibre. Nathan knew that Lord Logan had a heart for young people.

While Lord Logan would never directly and publicly criticize a father whom he suspected of beating a child, he had other ways of dealing with these men. He was often heard to say "It is a great tragedy when a man cannot lead his family. Beatings are a mark of a man who has not yet earned the respect of his family to make the best decisions for them."

These comments, coupled by his example, showed the people that there was a better way to win the hearts and loyalty of others.

Nathan had a room set up next to the stables. Although he was not family, Lady Christine had insisted that his room be furnished in the same manner she would have chosen if she had a son of her own. He had a comfortable bed, a side table, an oil lamp, curtains, a table and chairs, a washbasin, and a small library of books. Lady Christine had insisted that he be taught to read and write and learn to ride, fish and hunt. In addition, he also had a small stove, where he could prepare basic meals and warm the room in winter.

"Once a week, I work in the kitchens so that I can learn to cook. Lord Logan wants more than pottage when he is on a journey." He tried not to boast but felt genuinely proud of what he had become. While most of his clothes were work clothes, he also had a set of smart clothes for attending village functions.

"Every fortnight Lady Christine invites me for tea and teaches me table manners and how to treat a lady in a proper and refined manner. After tea, she would always send me off with a batch of special treats for me to enjoy in my room. I sometimes trade these with the other servants for things that I really want."

"Lady Christine told me that she believes that God sent me to them for a reason and that I should have the opportunity to improve myself in life." Then Nathan lowered his eyes and shyly told Nadine, "Lady Christine says that she wants me to be able to treat a lady as kindly as Lord Logan had treated her."

"I cannot bear to see Lady Christine suffer. I must see that she gets the care that she needs and find a way to return Lord Logan to her. I would not want her to feel the great sorrow of the lost family that I have felt."

"Did your village suffer from the illness?" he finally asked.

"No. My village was protected." Forever Gone Lake is our champion. It is said to suck the souls out of men. Few would dare take their chances. It keeps us protected from most diseases. Even our famous taxidermist's customers stopped coming in the time of the sickness."

"I think sometimes the things that we fear, or dislike, may be the things that God sends to protect us." Nadine was warmed by the thought of Nathan's great affection for his master and the Lady Christine and was determined to help them be reunited.

Nathan stared at the flames. The heat seemed to dance in a mesmerizing rhythm, twisting and curling. The light flickered across the trees in the forest, casting shadows. A sharp crackle of the logs brought Nathan's eyes back to Nadine.

"I should have been here to help," lamented Nathan.

"You are here," said Nadine.

"No, I mean, when the bandits came. I should have been here to help."

"I know what you mean. I am saying that you are here now. You are doing something. What good would it have done if you had also been captured?"

"I just feel so… so useless. It is like my family dying again. All I do is sit and watch. I do nothing." Nathan could not look at Nadine while he spoke. He stared at the flames.

Nadine fell silent, thinking about how she felt when the wall of fire roared between her and her family. Impotent regret was no stranger to her.

She moved closer, touching his shoulder, and she quietly said. "I feel your pain. But you are here now. You were spared for a reason. My parents, your new family…they need us. Regret has no place now." For a moment, their eyes locked. Nadine quickly looked away and poked at the fire with a stick. Sparks flew up in the air like fireflies dancing in the moonlight.

Nathan watched the way the flickering flames danced in Nadine's eyes.

They sat in silence.

Tiber lay quietly watching the flames dance, twisting and curling in the night air. Drawn by the light, a moth flickered by. Jumping up, Tiber's white paws flashed in the firelight in her pursuit of this new prey. Nathan smiled at the little cat's game. Then a sharp pain flashed through his leg as Tiber slashed at the moth that had come to rest on him. "Ouch!" he cried as he jumped away. "Nadine, your cat!"

Nadine could not speak. She was laughing too much.

"What a warrior you are Tiber," she said rubbing the little cat between the ears. "Even the great Nathan fears you."

"Humph!" sulked Nathan, rubbing his smarting leg. "It is no wonder that people think that cats are messengers of the devil," he grumbled.

"Or testers of a warrior's true courage?" teased Nadine.

Nathan continued rubbing his leg. "I think it's time to eat. Have you ever tasted roasted Tiber?"

"What?" cried Nadine. Now it was Nathan's turn to laugh. He shook a finger at Tiber. "That's what happens to naughty kittens who injure the cook," he mock-scolded the cat.

Nathan poked at the bubbling stew. He had used the eagle meat and infused it with roots and some of the chopped herbs he always carried on campaigns. The scent wafted through the air making Nadine's mouth water. Using some dry bread that Nathan had broken up to scoop the rich gravy, Nadine devoured the meal. It was delicious. She gleefully agreed to the second helping that he offered.

"Are all the women in your village as…. um… passionate about life as you are?" he asked with raised eyebrows.

"No. I cannot say that they are. My parents are always trying to make me more of a lady," replied Nadine, watching for his reaction.

"Well, perhaps the villagers should take some lessons from you," he grinned.

Nathan unrolled the furs and oilskins. "Let's get some rest. We have a long ride ahead of us tomorrow."

Nadine curled up with Tiber. Before long she was fast asleep. Nathan sat for a while watching the fire. Nadine flung off the fur in her sleep. He smiled. His father had many a morning stumbled, bleary-eyed, into the kitchen as he complained about the nocturnal thrashings of Nathan's mother. He reached over and covered her with the fur. Finding two large rocks, he pinned the furs down, to protect her from the night insects. His father had said it offered some relief from his wife's attacking legs.

Having Nadine close made him feel like he was home.

For the first time in as long as he could remember, Nathan slept a dreamless sleep.

He woke just as the forest leaves welcomed the sun's early morning embrace. In the quietness of the morning, he could hear a faint buzzing. "Honey!" he smiled in recognition. He sat quietly for a moment, listening for telltale sounds of intruders. He glanced at Nadine and smiled at the innocence of her still-dreaming face. Quietly gathering his tools and a smoldering stick from the night fire, he crept silently towards the sound of the buzzing.

The bees had formed their home in a weathered old tree trunk. Nathan waved the stick and released a whisp of smoke into the nest. A few lazy scouts flew out to investigate. With a cloth covered hand, Nathan reached for the sticky honeycombs. The first handfuls came away with ease. But then as the effects of the smoke wore off, the bees realized that the attack was real and gathered their troops for a full attack.

Pulling his searing hand away from the nest, Nathan ran as fast as he could to the river. The frigid morning temperature sucked out his breath as his body hit the water. The bees angrily buzzed their final warning before they returned to repair the damage he had caused.

Shivering, a sting-riddled Nathan bemoaned what it meant to be a man wanting to please the fairer sex.

Nathan lit the morning fire, with chattering teeth. He made a frame from sticks and hung out his drenched tunic to dry next to the fire. In case Nadine should awake, he left his breeches on but crept closer to the fire to keep warm. He then prepared the morning meal infusing it with the honey from his morning quest.

The fragrant smell of cooking gently roused Nadine from her dreams. She opened her eyes to find Nathan watching her. A glimpse of his muscular chest quickly made her look away. Nathan grabbed at the tunic scattering the frame of twigs and he hurriedly dressed his upper body.

Her face still flushed; Nadine made a fuss of Tiber. "Is it safe to look now?"

"Yes," replied Nathan, making a show of rearranging the cooking vessels.

Nathan boiled some of the crushed wheat from Nadine's provisions and mixed it with berries and some of the honey from his morning's adventures for their breakfast.

Nathan's face and arms showed the evidence of some bees

who had sought to punish the invader of their golden treasure. Nadine gave him one of her rare lopsided grins, that was reserved for when she was trying not to laugh and told him to keep still while she removed the stingers. Maireid, Nadine's older sister had experienced so many bee stings that Nadine had learned about removing the stingers by watching her father remove them from Maireid. The irony was that while Maireid never deliberately went looking for adventure, she was so often stung. Yet Nadine could not even remember if she had ever been stung. However, she knew that by leaving the sting in, there would be swelling.

Nathan was not a compliant patient at all. "Leave it" he cried, pulling away from her.

Nadine rolled her eyes. Why was it that boys and men always fought treatment?

"Nathan don't be stupid now. Some of these are on your hand. When they swell up, how will you be able to hold the reins? How will you be able to carry firewood? If the swelling slows us down, then both Lord Logan and my family will suffer."

Her arguments were sound, and Nathan could not find any logical counter argument, so he reluctantly submitted to the extraction. He gritted his teeth and despite one or two sudden expressions of pain endured the process without further protest.

He was still looking grumpy as he dished up breakfast for them. Even Tiber was enjoying some warm crushed wheat and honey that he had put out for her. As they ate Nadine felt a pang in her heart as she thought of her father, who also cooked so well. She tried to shake off the longing for her family and chatted to Nathan instead to lure him out of his self-pity. She tried not to smile, but she did think that it was silly that someone who was brave enough to care for sick and dying people could be such a baby about his own treatment.

After breakfast, Nadine checked the horse's leg. "His name is Brutus," Nathan told her. "Well Brutus, do you think you are ready?" asked Nadine, caressing his leg. "He is ready," she said. "But we will need to take it easy and rest him along the way."

Nathan wondered what the knights would say, hearing a village girl telling the stable boy what to do with a horse.

THIRTEEN

The Wolf

Eyes watched from the semi-shadows. Hunger driven eyes, searching. The memory of the night's smells around a cooking fire lingered in flared nostrils. Yellow eyes sparkled in anticipation. Her breath short, nervous, white bursts in the early morning air. Her dense cream and grey fur, once glossy, was matted and her ribs had begun to reveal themselves after the pups had arrived.

She lost her pack through the bandit's merciless hunt and her kin now adorned their shoulders in new fur-lined hoods.

She pawed the cold ground, eager, yet watching to remain

undetected. The humans were close, but she knew that they would not linger.

The night fire had roared, and the humans had slept so close to the fire that she dared not attack. But the many months of watching the bandits told her that in the early morning, mankind would mark their territories near trees that lead them away from the cooking fires. There could be a chance.

These humans also had with them a small creature that might take off the edge of the gnawing pains that filled her belly.

Her hungry mouth glistened with saliva. She could taste the kill as she inhaled its scent.

She had crept downwind so that the creature would not detect her. The male moved away to rearrange packages on the horse.

Alone and weakened, the wolf lacked the strength to bring down large prey by herself. With no pack, she did not have the herding strategy. But a small cat would be no match for a starving wolf.

Her speed, intelligence and jaws were her only allies. But this small creature would help her to nurse her pups for a few days. Darting back and forth, behind the trees, she waited for the female to move. Finally, the female left to go and relieve herself behind a tree. The small creature was staring at the dying embers of the cooking fire, her white neck an easy mark to target.

The wolf's paws merely kissed the ground as she flew to the spot where the creature sat. Sensing movement behind her, Tiber sprung away, her eyes wild with fright. With snapping jaws, the wolf lunged at Tiber. Missing her mark, she snarled. Her paw pinned the cat's tail.

"Tiber!" Nadine screamed, rushing forward from the trees. "Oh, God in heaven, save us." she cried.

The snarling wolf held fast to the crying prey's tail.

With spear in hand, Nathan raced towards the wolf. The wolf's eyes darted between Nathan and Nadine.

Nathan hesitated, knowing that these woods had a history of wolves with white-foam sickness. A human infected by white-foam sickness would eventually die. He'd had enough of sickness.

If the wolf was in the preliminary stages, it would not yet show the foam. Still, he hesitated.

Sensing his hesitation, the wolf's jaws snapped at the little cat.

"No!" screamed Nadine, diving onto the wolf. Her tail released for an instant, Tiber raced up a tree.

Now in battle with a worthier prey, the wolf snapped at Nadine. Nadine fought wildly, kicking, thrashing and screaming. Nathan felt powerless to attack. The wolf was a writhing target. One false move and Nathan would impale Nadine. The wolf snapped at Nadine's face, managed to bite a few tufts of her hair. Nadine wildly thrashed her arms, rolling over, trying to get away from the wolf. It snapped again, this time grazing her wrist with its teeth. Nadine's rolling body sent sparks in the air as she knocked coals from the cooking fire. Some of the coals landed on Nadine's thigh and she screamed in pain.

The wolf too had been burned and it yelped in pain. As the wolf rolled over with her belly to the air, Nadine saw the extended nipples. Nadine now knew why the wolf had come. She was alone and needing to feed her young. "Keep the wolf from me Nathan," she called.

"What?" he said, in a state of shock. "Keep the wolf away," she called again. Racing over the horse, Nadine pulled a fresh fish from the saddlebag and tossed it to the wolf. Baring her teeth, the wolf clamped its jaws over the fish and raced into the woods.

Nadine sank down onto the forest floor. Sobs wracked her body. She was an emotional pit of sorrow, pain, relief and shock. "Come, Nadine," Nathan's arm was a comfort against the cruelty of the world. She allowed herself to be led to the horse.

The horse's wide unsteady eyes reminded Nadine that she was not alone in the attack. She held her weary head close it its face and murmured softly to it. A peacefulness rolled over her.

"Brutus," she said softly. "It is alright." Running her hand over his quivering muscles, she soothed his fears. "She was just a hungry mother, wanting to feed her babies. She has no one to bring her food as you have." Cupping a small handful of oats, Nadine comforted Brutus until his body was still again. Sensing the calmness, Tiber descended from the tree and rubbed her body against Nadine's legs.

"Come girl," Nadine soothed as she picked up the little cat and held her close. The soft silky fur and the warmth of the animal's body brought light to Nadine's heart.

Nathan marveled at this girl. So fierce. Yet so tender.

A noisy beetle flew by and broke the spell. Tiber's white paw flashed as she tried to grab at the insect overhead.

Nadine laughed. The tension evaporated from her mind, leaving only the telltale ache of her muscles. Seizing the moment of lightless, Nathan declared, "It's time to go."

He was about to reach for Nadine, to lift her onto the horse, when she unceremoniously grabbed Brutus and propelled herself onto the horse. In stunned silence, he too mounted the horse, trying carefully not to knock against Nadine. "Hold onto me," he said. Unsure, Nadine uncomfortably placed her hands around his waist. Nathan frowned.

"Do you want to fall off in full gallop? Tighter, Nadine," he said more gruffly than necessary.

"Fine," she said almost squeezing the air out of him.

"I would like to get to the Medicine Woman, with some air still inside me," he sputtered.

"Oh, do make up your mind," retorted Nadine. "Can we go now?"

After some time, the forest opened to reveal a well-travelled pathway. A painted wooden sign showed that the village was just a few hours ride away and soon they began to see more travelers along the road. Luckily one of the travelers knew exactly where to find the Medicine Woman, and he happily showed them the scars on his leg, where she had removed a piece of wood that had impaled his leg after he had fallen off his roof while thatching.

"Many villagers said that I would lose this old leg of mine," he boasted to them. "Between you and me, if those barber-surgeons, would have done it, I would be dead, now I would," he whispered.

Nadine smiled. The barber surgeon's simple and almost barbaric forms of surgery caused many of their patents to die from loss of blood. Ironically these surgeons did not pay many of the taxes that normal villagers would pay, due to services to the people.

"As the fates would have it, our barber-surgeon had left some months prior to visit family and had not yet returned. I had to visit the Medicine Woman, I did."

Leaning in closer, he told them. "I have to tell you that lady scared the living daylights out of me. Her place is full of weird stuff. But she saved my leg. And look, I have this scar where the wood was. I can tell you; the ladies really like to hear this story around the fireplace," he told them with a roar of laughter.

FOURTEEN

The Medicine Woman

The Medicine Woman lived in a round hut at the edge of the village near the river. Her garden was filled with strange plants that Nadine had never seen before. Their approach was announced by a large colourful bird's squawk.

"Come on in, it's open," called a voice from inside. Nathan pushed open the beautifully carved wooden door and they stepped into a room magically filled with light and colour. The Medicine Woman glanced up from crushing herbs and saw the awe on Nadine's and Nathan's faces.

"They are called stained glass windows. A travelling artist from

Rome taught me how to make them."

"You look weary. Please come and sit here and soothe yourselves." she said pointing to two intricately carved chairs. Nathan marveled at the carpentry.

"Aren't they beautiful. They are part of my most treasured possessions. See the intricate patterns on the arms and legs? I personally love the embroidery on the cushion. It has all my favourite healing herbs."

Nadine ran her hand over the satiny feel of the thread.

"It is silk" said the Medicine woman. "A gift from an Emperor," Nadine hesitated.

"No, please do sit. A chair without someone to enjoy it, has no purpose. And please call me Elizabeth."

Nadine was surprised at how young the Medicine Woman was, with a glow to her skin that Nadine had never seen on any woman. Her emerald green eyes were framed by dark, long lashes and her fire-coloured hair was braided into a long plait down her back. A few stray curls of red hung on her forehead.

"What are your names and why have you come?"

"I am Nathan, and this is Nadine. We are travelling companions. I have come to see you, but Nadine must travel to the Dragon Whisperer in Holly Hill Cave," replied Nathan.

"Holly Hill Cave," remarked Elizabeth, with a look of surprise. "Imagine that."

Elizabeth produced two large blue and white painted bowls, filling them with warm water infused with soothing lavender. She instructed the travelling pair to put their feet into the water. The bowls, Elizabeth explained, were glazed. A potter from China had taught her how to make the glaze, paint the bowls with intricate patterns and then bake them to give the shiny painted finish that could hold water without leaking.

Elizabeth poured hot liquid into matching blue and white glazed mugs and topped them up with honey. A plate of freshly baked cookies infused with vanilla pods lay on the table between them. Warm happiness filled Nadine and Nathan. Even Tiber was treated to some warmed milk.

"Tell me your troubles," said Elizabeth. Her face filled with compassion, as Nadine and Nathan shared their adventures up to their arrival.

"Such troubles at so tender an age. Of course, I will do all that I can to help you."

Elizabeth questioned Nathan about Lady Christine's symptoms. There were so many questions, in such intricate detail. Nathan could not imagine how all these things could possibly matter. Nathan explained the strange moods, the burn like marks on her tongue and the itchiness, followed by irritability she often felt.

Elizabeth sighed and then after a few moments, a small satisfied smile began to emerge on her lovely face. "Yes, yes," she murmured, as she picked through several jars and scrolls.

Surrounded by scrolls she began to copy over portions from her scrolls onto a new fresh piece of parchment.

Nadine and Nathan stared at Elizabeth as she hummed a little tune. She seemed to be oblivious to their presence and had become totally engrossed in her work.

She tugged at the delicate leaves of some of the vast range of plants that were absorbing the sun along the windowsill. Then she arranged some small glazed jars and filled them with the various remedies that she had prepared. Finally, she put stoppers in the top of each jar. After melting some blue wax, Elizabeth sealed the jars and placed them in a small neat row in front of Nathan. A look of satisfied happiness radiated from her.

Nadine and Nathan stared in silence at the Medicine Woman. They had never seen ceramics before. Red wax seals were common on important letters, they had never seen the melting process. They marveled at the blue wax. It was like stepping into a whole new world.

"Nathan," Elizabeth said at last, wiping her hands on her apron. "You have been trained well by the cook. But it appears that Lady Christine's problems are caused by a reaction to some of the food that she eats. This means that she needs to stop eating certain food completely for a while and then only on special occasions after that. It will be hard for your cook to change her way of preparing food, so I am writing the ingredients for many delicious foods that will help balance her system."

"This condition that Lady Christine has affects many parts of her body. Her digestive system has slowed down, making her keep toxins in it for longer. Her moods are also affected as well as the parts of her body that she needs to have a healthy child. A lot of people do not know that too much of certain kinds of food and not enough of others can change the way that we think. Inside your body there lives a type of warrior, whose purpose is to fight off illness. Some foods make the warrior strong. Some make the warrior weak. When you eat the right types of food you will have a strong warrior."

"Some of the baked and sweet things that we eat weaken our inner warrior. Many cooks of Lords prepare foods full of treats that make their lords and ladies love them but do little for their physical and mental health,"

"I think in time, Lord Logan may well have a child with the lovely Lady Christine," she said with a soft smile.

"You must give these herbs to her every day until her cleansing is complete. She must also stop drinking wine for a while. But do not let her drink water from a river. Use a jar to collect rainwater and keep it far away from any other water."

It was well known that human waste that was not collected by the compost merchants was washed away into nearby rivers. Many commoners and even some nobles did not know that this was a problem. It was the way that dysentery was passed onto people. River water near inhabited areas was foul and that was why most people drank wine.

"She must only drink the rainwater you collect, for she will need to drink many cups of clean pure water until her cleansing time is over. Do you understand Nathan?" she asked, looking directly into his eyes. Still in awe of this strange woman, Nathan, could only nod in response. Then she cut off a piece of a fat, juicy looking plant, and put it into a small jar with water and a small bit of soil.

"Open this jar each day to give it some sunshine and then plant it when you get back home. When the plant begins to grow, take small cuttings, dry them into crystals and give them to her with the rainwater. They will taste very bitter, so she may want to eat a small bit of fruit afterwards to make the taste go away."

Nathan glanced as the row of jars. He imagined seeing Lady

Christine's joy, as she shared the news of her pregnancy. The idea warmed his heart as his eyes glistened at the visualization.

For a moment he looked at Nadine, who had gleefully finished almost the entire bowl of vanilla cookies. He stared in shocked disbelief. A small guilty smile played at the corner of her mouth.

Brushing the crumbs from her face, Nadine quickly asked "And what of the Dragon Whisperer?"

"You are most fortunate to come and visit me today, because you see, at Holly Hill Cave, there is a nasty plant that produces the most dreadful rash. As the Dragon Whisperer chooses to live there, he often meets this plant and comes to town once a month to get a jar of my ointment, which removes the itch. He is in fact due to arrive in the morning. So, you may rest here for tonight, so that you may be refreshed for when he arrives."

Nathan's stomach growled in protest at the absence of cookies. Upon cue Elizabeth replenished the bowl and winked at Nadine.

"Now let's take care of your horse," Elizabeth said.

"My, what a magnificent animal," she exclaimed. "Such a majestic form. You have cared well for him Nathan. His coat must shine like an ebony mirror in the sun. After he is watered and fed, I will get one of the local stable boys to clean off that travel grime and have him fit for a King's inspection in no time."

The sensual glint that played in Elizabeth's eyes, told Nathan that she was an accomplished rider who found joy in the full gallop of a fine horse. He smiled at the thought.

Grabbing Nadine by the hand, Elizabeth strode off briskly to her hut. "Come let's get the two of you rested. In the center of the hut was a trap door. Below the surface were several rooms, plus a communal area with shelves of books and wooden carved tables and chairs. Elizabeth had decorated her walls with a rich red clay from a nearby river and had hung large painted and glazed discs with colourful patterns, Nadine would have never had thought that there could be such a comfortable home underground. Tiber curled up in a small fur lined basket.

"I always keep a few spare tunics around for travelers," she said happily rummaging through a kist. "Ah, this will be perfect for you Nadine. The blue embroidery will go nicely with those exquisite eyes."

"And you Nathan, mmm, I think that this will do very nicely, for those broad shoulders of yours. Now for modesty's sake, Nathan, do come up and help me prepare for our evening meal, while Nadine freshens up. Nathan prepared the fire, as Elizabeth rubbed olive oil, crushed garlic and pressed rosemary onto a leg of lamb."

She kneaded some bread and placed her creations into a ceramic container to bake on the fire. "You live like a queen," remarked Nathan at the rich menu. Elizabeth leaned in closer. "Let me tell you a secret. A gifted healer pays no taxes." She winked. "Plus, when the villagers have no coin, they find other ways to pay me. Who needs coin when you have a beautiful home and plenty to eat?"

The sound of the trap door squeaking open announced Nadine's arrival. The sweet smell of cocoa butter wafted through the room. Nathan could not help himself, closing his eyes and deeply inhaling the delicious scent.

"Off you go, Nathan. It's your turn" Elizabeth urged seeing the look on his face.

"Sit here," she ordered Nadine. "Now let's get rid of those

tangles in your hair. You probably have not brushed it since the dragon took your family."

"My mother or sister would always brush my hair," replied Nadine softly. "That is indeed a joy of mothers and sisters." said Elizabeth looking at her handy work. "I should like to meet your mother. I think that we may have a lot in common," Elizabeth mused.

With their feast now ready, the party of three joked, laughed and danced. But Elizabeth was adamant that they retire early to be rested for the next day.

Before bed, Elizabeth taught them soothing songs that she used for children with fever or people suffering from nervous disorders or men who had sustained severe war wounds.

She showed each of them to a room with a bed, side table, candle, washing basin and jar, so that they could refresh themselves. The bed coverings were richly decorated with embroidered patterns. Nadine had never seen such decorations and wished that her sister was here to see the room.

Maireid loved decorations and would spend many hours with travelling merchants who carried with them decorative cloths. Her sister also loved tidiness and order and well-furnished rooms. Nadine now felt a twinge of regret for tormenting her sister so much when she rearranged things in her sister's room. She vowed to be more respectful of her older sister when they were reunited.

"Good night Maireid," Nadine mumbled as her exhausted body succumbed to the warmth of the feather mattress.

FIFTEEN

The Dragon Whisperer

In the morning, Elizabeth awoke Nadine, gently rocking her shoulder. "Quick, Nadine, you must prepare yourself for the Dragon Whisperer. Inside he has a kind heart, but on the outside, he is a stern looking man prone to outbursts of anger. I think the combination of being terribly old and living alone, has made him rather grumpy. Plus, most of his conversations are usually with fire-breathing dragons, so he is not accustomed to regularly having normal conversations."

Elizabeth prepared breakfast for Nadine and Nathan and made Nadine a special drink that would help soothe her nerves, but still allow her to keep her wits about her. She had reminded Nadine that this encounter with the dragon would be vastly different from her first one.

As they were finishing up, there was a loud roar, followed by a thud. Nadine's heart first felt like it had stopped and then began racing again. Her body reacted to her mind, as it recognised the sound of a dragon. She closed her eyes and swallowed hard. The memory of the heat of the fire on her face flooded her mind and she struggled to settle her thoughts. Nadine glanced fearfully up at the window to see a rather old man climbing down from an enormous copper coloured dragon.

Although the dragon looked very fearsome indeed, with brilliant yellow flashing eyes and sharp yellow tinted talons. Nadine was relieved that it was not bellowing fire. It calmly sat down and gulped down fish from the large bowl that Elizabeth and put outside in anticipation for her unusual guests. Using the mind-focusing techniques that Elizabeth had taught her, she managed to center her thoughts and calm her mind.

The Dragon Whisperer used his intricately carved ebony staff to pound on the door. "Medicine Woman, it is I, the Great Dragon Whisperer, open up!" he roared. Inside the house, Elizabeth rolled her eyes, sighed, straightened her skirt and opened the door.

She gave a small ceremonious curtsy and guided to the Dragon Whisperer to the table and chairs. The Dragon Whisperer looked down his enormous nose at Elizabeth and sat down in the largest chair like a king waiting for a lowly servant to be at his beck and call.

"I am here for my remedy, Medicine Woman."

"Here it is as agreed, Great Dragon Whisperer. But before we conclude our business, I have need of your expertise," said Elizabeth. The Dragon Whisperer narrowed his ancient looking, steely blue-grey eyes, that were topped by wild hairy white and grey eyebrows.

"You may speak," said the Dragon Whisperer, looking as if there was some greatly suspicious act underway.

"I have in my care two young people, who are on a great and noble quest and need a man of your vast talent and wisdom. If it was only the plight of these two young people, I would not have bothered a man of your importance at all. But the future of two entire villages is at the mercy of your decision to help or not. I believe you to be a man of great wisdom, who values justice more than anything else."

This rather flattering approach produced a glint in the old man's eyes and Elizabeth sealed the deal by placing a large mug of her own well-known and appreciated honeyed beer in front of him.

"You may present them," boomed The Dragon Whisperer, arranging his great copper-coloured robes more neatly around him. His robes matched the dragon and provided some camouflage while travelling with the great beast. They also gave him an air of authority, for not many people could prepare such a robe or even find the dyes to colour it. For as long as anyone could remember, he had been called by his title, and not by name. There was not a single living person who even knew if he had ever had a name.

Nadine, quite accustomed to addressing elders, could not help but tremble a bit in front of this great and fearsome man. She used the breathing techniques learned from her mother, and comforted by Elizabeth's presence, she pressed on.

She remembered to curtsey as Elizabeth had taught her, but the steady and defiant look in her eyes, made the Dragon Whisperer realise straight away that this was no ordinary girl. Her determination and bravery shone through her nervousness.

Nadine held nothing back. She explained every detail, including her observations about the mother dragon. Nadine's exquisite blue eyes, framed by the longest lashes the Dragon Whisperer had ever seen, sparkled as she told of her adventures.

As Nadine spoke the Dragon Whisperer glanced at the boy. His eyes narrowed for a moment. Nadine paused her story as she noticed that his gaze had shifted. His brow furrowed into a brief frown and equally as quickly there was an expression that almost looked like shame, and then it was gone. Nadine sensed that memory had touched the great man and then just as suddenly as it had appeared, it was gone and once again the sternness in the old man's expression was set. There was no time to ponder its meaning. The old man's intense eyes were fixed on Nadine, willing her to continue with her tale.

The Dragon Whisperer was impressed by the girl's ability to empathise with the mother dragon, who was clearly the cause of the loss of Nadine's family. To Elizabeth's great surprise, he took Nadine's small hand in his enormous weathered one and looked deep into her eyes.

"Girl, you have a special gift. You can sense animals' true spirits and needs. I see this in your empathy for the great dragon, the special care you take of your cat and your ability to calm a frightened horse. You have great courage and have travelled a great distance to save not only your family, but your entire village, and for this reason, I will help you."

"Now I need you to sit very still. You may have heard that I can see through a dragon's eyes. But I can also see a dragon through a human's eyes if they are a gifted one like you are."

"This may be hard, but I need for us to sit quietly here together until I am able to see her through your eyes." Nadine sat unflinchingly and stared into the Dragon Whisperer s eyes. For a long time, the old man did not move at all. Then a spark seemed to appear in his eyes, followed by a great sadness.

"My dragon knows of Muquin. Her mate was killed in the Dragon Wars," explained the Dragon Whisperer.

"The Dragon Wars?" quizzed Nadine.

"The warlords of ancient times uncovered the secret of the dragon and human pairings. A dragon that is taken when it is a hatchling can be trained to the will of man. A hatchling will bond with its captor. For the warlords, this can produce a destructive weapon that can destroy mankind."

"Dragon Whisperers like myself were gifted with the ability to communicate with Dragons. In the beginning, there were four of us. Each with a special gift. Our purpose was to protect and guide the dragons. To act as a sort of mediator between humans and dragons."

"Why would humans need that?" asked Nathan.

"Dragons are misunderstood creatures but have many qualities that humans have. Like humans, they build a home. Like humans, they have a bond with their offspring. And like humans, they will defend their homes."

"But if provoked, a dragon can destroy entire villages within minutes." said the Dragon Whisperer watching Nadine carefully.

"For a warlord, a dragon fuels their lust for power. Imagine being able to exterminate your enemies without the costs of feeding an army?"

"Money?" Nadine was confused.

"Coin girl. For a warlord coin, plunder, treasure, call it what you will, means more power, more control." said the Dragon Whisperer.

"Is that why the Bible says that love of money is the cause of all evil?" asked Nathan.

"Some say that. But be clear of what you are reading. It is only the love of money, not money itself that is the root of evil," checked the Dragon Whisperer. "Coin like dragon fire is only a tool. Only the one who commands it can change how it is used.

You can cook your meal with fire. But you can also burn a village with fire. The text speaks of the love of money being evil. Money itself is not evil. In the hands of the Medicine Woman, coin can buy ingredients for my ointment. In the hands of a warlord, it can pay for poison."

"But back to the point, we have little time."

"The Northern King seeks to imprison this hatchling and train it like the dragons of the Dragon Wars. This must not happen. A hatchling is only born every 100 years. So many dragons died in the dragon wars that there are not enough dragons alive to harness in combat against the Northern King."

"A dragon cannot mate with a different kind of dragon. They can fight alongside each other. They can be companions. But they cannot mate. Their unions produce no eggs.

Like the Dragon Whisperers each have a gift, each species of dragon is created for a specific purpose.

"Why is that?" asked Nadine

"I cannot say," replied the Dragon Whisperer. "But when Muquin's mate died, he took with him the seed to keep the Silver Wings alive. For Muquin to have a hatchling meant that they must have mated during the times of the wars. Her hatchling would have been a way to celebrate the life of her mate. He was fierce and very loyal. He died saving her."

"Her Dragon Whisperer died in the wars as well. Each Dragon Whisperer has a secret hiding place for memory. Before they die, they pass it onto the dragon. It is the last sanctuary for a dragon and is unique to them. The Ancients helped them forge these places for the dragons. The Dragon Whisperers had other allies as well. They knew that a war would destroy both mankind and dragons and they fought to keep the dragons away from the warlords. A dragon with a darkened heart could destroy the world."

"The Silver Wings were said to be the most beautiful of all the species. They had eyes like the crystal blue of the uncharted waters. Their wings sparkled like the sun kissing the seas."

He paused for a moment.

"And when they die, their remains split up and fly to the night sky to create star formations."

"The heavens burst open when Muquin's mate died. To the east, you can see his formation. A dragon will speak to its mate after the formation is settled. But its new voice takes many decades to form. Muquin can see it but she cannot hear him yet. She would have had to raise the hatchling without his wisdom and now it is gone. She is all alone."

"Sometimes my dragon does see her when he hunts. But she does not open her mind to him."

"Then how does he know what happened to her hatchling?" asked Nadine

"He does not. Only I do," said the Dragon Whisperer with great sorrow.

"My Dragon could feel her open her mind when she was searching for the hatchling. She did it to try and telepathically find it. It made her mind easier to read. He knew that she was searching, and he could see through her eyes."

"I don't understand, why only you know then," Nadine questioned.

"I can read the thief," replied the Dragon Whisperer.

Nadine eyed him suspiciously.

"So many questions" grumbled the Dragon Whisperer.

"Now girl, tell me of the dreams," the Dragon Whispered pressed.

"What dreams?" asked Nadine

"You know what I mean. The dragon dreams that have come to you. The voices. The visions." The intensity of his stare frightened her.

The Medicine Woman reached to the Dragon Whisperer. He glared suspiciously at her tender hand on his shoulder.

"She is frightened. Be gentle," said Elizabeth.

"Very well," he replied gruffly

"You have the gift. I can see it clearly in you."

"Your father, your mother, do they have it?" he said grabbing her wrist. Nadine pulled away.

"Stop it" cried Elizabeth. "Do not speak in riddles. Tell her clearly what you mean. And you will do it without touching her."

The Dragon Whisperer gave a snort in response.

"Where are your parents' kin?" he asked.

"My mother's kin are from the middle Marsh Lands. My father speaks little of his family, but I think that they come from the west. He left as a squire when he was young. I never met any of my father's parents. But my mother speaks of her mother," replied Nadine rubbing her wrist.

"I can see that you know nothing," he spat.

"Once there were four Dragon Whisperers. Each with a unique gift. This gift is passed down through generations. But having the gift does not make one worthy," he said searching her eyes.

"For those who lived with their family, they could be trained. But wars often bring separation. Like with your father who never saw his family again. These separations stop the passage of wisdom."

"Someone with the gift may go many years without knowing it. But the sight of a dragon will always call to the gift. Sometimes even the sound of its roar will call to the gift."

"For some, the gift lies in their blood, but never rises to a purpose. Especially if their heart is darkened. But for the true of heart, the gift always leaves signs. You have these signs."

"What signs?" Nadine asked.

"The kitten you have. The villagers would not have easily accepted her. But you adopted her. The starving wolf... Others would have killed her. But you fed her. Those who are worthy will always seek to help the creatures of the earth," he replied with restraint.

"But I killed a bird," she said.

"Yes. But you did it to save your kitten."

"We all have choices. Those who are worthy do not fight because of greed or lust for power. They fight for justice. For what they believe in."

"When you first heard Muquin's roar, there would have been voices. Think back, what did you hear? What did you feel?"

"I was afraid. No. I was terrified. But I told myself to think. To calm myself," she said furrowing her brow.

"Is this normally how you talk to yourself?" he quizzed.

"No. I never hear myself talk to myself. I just do things," she said with a puzzled look. Or, I think of what my parents would have told me to do. Or what I have learned from the Bible."

"Indeed." Finally, the girl's mind was starting to reason, he thought.

Seeing the look, Elizabeth gave him a stern frown that belied her gentle nature.

"Then what of the dreams? Have you dreamed of dragons?" he pressed again.

"Yes," she said

"What were they? Tell me everything," he demanded.

"I dreamed of two dragons twirling in the air. Then one exploding into a group of stars," she said.

"It is the Silver Wings." he exclaimed; his eyes suddenly wide with wonder. He looked at the Medicine Woman. "She feels the Silver Wings."

Abandoning his promise to be gentle, he grabbed her by both shoulders. "I have waited a long time to find one of your kind." he cried

A grin threatening to explode into laughter crept over the width of Elizabeth's face. She had never seen even the tiniest glimmer of joy or humour in the Dragon Whisperer. But this fresh look shed years off his age. His eyes sparkled and a vitality soared through his body.

"There will come more." he scrabbled through the bag. He tossed out a cloth bundle secured with string and wax.

Suddenly he stopped.

"Your parents, did they teach you to read and write?" he anxiously asked.

"Yes, they did."

Closing his eyes, he sighed.

"Very good," he said.

Drawing a simple dagger from his robes he cut the string and broke the seals of each bundle. Inside were four small volumes. Each a distinct colour. He drew out the silver one. The volume had the feel of leather, but the covers were carved or burned with patterns that were filled with silver detail. Opening the book, he presented it to her. A book with blank pages.

"This is yours. You must record your dreams. When the time is right, they will build together."

"Do this every day without fail. Without fail, do you hear me?" he demanded.

"Yes," she replied fingering the pages of the volume.

Let us get on with your training.

Turning to face Nathan, the Dragon Whisperer sighed and said, "My dragon knows the way to the Bandit's lair where Lord Logan is being held. I will assist you with fire powder and the Medicine Woman can assist you with sleeping potions. If you can get into the lair and get a message to Lord Logan, warning him and his men not to drink anything, you could get the bandits to fall asleep and then create a diversion with the fire powder to get Lord Logan out."

"I am sure that his men will help you with the rescue of the little dragon, but only Nadine can return the baby dragon to its mother. Because only Nadine will have a tender enough heart to help subdue Muquin without being burned up by the mother dragon's wrath."

The Dragon Whisperer took out a small bag of powder and looked at Elizabeth. "This powder is immensely powerful, when thrown on the ground, it produces a small explosion surrounded by a lot of smoke. They need to test it to see its true power, but not in your home." Again, came the look of shame, but no one dared to ask any questions. Even Elizabeth did not recognise this expression on the Dragon Whisperer's face. He had always worn a stern expression. His sense of fairness had on many occasions displayed his character, but few people could endure the intensity of his personality for too long. It made him a very isolated old man.

Elizabeth nodded in understanding. "There is a small quarry a short way from here. The only villagers that ever go there are the workers, and as today is the Festival of The Wild Boar the workers will be at the feast. They can safely test it today," replied Elizabeth.

"Let's go there now," said the Whisperer.

With a fistful of the fire powder, Nathan twisted his body to propel the powder forward. Upon the stone, the fire powder erupted with a burst of sparks and flames. The pungent smell from the emerging smoke stung his eyes and blurred his vision.

Coughing and gagging, Nathan ran back. "You are too close

and too eager," scolded the Dragon Whisperer. Nathan glared at the older man.

"He could have told me," muttered Nathan under his breath. Though his face remained unmoved, a glint of humour threatened to emerge in the Dragon Whisperer's eyes. His hearing was acute.

"How then would you have learned the lesson?" he asked. "Now the girl!"

Fearing the powder, Nadine took only the smallest portion. Her results produced only the whisper of a spark.

"You doubt yourself. In your fear, you would have been captured as well, with all your assailants laughing at your little girl tactics."

Nadine's eyes flashed in anger. "Then tell us, what is the right amount," she yelled.

"Very well, we don't want you wasting all of it." sighed the Dragon Whisperer, as he divided the portions.

"This portion will create a diversion. Loud enough to be heard and not seen. This is used from a distance, to make them come to you. This portion is when you are confronted, and you want to disappear into a cloud of smoke."

"Using an arrow, you propel the last portion forward," the Dragon Whisperer shouted, "and this when you want to create chaos."

A blast erupted in the distance. The smoke reached high into the air, as eruptions of flames flared up in the distance. Villagers began to emerge as they sought the source of the commotion.

The Dragon Whisperer hastily led them away from the quarry.

They quickly entered Elizabeth's home away from curious eyes.

"Well then Medicine Woman, prepare the sleeping potion, there is not a moment to lose. While you are making your preparations, I will prepare the young people and speak to my dragon. I may well dine with you tonight before I return to Holly Hill Cave. You know, human beings can only go without food for a certain time and the faster these children get back to the villagers, the better."

Elizabeth had not spoken of this to Nadine before, for fear of distressing her. But now Nadine's eyes frantically flew to Elizabeth's face, searching for an answer.

"It is true Nadine. While the body could probably endure no food for about three weeks, the maximum amount of time one can survive without water is about seven days."

At these words, Nadine felt the sting of tears, as she thought of her baby brother Mikael, who never seemed to stop eating. It was now a few days since her journey began.

SIXTEEN

The Meal

The dragon's radiant copper glow merged with the rays of the sun as the Medicine Woman and the Dragon Whisperer watched Nadine and Nathan disappear riding on its back.

Elizabeth stared into the distance for longer than necessary.

She had to admit that the company of the Dragon Whisperer filled her with dread. Their interactions had always been tense and minimal. He came for the ointment and hastily left.

Now he wanted to dine with her. Her normal relaxed manner was now frozen with indecision.

"Are you going to stand there the entire afternoon?" he grumbled.

Elizabeth gritted her teeth in impatience at his impossible demeanour. She was an independent woman, a healer whose reputation had spread beyond the continent. And here was this grouchy old man ordering her around like a worthless apprentice.

He was already inside and seated in her favourite chair by the time she arrived at the door. Grabbing a handful of lavender from a pot near the door, she crushed the leaves and inhaled deeply.

"You may begin to prepare the meal," he ordered, his presence filling the room.

The crushed lavender fell to the ground and took with it the remaining shards of her patience.

"Dragon Whisperer, you may well be the Lord over the great beasts of the sky. But in this place, my home, I am Queen. If you wish to dine with me, you would do well to remember that once long ago you had a mother whom, I presume, taught you good manners," she said, daring him to defy her. She was greeted with stony eyes.

"Very well" he replied stiffly. "What are your terms?"

"My terms!" she cried in desperation. "For pity's sake… do you not even know how to have a normal conversation. Or is your disposition always as scaly as your dragon?" The words burst out. But because she knew it was an awfully long walk back to Holly Hill Cave, Elizabeth immediately softened.

"Forgive me. It has been a long day. Here let me pour you some of my own special brew," she placed a large vessel of sweet-smelling warmed honeyed ale next to him. With narrowed eyes, he tentatively tested it. "This will do nicely," he said.

Knowing the Dragon Whisperer preferred a simple life, Elizabeth prepared a version of a peasant meal. A jar of pea pottage boiled on the coals, while a peasant's barley flour and rye bread baked. Fresh river salmon sizzled while she ground sorrel and salt for the sauce. The only high-born dish was a custard tart infused with saffron.

For the first time in decades, the Dragon Whisper found himself enjoying the company of a woman, although the years of solitude had stripped him of the art of simple conversation. He stared blankly at the cooking fire.

The sound of Elizabeth's voice jarred him back. "There is something that you know that you are not telling me," she stated.

A troubled look passed over his face.

"I fear great danger. The Northern King is not to be trifled with."

Elizabeth coaxed. "There is more."

"King Radolf is breeding an army. Unlike anything we have ever known He is a brutal man, prone to cruelty that we have not seen in many years.

Once before there was a warlord who sought to harness the power of the dragon. It was then that the first dragon wars erupted. There were many casualties. Entire colonies of peaceful dragons perished. He wished to exterminate the Dragon Whisperers."

In the same way Dragons can be turned, Whisperers can be turned. Those who remain in the community can withstand a spiritual attack. They draw strength from each other."

"And those who do not?" asked Elizabeth.

"Separated and given enough trauma they will turn," replied the old man.

They sat together staring into the fire, their silence heavy with unspoken words. Elizabeth was torn between her concern for Nadine and knowing that The Whisperer needed to search his mind.

"The meal is almost ready," Elizabeth's announcement broke the uneasy tension.

"But I do have a rule in this house. All guests are to wash their hands and move the hair from their faces before dining," she said placing a bowl of warmed water fragranced with lavender oil beside him. She poured the water over his hands and rubbed the oil into them.

He gave her a startled look.

"Be at ease. It will help hasten the healing of the itch in your skin," she said.

His hands were larger than she had imagined. But then they would need to be large to command the beasts of the sky. As she touched them, she felt some of the power that they wielded. "Remain seated," she ordered. With a comb, she loosened the tangles of his hair and trimmed his fearsome eyebrows.

As she secured his hair with a leather strip, she announced "There you go. Fit for a royal banquet."

For a moment their eyes met. His guard took leave and suddenly she saw what she had never seen before. The sternness was replaced with a vulnerability she had not encountered before in a man.

She saw a man who had known great love. But whose heart had been struck down by some massive tragedy. Then again came the look of shame she had noticed earlier.

She turned quickly to allow him the dignity of privacy for his moment of weakness.

"Now let us eat," she said, laying the meal before them.

For a moment the man returned to the joy of his younger years. A time of family. When the love of a good woman had pushed him to be the best he could be.

He watched the sway of her hips, as her skirts danced around her form. How the light of the fire framed her face. The chatter of her voice filled him with a happiness he had forgotten. Her waist was so tiny that his hands could easily encircle it.

Perhaps just this one night, he could forget about the war. Forget about the King. And forget his failure.

To her surprise, he laughed. It was a deep rich rumble that lit up his eyes. There was a sensuality about his mouth that emerged when he was playful.

A woman of understanding and education was a rare find for the Dragon Whisperer. But he imagined that the same could be said for a woman like Elizabeth. There would be few husbands who would tolerate the endless flow of patients and the hours of study. She would need a man confident enough in his abilities to not feel threatened by her. She was a mix of passion and tenderness. Harshness and peacefulness. Strength and beauty.

No woman had ever sat alongside him on his dragon. But the memory of Nadine and Nathan soaring together, made him wonder.

The return of his dragon broke the spell. Regret filled his mind. No, he was too old. His time had passed and now he would return to his cave. Alone. To wait for the reckoning. The time when his personal demons would return to torment him.

Elizabeth saw the stone roll over the place in his mind that had opened to her.

She wrapped her shawl a bit closer. The Dragon Whisperer rose to leave. "I thank you for the meal," he slowly said.

She simply smiled and quickly opened the door.

Within seconds the Dragon Whisperer had mounted his dragon and disappeared. A silhouette against the moon.

SEVENTEEN

Muquin's Choice

Muquin gazed at her prisoners. Once she had fought for them alongside her Dragon Whisperer.

Megadeus had urged her to help them. Their last fight had been about these people.

"Mankind is a cruel and greedy species," she had protested.

"Not all of them are. They are like us. Our kind has also suffered from darkened hearts," he had argued.

"Yes, but do we try to exterminate our own kind? Do we fight the Copper Fire Dragons? Do we slay Emerald Forest Dragons? No. We are allies with the Crystal Water Dragons. We will fight one who turns on our kind, but we will never destroy a species. Did you know that in the villages they sing songs about slaying us? They train knights to claim us as trophies. It is disgusting."

"Muquin, listen to me. The Warlords have captured a hatchling and turned its heart. These things you say we do not do; this dragon will do to us. He is under the command of the warlord. He will destroy mankind, and those he does not destroy, will turn on us and kill us all. The fear will be unmanageable."

"Leave me to my peaceful nest. Let us grow hatchlings together Megadeus. Leave these people to fight their own battles," she pleaded. "I want no part of it."

"Peace? Muquin. There can be no peace if we do nothing. Our hatchlings will never be safe. Mankind's children will also suffer. Their young and those too old to fight will perish. There will always be a warlord that rises to steal one of our kind if we do nothing. My love, fight alongside me for the sake of our species."

Megadeus understood her fear. He wanted nothing more than to live in their nest and teach his hatchlings to fish and hunt and dance in the moonlight. He would share with them the wisdom of those who had gone before.

But he would not bring them into a world where they would constantly live in fear.

"Our Dragon Whisperer will teach us the ways of mankind. He will help us to see them as they really are, and he will be our ally."

"I care not for their young and old. I have lost too many of our own kin to mankind. We are the last of the Silver Wings. Do you not see that?" she shouted.

"Muquin. You sadden me. There is great love in the hearts of many of mankind. Do you not see how tenderly even the strongest of their warriors hold their new young? How their clergy find ways to feed those who suffer without food. Your eyes perceive only their actions born out of fear. But there is goodness in mankind. Let us help them fight off the warlords who seek to control them and us."

The tenderness of his touch and the richness of his voice always softened her heart. She would do as he asked. But only because she would not sit idly and wait for him to be slaughtered by these treacherous people. She would be the eyes for his back when their knights tried to corner him.

Megadeus had never lost a battle. He was the fiercest of the warriors. But he did not have a treacherous heart and she had seen how treacherously mankind had laid waste the lives of so many of her kin.

In the end, it was not mankind who caused his death.

She had done it. As surely as if she had torn out his heart herself. She had flown directly into the line of sight of their dragon killer. She had not seen the spear bearer. But Megadeus had.

He had flown into the line, pushing her roughly out of the way. The spear had pierced his heart. His crystal eyes closing into darkness. Their love silenced forever.

She watched her prisoners suffer. Megadeus's words of tenderness about the mothers and their young pulled at her heart. But she had also seen them trample their young to save themselves when they had first entered the tunnel.

"Let them perish," she thought. "I care not for them. I care only for my hatchling. I suffer without him."

The baby in the tunnel cried endlessly. Without food and water, the mother could not make the milk to feed it.

Muquin turned her head away in shame. Her mate's words "You sadden me," flooded her mind.

No, she had to get away, lest his words turn her now.

Unless she had her hatchling back with her, these people could continue to suffer. She could not back down now.

Should she find a way to retrieve her offspring herself, she would release the villagers for Megadeus' sake. But while the hatchling was held captive, the prisoners would remain here.

Muquin cloaked her form and stepped into the hidden passage. She opened her mind, willing the hatchling to read her telepathic call, and flew into the sky. But the hatchling could not hear her.

Only Nadine's tortured dreams could perceive the images that now replayed in Muquin's mind.

EIGHTEEN

Suffering

Maireid ran her tongue over her cracked and dried out lips. She knew that it was a vain exercise, just serving to make the dryness worse. She watched over her sleeping brother. But her eyes were dull.

The smell of human faeces and urine was overbearing. The three leaders had guided the people to keep their waste away from the main group. But there was very little ventilation.

When her mother left the note for Nadine, she had shared her mother's faith that her sister would find help.

Now despair clouded her mind. She wondered if Job felt this

way. Maireid had learned of Job and his suffering from the traveling Friar. It was the story of a man who once prospered but lost all his possessions and family. Events the enemy had planned. She hated the story. Now Job's suffering was no longer a Bible story. It was her life.

Her father suffered. His wound oozed. The remedies that her mother would have used lay in their home. The burned skin tightened and shortened. His movements grew strained.

Their rations were long gone. She had shouted at her brother when he had wailed to his mother that he was hungry. It made her feel so guilty.

She glanced at a mother, with a near-lifeless infant at her breast. "Oh, God," Maireid pleaded in her mind, "Where are you? Where is Nadine? Will you not rescue us?"

She looked at her mother, who was stroking her father's arm, while cradling her brother in the other arm. Maireid felt so alone. As the eldest, they always expected her to be mature. To be strong and to be positive.

She envied her baby brother. He snuggled up in their mother's arms. Maireid wanted comfort, too. She knew that her brother's need was greatest and that her father was ill. But she could not bear the suffering any longer. Once there had been tears in her body. But they were all now spent. Nothing came from her eyes, even though she felt like crying.

Then came the sound of the dragon returning. With a thud, Muquin's body hit the ground. This time there was something different. Her body glistened. Rain. Muquin was sopping wet. Maireid could see the water dripping down off the dragon's great body and forming small pools in the pockets of rock around her.

She reached into her pocket and pulled out a leather pouch. It was watertight. Maireid had observed her mother moving around the dragon and now knew when the dragon was asleep.

Her plan would require several trips. To save her family, she would risk it.

Maireid crept past the dragon. When she reached the first tiny pool of water, she cupped her hand and drank some. Closing her eyes, the cool liquid filled her with pleasure. Guilt pushed the feeling away. No. Mother said, "To care for others, you must have some strength yourself."

After a few handfuls, she began to scoop some water into the pouch. Her hands were her only tool. Water spilled over the sides of the pouch. Still, she measured out at least twenty handfuls.

The scales of the dragon's body could hold a lot of rain. She smiled at her mother's teachings about gratitude.

"Mother," she whispered as she touched her mother's cheek. "I have rain." Her mother's eyes opened listlessly. She stared at Maireid unable to take in what her daughter said.

Maireid put her finger in the pouch and lifting it out with a drop of the rainwater covered her mother's bottom lip. A spark of recognition fluttered into life in her mother's dull blue eyes. Maireid scooped some out with her hand and let the precious drops trickle down into Dorothea's mouth. She measured out the ration she had counted for one person.

Dorothea shifted Mikael. "Mikael be silent now, boy." Maireid fed Mikael his ration. They woke Nicolous. Relief overflowed. With it came guilt. Others suffered.

Dorothea dared not ask Maireid to go again. But she saw the mother with the dying infant. Maireid knew what she must do. She crept again to the puddles. This time Dorothea helped. Together they harvested what they could.

They gave a pouch to the mother and urged her to keep this a secret. The young woman clung to Maireid's hand. Her eyes held the silent relief that came at the end of great despair. It would be over an hour before her breasts would once again provide milk for her baby. But with all the rainwater now gone, they eased back into their lives of lack. For a while, hope was restored.

They prayed that Nadine would get help to them. That they would return home. Free to sing and dance, the grass beneath their feet and warm sunshine on their faces.

NINETEEN

The Search

Muquin knew vengeance was not the way. Silver Wings were set apart. She knew she had allowed the pain of her loss to distort her purpose.

"Megadeus. Where are you now? How long must I wait for you to speak?"

But she did not need to hear his voice. She knew what he would say now. She watched the village mother again. Dragon mothers hunted for the first feed for their hatchlings. The first feed created the desire to hunt. A hatchling would suffer without its mother, but the first feed would enable it to find its own food.

Humans used their bodies to create nourishment. If a mother went without food, she could not create the food for her young. A new human life left unattended would die.

Her thoughts came fast, one after the other. A human had found her hatchling, of that she was certain. She could feel that her hatchling had not yet reached the life-force stage of flight. It was still safe; and true hatchling suffering had not been transmitted to her. But she was suffering without him.

Megadeus was the leader of their kind. Silver Wings were the carriers of wisdom. They passed it down generation to generation. Her Dragon Whisperer told her that many humans used a book to record lessons. Lessons from their spiritual leaders.

Some humans could not read the markings in these books. People called priests taught the humans. Humans taught their children. He told her that humans taught not only with words. They also taught through the kinds of lives they lived.

That is what the Silver Wings did. They taught other dragons. By human terms, would they be priests? What kind of priest would she be? Megadeus had been their leader. Even when humans destroyed so many of their kind, he did not hate. It would not please him to see her actions now.

He would never condone this suffering. None of these people had taken her hatchling. Yet, they suffered now. The human offspring suffered the most. The infant would not last. She had brought the rain for the people. She had feigned sleep, and watched the girl harvest it. Now she saw the nursing mother hold the offspring to her chest. The creature sucked at her.

The life bond they shared amplified her loss. Muquin turned

away, and cloaking her form, she stepped out of the entrance, and took to the skies.

"Megadeus, teach me how to track without the bonding ceremony. Why do you remain silent?"

She flew above the path to the village, following her instinct to go north, to the castle on the hill. But she felt blocked. A barrier of great power was cutting her off. What was it? She opened her mind wider. A risk. An open mind would invite forces she did not know. Megadeus had possessed the power to resist. But female dragons without a hatchling did not train in The Way. They remained innocent until the first hatchling. The mind needed to be pure as first hatchlings were sacred. Purity protected the hatchling from forces that tried to penetrate a mother, but it also made them a target for dangerous forces. Female dragons kept their minds pure only until the hatchling arrived. If Megadeus was alive, he would have begun her training now. But right now, she was too weak to fight the block.

Even in battle, Megadeus had instructed her to keep her mind closed. He trained her in strategy. But not in mind forces. This purity provided some safety for her hatchling. A warlord needed to find a powerful force to turn a pure hatchling. A firstborn. However, given enough trauma, the hatchling would turn.

Megadeus had not told her how much time she would have. Every day she searched. When her mind opened, she saw things she did not know. Mist rising from a lake. An eagle bearing down. A snarling wolf. Fire burst from the ground. A book with a dragon. Something else was searching, but for what? Someone else suffered.

For years she had been alone. Hidden in the tunnels. But now she felt a call pulling at her. What was it? For a moment the sky darkened. The sky turned Copper. The vast form of a Copper Fire Dragon soared above her. "Muquin, I am Zairdenth," she heard. Muquin shut her mind. He was of the betraying kind. She needed to be more careful. How much did he see? She realized he had read her before. Once. After she lost the hatchling. But she had been too distraught to recognize the reading.

Zairdenth seemed different to the betrayer. The betrayer was dark. Zairdenth had the rich glow of a true Copper Fire Dragon, his powerful body a magnificent example of the forgers of villages. She sensed his searching. His orange luminescent eyes were filled with purpose. But what did he search for?

Then she realized. Zairdenth had been searching for her. Why?

TWENTY

Lord Logan

The mighty copper coloured Zairdenth rose steadily and high into the air, carrying Nadine, Nathan and Tiber. Nadine had half hoped that the Dragon Whisperer would join them, but the old man had told her that Zairdenth would not be able to take all of them, so he would remain with the Medicine Woman until the dragon returned.

Nadine felt the lurch of her stomach as she adjusted to being so far off the ground. The powerful dragon's wings beat just a few times until it had gained momentum and began to glide on the air. Just like the quest they had all started on, it took much more effort to start than to glide. Now with courage in their hearts, they moved towards the bandits' lair.

Nadine felt the pure adrenaline of flight and laughed out loud at the heights they climbed to. She loved to climb trees, but this was higher than she had ever been, and the view was unlike anything she had ever seen. She felt exhilarated and free. She wished that she could fly like this every day. She felt powerful. As if she could do anything. The trees merged into a beautiful landscape with the river flowing beside it. Nadine began to take in her surroundings as she marveled at the sheer beauty of the world from this vantage point.

In the distance, the bandit's lair began to come into sight. Nadine and Nathan could clearly make out the old Ancient 's ruins and the stone altars that they had built so long ago. Nadine was surprised to see everything was primarily made of stone. She saw the series of massive stones that had symbolic carvings on the outside.

The ruins were of a form of architecture that Nadine had never seen before. The structures were symmetrical. A form of design borrowed from another culture in a distant time. Some of the stones had collapsed on the ground, leaving crushed rock and debris lying around.

Many of the remaining walls were now partially covered with a densely green creeping plant. Nadine marveled at how this structure could have been built so close to her home. But then she thought of the river that ran close to the ruins and that perhaps their provisions may have been transported along the river.

As Zairdenth slowed, Nadine took out the map that the Dragon Whisperer had drawn from his vision through his Dragons eyes. Nadine and Nathan saw that the map was a perfect drawing of the bandit's lair. But she would have to get into it to discover the layout for herself.

The dragon slowly glided around the area, giving Nadine and Nathan time to discuss their plans while observing the area from a high vantage point. With the use of the map, she and Nathan could plan their exit route. From this point, they could also see where the bandits kept the horses.

"Nadine, I think that the river would be our fastest route of escape," suggested Nathan.

"But then we won't be able to take the horses," replied Nadine. "And riding may be the fastest and safest way. We have no way of knowing how fast the river flows or if any of the party will be injured." It was a difficult choice, as each option had its own benefits.

"How many men does Lord Logan have with him?" asked Nadine.

"Including Lord Logan, there are five men" replied Nathan. "He wanted his party to be small enough to travel swiftly and draw as little attention as possible." Nadine and Nathan considered the different options once more.

"If the men take the horses and keep an extra one with them, we can take a raft down the river and meet up with them later," suggested Nadine. Nathan nodded silently, letting the idea simmer in his mind for a while.

"Mmm, splitting up may mean a better chance of safety for more of us, and certainly Tiber can deal with the river as she has travelled by water before," said Nathan.

"On the other hand, if the raft is large enough, we may well be able to get all the horses and men on board. That is, provided we can keep the horses calm enough," added Nadine

Together, Nadine and Nathan decided it would be a clever idea for the Dragon to drop them near the ruins at night when there was little chance of being spotted by the bandits. They would also need to remain hidden for at least one day to be able to plot the bandit's movements. For them to get the sleeping potion into the food and water, they had to see where the provisions were stored. Nadine was acutely aware that every night they spent waiting added an extra day to her family's woes in an uncertain environment without food and water.

Nadine and Nathan decided to observe where the guards were stationed. Even bandits needed to have lookout posts, to see if there were approaching soldiers or potential victims. Nadine had been taught not to be superstitious, so the threat of evil spirits that the bandits had tried to imply, did not frighten her. But they both knew that being discovered would completely ruin their plans to rescue Lord Logan and his men.

Shortly after nightfall, the dragon silently glided down towards the ground, and Nadine and Nathan had to drop down a short distance to the ground. They could not risk the sound of the dragon landing. Its sheer size would have created a mighty thud as its giant body came to rest on the ground, and they needed to make as little noise as they could. The enormous Copper Fire Dragon swooped down as low as he could within the treed area, allowing Nadine and Nathan to slip down to the ground. The little cat, Tiber, remained tucked into Nadine's bag and didn't make a sound. Then the dragon turned skyward once again.

Nadine and Nathan ran quickly to the trees and climbed a large oak tree; one of the Ancients' sacred trees. They positioned themselves to observe the bandits in their routine. The Medicine Woman had given them special herbs to place under their tongues to help them stay awake longer than nature intended and to keep them alert.

Nathan and Nadine knew that lighting a fire would put them at risk of being discovered. So, they kept themselves warmly wrapped in the furs and chewed on the dried meat in silence. Nathan had shown Nadine some of the hand signals that Lord Logan's Captain had taught him to communicate during hunts and battles. This allowed them to remain silent during their observation of the bandits and communicate only with their eyes, head movements and gestures.

When the moon was full and high in the sky, an owl swooped down onto a nearby branch with a field mouse in its beak. The sound of the bird startled Tiber and she made a soft meow. She popped her head out of her hiding place, and seeing the owl with its mouse-prey, decided to investigate. Tiber ran across the branch, her small white paws flashing in the moonlight. As she dashed towards the owl, the squishy body of an unseen caterpillar on the branch caused her to lose her footing and she fell off with a cry of fright.

Tiber managed to hook onto another branch with her claws during her decent, but now her white belly stood out like flash of white light. Her startled cries alerted the guard. Nadine sucked in her breath and her frightened eyes darted wildly from Tiber to the guard. Her instinct was the rescue the kitten, but she dared not move. Nadine's stomach and throat tightened, and the cold prickle of fear moved up her arms. The whites of Nadine and Nathan's eyes were enormous as they stared at the approaching guards. Neither of them dared even breathe.

Tiber's rear legs dangled off the branch as she tried to claw her way back onto the branch. Finally, one of her back legs swung up and hooked into the bark. Her claws finally found a holding spot and she managed to claw her way back into a balanced position. But the guard was still making his way towards the tree. Nadine and Nathan both knew they were no match for a battle-hardened bandit.

Nathan was the first to act. Using his sling shot, he launched a pebble in the direction of a tree on the other side of the grove. His movement startled the owl, and it took off into the darkness, still clutching its prey. The guard heard the noise of the stone as it rustled through the leaves and struck the tree. He moved off in the direction of the sound, but when he saw the owl fly overhead, he relaxed and made his way back to his station. Nadine and Nathan simultaneously let out a breath. Nathan drew his finger across his forehead and flicked it downwards to indicate his relief. Nadine vowed to give that kitten a good talking to. They had only just escaped being detected.

Dawn brought the sound of chattering birds, Nadine and Nathan realized that they had both briefly nodded off. As the camp came alive, they kept an eye on every movement. They thought that they had counted 12 men. It was important to see where the guards stood, and when they changed shifts. At the edge of the river, there was a large raft and a stone jetty where the original druids must have ferried across to the other side. Nathan said that the raft might be able to hold five or six horses at least. The river was flowing quite swiftly and if they could get the men and horses onto the raft, they had a chance to get away from the bandits quickly. They waited. And watched.

Two of the bandits had gone to the river to get water. The water for the horses was stored in the trough and the water for the men was kept in a bucket, from which leather pouches were filled. These were hung on hooks near the entrance of the ruins. Each man was allocated his own water pouch. The prisoners received one bucket of water a day, which was taken downstairs to where the prisoners were being held.

The guard they had seen the previous night threw himself down next to the fire, waiting for the morning meal. His bulging biceps carried the kill marking of the Warriors of Contron. They were a loathsome and violent people who carved marks into their arms with each kill.

His neck was adorned by a string of wolf teeth and hefty leather straps on his legs held daggers, a favourite hand to hand combat signature of the Contron.

Warriors of Contron were legendary in their ruthlessness. They were sought after as mercenaries. Nadine's father had told her that they could never be trusted. Too many of them had led a revolt against their employers.

Sometimes a surviving Contron who displayed the silver hair-crown of old age would sell his skills to train other warriors. They were ruthless tutors, who would not hesitate to kill their students if they found a weakness in their stance. It was said that King Radolf had a Contron tutor.

Contron children were seldom children borne of love. They were the offspring of women claimed as spoils of war. The lust for war never waned and a warrior never remained long enough to create a home.

"I do not feel right about this," he said, prodding the flames with his sword. "There is something in the air. I can feel it." He sniffed, like a hunting hound.

"Do you tire of this lair?" smirked the Bandit King. "Is it too tame for you? Do not cluck like an old hen. Soon we will have our ransom and you can go and find some village to attack!" He slapped the warrior on the back.

The Contron sneered. "And you grow lazy and fat," he replied using his dagger to prod at the leader's belly. A crimson mark spread from the tip.

"Watch yourself! Remember that it was I who dragged you bleeding from the battlefield," said the leader, inspecting the wound.

"Yes, and you robbed me of a Warrior's death. Now I sit in this abandoned wreck of place and babysit Lord Logan and his pathetic men," he grumbled, spitting into the fire.

"Go and hunt another wolf," said the Bandit King

None of the group ever used names that could lead to their true identities or their clan. No two of his men were from the same tribe. He had chosen them carefully. Each man had suffered the loss of kin or clan. They had no one to go back to.

"They are all gone," moaned the Contron. "I have nothing to kill. Give me one of those weaklings down below to play with." he sneered. "My arm itches for another mark," he said, pulling at his beard.

"Soon enough you will have sufficient coin to start your own war party. Then you can take your pick of the surrounding villages and go breed more Contron Warriors. Now eat and get below for your rest," retorted the Bandit King.

Theirs was an uneasy alliance. But the Contron knew he would not have lasted the winter with such a battle wound.

His kind lived to die. It was their glory. Rescues were for weaklings. His clan would quickly turn on weaklings. But now he had a blood oath to the leader of the bandits that he still waited for the opportunity to redeem. Luckily for him, his entire clan had perished in the battle. There would be no clan execution. Only he had survived, through the intercession of the Bandit King.

But with this ransom game that they played, preying on the wealthy, he had few opportunities for a real battle. The Bandit King never allowed an unnecessary kill. He was a strategist. Show enough strength to subdue. Send a message to the families. And safely release the prisoners.

Soon the Bandit King would be able to buy his way back to the life he once had. The Contron was his mascot. His scarred face and ruthless nature kept the prisoners compliant. But he could not be harnessed for long. Once his blood oath was fulfilled, he would leave.

The Contron's agitation could not be ignored though. He had an uncanny instinct for danger. This had been proven true too many times to ignore.

The Bandit King smeared some of the herb-infused fat on the small puncture wound left by the sharp tip of the guard's dagger. It was superficial. but even the smallest wound left unattended could bring an infection. Men perished from fever just as surely as in battle. He would take no chances. He ran his fingers up to the hardened lines of his torso. "Fat! I think not my friend," he muttered to himself.

Today, he would inspect the prisoners himself. He was not a cruel man. He knew something of loss.

The Bandit King watched Lord Logan's face from the stairs. This was a man worthy of his men's loyalty. Justice came at the hand of a man like this. He would fight with the ferocity of a wolf. But like a wolf, he would lead for the preservation of his pack and would be tender with his mate.

The Contron would think a man like Lord Logan was weak. But that is why the Contron had never built empires. They were brash violent men, who lived on instinct. Men like Lord Logan lived on cunning. But the way they valued justice and the call of a higher purpose is what drew men to them.

Once the Bandit King had believed that he served a just man. A man worth fighting alongside. But now all that lay in ruins, in a Kingdom he could never return to. In a different time, perhaps he and Lord Logan would have spoken of the dreams of men for their families and dreams of their lands. But not now. There were no chains or restraints on Lord Logan or his men. The impenetrable walls enclosed them. Small carved ventilation shafts at intervals provided air for the prisoners.

Lord Logan turned and looked at the Bandit King. For a moment they held each other's gaze. The Bandit King's face was a mask of nothingness as he turned away. He walked quietly back to the fire.

Φ

The observations of the two friends up in the oak continued. They saw a cook who prepared porridge for breakfast and scooped it into bowls, first handed out to the men who were not on guard duty. Later the men who had eaten swapped places with the guards, and after that took food to the prisoners. It was clear that they changed guard at mealtimes when the sun came up and when the sun went down. Then they changed again when the sun was high in the sky, and once more in the when the moon was at its highest point. The guards changed four times, by their count.

Nadine's father had once told her that the best time to go into a camp was in the middle of the night, or just shortly before sunrise, because the guards would be more likely to be sleepy at these times. Because people feared the old Ancient's ruins, and would not approach this place, the bandits only kept one guard during the day.

Next day, Nathan took some of the sleeping herbs the Medicine Woman had given them and ground it into a paste, which he smeared onto small pebbles. These were left it in the sun to dry. Shortly before nightfall, he took his slingshot and aimed the sleeping-potion-pebble into the water bucket they had observed earlier. The stone flew silently through the air, hit the wall and plopped into the bucket. Nadine watched silently, waiting for the moment that the men and guards nodded off.

Φ

Fire powder could spook the horses. Nadine harnessed the six horses together and silently led them close to the river's edge and tied them near to the ferry. She placed the hay baskets over their heads so that the food would comfort them.

One horse remained close to the ruins. Grabbing one of the bandit's cloaks, Nathan pulled it over himself. He moved close to the hole in the ruins nearest to the prisoners, and unwrapped the wrist pouch that Lord Logan had given him to keep messages in.

He had written one word on it, "River." Peering through the hole he saw Lord Logan. He dropped the pouch directly over Lord Logan's head, trying desperately to throw accurately. It found its mark, landing on his Lord's nose.

Lord Logan recognised it immediately, opened it and saw the word. "River." He began to make silent gestures to the rest of his men. Nathan had gathered some sturdy sticks and slid these through the hole, which Lord Logan's men grabbed before they could hit the ground and alert the guards. These would serve as their weapons.

With her nerves on edge, Nadine prayed that their plan would work. She waited for Nathan to position himself near the stairs that Lord Logan would use to ascend. She eased the lizard she had captured amongst the stone walls and placed it at the feet of the remaining horses. Then she ran swiftly to the river.

The angry lizard began to hiss and frightened the horses. By then Lord Logan and his men had reached the top of the stairs armed with their sticks. As the horses began to show their fear one of the guards began to stir. Nathan thrust a small pouch of fire powder into each man's hand and then threw his powder to the far side of the ruins directly opposite the horses.

TWENTY-ONE

A Time to Rise

Sleep would not come. The Contron was restless. He was bothered by the kind of quiver his kind usually felt before a battle. Although it was not his turn, he chose to scout the perimeter of the Ancient ruins in the cool night air. The Bandit King insisted that his men were well rested. No one was ever allowed a double shift. But the primal call of battle had engulfed the Contron's senses.

The Contron sniffed again. There was something in the air he could not make out. A memory. He stumbled over a rock. The torch jolted out of his hand. He grabbed for it, scrambling over the rough ground, lest it caught on the dry autumn grass. The torch scalded his hand.

The smell of burning flesh filled his nostrils. For a moment he just stared at his hand. Then he turned and glanced at the tree. Burned flesh. The tree reminded him of healing balms which could mask the smell. But a fresh wound only days old would permeate the air. The sweetish smell of burned flesh had given away many a villager cowering from the advancing Contron.

Then his heightened senses detected something else - the musky smell of a female who had not washed in some days. His hungry body responded immediately. It was not food that he needed: it was the screams and thrashing resistance of one of his most desired spoils of war.

Somewhere in their camp, a female was watching and waiting for him to claim her.

He would find her. He sniffed the air again, and his breathing quickened. He extinguished the torch and unsheathed his dagger.

On another night a cloudless sky would have revealed the beauty of the stars that silently watched Nadine. But tonight, the moon flashed on the smooth creaminess of Nadine's cheeks. There was just enough light to reveal her slim form racing toward the river. The Contron let out a small grunt.

It had been many months since he had felt the skin of a woman yielding to his will. The Bandit King did not allow any women near the lair. He said they dulled a man's senses. Yet, the Contron had never felt more alive.

His powerful legs easily covered the distance between them. Easing behind the tree, he waited. Women had a sense. They could feel danger upon them. He savoured that glorious moment when they turned. It was always the same. They would feel his presence. Then they would feel the stirrings of fear. Their inner voice would try to quell the fear with whispers of doubt. Perhaps it was nothing. Then they would look again. After a few moments, they would turn back to their task. Then he would break a twig.

They would turn in a panic back again. He would then step out of the shadows, the glint of his blade flashing in the moonlight. Like a frightened rabbit, they would stare at him, their legs unable to move despite the panic that showed in their eyes.

The moment would cause his excitement to rise to a frenzy and the hunt would begin.

Nadine did not disappoint. She was afraid. She had never seen such a giant of a man. His body was grossly swollen with hardened muscles and she was sure could snap her as easily as the twig she had just heard.

Her thoughts were jumbled, but she knew she must not give away Nathan's position. The Contron's blood lust gleamed in his eyes. She realised that Nathan could not rescue her from this man. Her only hope was that Lord Logan and his men would come quickly.

"Run," whispered the Contron. "Run, little deer," Nothing excited him more than to have them flee.

Her instinct was to flee. "Stand still Nadine," came the voice. She hesitated. Could it be the voice of the Silver Wing that the Dragon Whisperer had spoken of?

Her erratic eyes confused the Contron.

Instead of running, she slowly backed away, clutching the

pouch. "What was in that pouch?" he wondered. Time stretched between them for a moment.

Then he pounced. His bear-like frame covered the distance with just two powerful strides.

Nadine screamed.

She did not mean to. It would give away their position. But she could not help herself. His body crashed down onto her. Tiber scurried out of the bag and into the tree.

This was no wolf. His powerful body crushed her beneath its weight, and he grabbed her arms to force them down.

There was no way to get him off her. Nadine thrashed and sobbed. But slowly his power weakened her, and she felt her limbs betraying her as his will proved to be too powerful for her to resist.

Nathan was about to throw down the exploding powder when Nadine's scream of panic pierced the darkness.

Lord Logan heard it as well. The men raced towards the sound. Rage tore through Nathan.

The Contron grunted with laughter. He tugged roughly at Nadine's tunic. Nathan was filled with disgust and loathing. He pulled the dagger from its sheath, his knuckles white with effort. He charged. Instinct made the object of his wrath jump up. But Nathan's blind hot anger drove him, and he hurled himself into the Contron, setting the beast of a man off balance.

Their bodies locked together as the energy of Nathan's charge propelled the warrior back into the tree with a crack that echoed through the night air. Dazed and disorientated, the Contron roared with anger and gripped Nathan's knife arm, trying to drive him down to the ground. Blood gushed from the gash on his head and dripped onto Nathan's contorted face.

Seeing the blood, the Contron snarled and brought his massive fist smashing down towards Nathan. But Nathan was leaner and swifter than this brute of a man. He twisted away. The blow shattered the Contron's hand as it landed with a crunch on the rock.

With flared nostrils the injured warrior launched at Nathan, his dagger ready for the kill. Nathan saw that the blade sat uneasily in the warrior's weaker hand. They circled slowly; the ground grew slick with the Contron's blood. Then Nathan dropped, and sliding down on his knees, he whipped past the taller man, slicing a groin wound.

The Contron stopped and stared at blood pumping from the top of his leg. A look of confusion spread over his face. He dropped to his knees. Without hesitating, Nathan lifted his dagger high and buried it into the side of the warrior's neck.

He stepped back and spat at the Contron's now still body.

No more was he a victim of death's thieving ways. Today he had wrestled with death and won.

He looked up and saw Nadine staring blankly at the lifeless body before her. Nathan removed his cloak. Crouching beside her, he covered her torn garments. Nadine steadied her trembling body on Nathan's arm.

She walked silently towards the corpse. With her foot, she pushed his body. The grotesque, bloodied face stared at her with unseeing eyes.

"You and your kind," she spat. "Bear witness to my vow. I will never let men like you control this world. You who prey on those who are weaker. I will fight to my last breath. I will find a way to let justice win."

The whoosh of an arrow broke the silence as one of the bandits fired sluggishly at the group. The sleeping potion was wearing off.

TWENTY-TWO

Departures

With the bandits coming to their senses, Lord Logan's men moved swiftly. They untied the ropes and with a mighty thrust of the sticks, pushed the raft away from the riverbank to begin the journey downriver. The raft was not really designed for so many people as well as horses, and soon the horses showed their agitation with short snorts, quivering and the pawing the raft.

Breathlessly, Lord Logan enquired. "Where are the rest of the men, Nathan?"

"There are none, Lord Logan" replied Nathan. "Just Nadine

and I, and of course Tiber," he said with a grin, as the little kitten popped its head out of Nadine's satchel. Lord Logan's eyes widened with surprise. Just these two young people and a cat.

"Well done lad. Well done indeed!" Then he reached out, took Nadine by the hand, bowed and kissed her hand, in the fashion that a gentleman greets a lady. "My Lady Nadine, I am indeed indebted to you," said Lord Logan. Nadine blushed and gave her special grin; a grin reserved for when one of her plans had ended as well as she had intended.

The river flowed swiftly and after they had travelled far enough to be sure that the bandits would not be able to catch up, they steered the raft closer the riverbank with their sticks. One of the men jumped off the edge and secured the rope to a tree. With the rope as a guide, two of the other men moved toward the bank and began to pull the raft ashore.

Nadine and Nathan helped guide the horses off the raft onto land. They then saddled up and kicked the horses into a brisk canter to cover as much ground as they could before sunrise.

They did not stop until the sun showed its morning rays from behind the trees. They dismounted stiffly, stretching their hands and legs. Nathan began to prepare breakfast for the men. He made crushed wheat with some of the dried berries that Elizabeth had given to him and added a little of his wild honey store. The men sat silently eating, thinking about their last few days. Lord Logan broke the silence by enquiring whether Nathan had journeyed back to Lady Christine at all.

"No, Lord Logan. Sadly, I have not. On the very same day that you were taken, Nadine and I discovered each other. Together, we journeyed to the Medicine Woman to get Lady Christine her remedy. Then the Dragon Whisperer drew a map for us, and his dragon brought us to the Bandit's Lair and now, here we are."

"You have already found the remedy? I can scarcely believe it. My dear Lad. God's hand has indeed been with you," exclaimed Lord Logan.

"Now Lady Nadine, for your great courage, you must be rewarded. How may I be of assistance to you?"

Nadine explained how her family and all the villagers had been taken prisoner and how she would have to travel to the Northern King to try and rescue the baby dragon and return it to its mother. Lord Logan nodded solemnly. This was truly a dangerous quest, for the Northern King had a great army, but more that was known to be a cruel and ruthless man.

He also knew that if the King was able to harness the power of the growing dragon, then no village would be safe. This would be a dangerous and tricky quest. But if successful, one that legends were made of. One where heroes would be made and talked about for generations thereafter.

But first, he longed to see his wife and bring her the remedies that Nathan had sought out. Lord Logan knew that he would then need to help Nadine in any way that he could.

It was only the following day that the party reached Lord Logan's lands. Another party of his men greeted them. The Captain instantly recognised Lord Logan and was overjoyed to see him. He was, in fact, heading out with the substantial ransom that he had worked tirelessly to raise from the people. The people who loved Lord Logan for his kindness, generosity and leadership.

Lord Logan did not allow creditors or tax collectors to take children or seize lands when the people could not pay. Rather Lord Logan implemented a rule that villagers owing money to others, would work for one day a week for their creditors, without wages in repayment. He set officials over the people who would record the amounts owed and the days required to be worked in order to repay the debt. In this way, both the creditor and the people could be satisfied.

This provided a fair solution. In a land where cruelty was commonplace, it had set Lord Logan apart from other leaders. It made his territory a prosperous place to dwell in and a sought-after trade partner. Lord Logan believed in the principle that everyone should carry their own load, but also that we should help bear one another's burdens. The burden of debt could be very heavy, sapping the joy out of life. But Lord Logan had brought love and hope to his villagers.

Dismounting, Lord Logan and Captain Julian embraced as brothers would. "What a sight for sore eyes you are, Captain Julian," exclaimed Lord Logan. "Tell me of the Lady Christine, how is she?"

"She is as busy as ever. She spends much of her time trying to soothe people and deal with issues of justice - things that you would normally do, to keep the people, calm. Yet, at night she suffers dreadfully, so I am told by her ladies. She will be overjoyed to see you. But, please do tell me of your escape."

"Captain Julian. May I introduce you to the lovely Lady Nadine, who together with Nathan here became our rescuer," said Lord Logan. A great hearty laugh roared out of Captain Julian, who slapped his thighs in delight.

"Oh, what tale you tell, Lord Logan. Even after your ordeal, I see that your sense of humour is intact." Nadine glared at him with fierce blue eyes. But Lord Logan quickly defended her honour.

"I do not jest Captain Julian. This courageous pair did indeed plan and execute the rescue. And now we must return the favour by planning a campaign to the Northern King's territory."

"But first, lead me to my bride."

Captain Julian's strong jaw visibly flinched at the sound of the Northern King's name, and the knuckles of his huge hands turned white as they gripped the hilt of his sword. Not wanting to reproach Lord Logan in front of the men, he held his tongue, but there was a hardness that set upon his normally humour filled, warm brown eyes.

TWENTY-THREE

Lady Christine

Lady Christine sank down onto her chair in the great hall, clutching her handkerchief. She was utterly exhausted. Her normally fair skin looked almost ghostly white and fatigue clouded her light blue eyes.

Her hair which usually glowed with golden strands, was dull and untidy. She had not kept to her normal beauty routine because the vast volume of work that had been required in Lord Logan's absence. Just that morning she had snapped at her ladies. "Leave it!" she yelled, throwing the comb to the ground. "I have no time for such trivial petting."

The ladies complained to the cook. "The mistress is once again in a foul mood. I don't know how much more of this I can bear. I hope Captain Julian returns soon with Lord Logan so that she can once again be her normal self."

Lady Christine was naturally a kind-hearted woman, but the strain of the last few weeks had begun to wear her down. She struggled to concentrate on the day's activities and listening to the people's fears and complaints drained her even more.

She had called the jester several times in the past few days to help settle her nerves. How she longed to see Lord Logan, who could sense when her moods would turn and was always quick with soothing words or great big hugs that were tender and strong at the same time. She longed to feel his arms around her and bury her head into his chest.

The people were troubled and longed for their beloved leader. While Lady Christine was kind and well-loved, she was no warrior and without Lord Logan, she could not hope to defend the villagers against enemies who envied their prosperity.

She could only pray that Captain Julian would be able to negotiate the release of her husband with the ransom the people had so willingly given. While the neighbouring Lords controlled their people with fear, Lord Logan was a leader who the people would willingly sacrifice for.

Lord Logan had left to find the Medicine Woman he hoped would help cure her of her recurring illnesses. Perhaps even one day enable them to have a child of their own. She felt guilty that the people were now living in fear because their Lord had abandoned them to look for a remedy for her.

The Lady Christine had, over the years, held so many of the villagers' babies, and her longing had grown stronger with each year. After Nathan's arrival, she had filled some of the void, but even the stable boy's special bond with her could not still her desire for a baby of her own. Now the promise of a child was one she would gladly abandon if she could just have Lord Logan safely return to her.

The strident sound of the trumpets blared nearby, and the hunting dogs all leapt up at the same time and ran barking into the courtyard. Lady Christine's fatigue vanished, as she jumped up, lifted her skirts and ran, in a very unladylike fashion, towards the courtyard.

At her first glance of the rather shabby looking Lord Logan, she began to sob uncontrollably. It was this lack of restraint, that made the villages love her even more. She was willing to be a true human being and quite unlike the distant and aloof wives of the other Lords.

Lord Logan ran to Lady Christine and lifted her off her feet, swinging her around in his strong muscular arms as if he had not seen her for years. At least a head taller than her, he tenderly kissed the top of her head, smoothing down her messy hair with his long fingers.

"I see that you have been on a grooming fast," he laughed.

"Only to make you feel dashing next to me she smiled," rubbing some ash off the side of his face.

Once back on her feet, she hugged Nathan with such a fierceness that he thought that she may well snap him in half. It was then that Lady Christine noticed Nadine. Although smiling at the joyous reunion, Nadine was filled with longing for her own family.

"Darling," said Lord Logan, with his warm brown eyes smiling at her, "May I present our latest champion, Lady Nadine." Lady Christine smiled at the respectful and caring way that her husband referred to Nadine. He was known for treating the young with profound respect, as if sensing the leaders that they would one day become.

"Sadly, my beautiful bride, we cannot stay long. Lady Nadine was key to our rescue and we have promised the help her journey to the Northern King to help rescue a dragon hatchling, so that she may have her family and all her village released by the dragon's mother."

At the mention of the Northern King, Lady Christine glanced fearfully at Captain Julian, who quickly looked away. To Nadine, the exchanged look did not go unnoticed, but she remained silent, waiting for a better time to enquire about that look.

Lady Christine insisted that Nadine be brought into their home to be bathed and dressed in the best that they had available.

Lady Christine waited until Lord Logan was being attended to by his servants. Then she marched to Captain Julian's quarters, without any thought of a chaperone.

"How could you?" she cried. "Did you bring him back to me, just for him to be slaughtered, by that tyrant?" With this, she gave him an unholy pounding on his chest. Captain Julian involuntarily grabbed her wrist and then suddenly remembering his position, dropped his hand to his side.

He turned to face her, she could see the trapped look on his face and was immediately ashamed of her behaviour. "We agreed for both our safety never to reveal our secret," Captain Julian reminded her.

"What would you have me do? Blurt out the reason why he should not go? Where would that leave you and me? You could have at least told him to send someone else. Someone who is more rested, who has not been held captive for all this time," she snapped back.

"You of all people, know that I could not. For him, this is a matter of honour. He gave that girl his word. She too has suffered. Her family has also been held captive. Would you have her go with people who are not as committed to the task as Lord Logan?" Lady Christine sighed in resignation.

She was acutely aware that it was Captain Julian's sense of honour to which she owed her very life and she could not deprive the girl of that.

"I am sorry Julian. I have not been myself these last few days. I am indebted to you once again. I thank you for all that you mean to this family. We have both suffered loss and I know that you would never be careless with our lives."

Captain Julian could find no words, his memory flooded back to when he had first lifted Christine' frail and bruised body into his arms. Her eyes were then full of despair and loss. He had brought her to this place at great personal risk to them both. Their safety had been in their secrecy. But now that too seemed to be at risk. Could he keep her safe this time? As she left, his eyes darkened with the memory of what they had left behind.

Φ

After a delicious soak in a hot bath with washed and perfumed hair, Nadine descended the stairs to the great hall, in a beautiful sapphire dress that she never dreamed of wearing. Nadine's eyes were framed in an olive complexion, and with the richness of the sapphire dress, she glowed with a rare beauty that belied her youth. She marveled as the wonderful feast was laid out for the victorious party. Many a head turned to look at her. But Nadine was immune to the stares of the group, her thoughts only on the huge feast laid out in the hall.

After the celebration dinner, Lady Christine led Nadine to a guest room, perfectly furnished for a young lady. She brought a candle to the side of the bed and got Nadine settled in the beautiful bed. Nadine could remain silent for no more.

"I am so sorry Lady Christine, but why did you and Captain Julian look at each other and then away when Lord Logan spoke of the Northern King? I must know what sort of man he really is and what sort of secrets you hide if I am to go into his Kingdom."

Lady Christine sighed and for the first time in many years, shared the story of herself and the Northern King.

"Nadine, for many generations women have been used as political tools. When a Lord or King wishes to create a treaty or peace with a politically important county, they will offer their female children as brides. Many years ago, my father entered into one of these agreements with the Northern King. This meant that I was to be married."

"Shortly before the wedding, my parents and I travelled to the Northern King's land to prepare for the wedding. A portion of my father's army travelled with us. While we were gone, members of the Northern King's army arrived in our country and slaughtered many of our nobles."

"The King locked my parents in the stronghold and told me that if I were to leave that he would have them killed. The Northern King is a vile and cruel man. He takes what he wants in the most brutal way and rules his kingdom through fear. He is powerful and greedy, wanting to gain control of everything he sees.

Captain Julian worked as a guard in the prisons at the time. He watched as my parents were slowly starved to death. It was a cruel and unnecessary death. The night that my parents died, the King paid me a visit with the intension of taking my virtue. But his men called him away because of a skirmish outside the castle. To my horror another man entered the room and pressed his hand firmly over my mouth. It was Captain Julian. He begged for my silence; he did not want to alert the King. He had heard the men from the returning war party boast about killing the nobles in my land. He knew that it was a just matter of time before I would either be killed or locked away in a tower. If Captain Julian had been found out, he too would have been killed."

"We vowed the get as far away from the Northern King as possible and never reveal to anyone what our plans were. For weeks we travelled. Captain Julian had lost his love to the great plague and had vowed to never love again. But he cared for me as a brother would. And so, when we arrived in Lord Logan's lands, we told everyone that were brother and sister."

"I have never spoken of it to anyone, for fear that the Northern King may trace me and harm the people whom I have come to love. I have had to give up my birthright as the future queen of my father's lands. But in that, I have met and married a man who is nobler in heart than many of the Kings I have known. He treats me with such love and understanding that this life is far better than that of any Princess, who is but a political pawn in the hearts of Kings."

"Now I see that you also have compassion in your heart and that you too will risk a great deal for those that you love. I am asking you to keep my secret, so that I may continue to protect those that I love."

Nadine understood the gravity of the situation. But it angered her that Lady Christine was being denied her birthright because of the King.

"Why did you not fight back and take back your Kingdom?" demanded Nadine. "Surely as the rightful ruler, you could find an army and go back and claim your rights. If I were Queen, I would be like Queen Esther, who had all her enemies' sons executed. She was steadfast in the face of death and approached the King without being summoned, facing certain death unless the King reached out with his scepter."

Lady Christine smiled at the girl's enthusiasm.

"You are right, Queen Esther was very brave and did save all of her people. But remember that she too lived under a secret identity until it was her time to reveal herself. Also remember that Queen Esther had the backing of her husband and was already a Queen before she made her move," explained Lady Christine, "Although she had to grow into her leadership role." she added.

"But Lady Christine, have you not grown in your leadership? Look, these people are now your people. They love you and would follow you," added an exasperated Nadine.

"In time perhaps. But why put that pressure on them. They are a peaceful people. There are no real warriors here. If they were to fight it would be for their own homes and families. I have seen the devastation of war and I would not want these people to suffer as my people once did."

Nadine sensed that Lady Christine had no desire to reclaim her Kingdom and it worried her that all those nobles had died in vain. Nadine was about to protest further when she thought of her mother's eyes. She could imagine her mother shaking her head and saying, "Nadine, now is not the time."

"There is never a right time," Nadine thought obstinately. She hated the Northern King without having ever met him. If she was a Queen, she would never let a tyrant like the Northern King take away what was rightfully hers. Never.

TWENTY-FOUR

Timing

Timing. Only those who owned it would conquer. The fastest predator of the skies knew this to be true. The King's falcon rose up on the chilled silent breath of the earth, its sleek body searching for prey. The falcon's body was primed for the kill, slicing through the air with razor-sharp talons ready to sever the spinal cord of other creatures of the air with a single strike.

A sparrow who had missed the winter flight graced the crystal skies. With an explosion of feathers, the diving falcon ripped the life from its unsuspecting prey.

Far below the King signaled to the bird. Plummeting to the

earth at staggering speed, the falcon delicately landed to present the kill to its master. King Radolf lifted his hand to indicate to the bird that it may eat. The falcon's beak became a slashing tool that ripped flesh from the kill.

King Radolf watched in silent satisfaction. Yes, timing is everything.

The King timed his days in precise routine.

He rose before dawn and he trained before he broke his fast. Armies cut off from provisions needed the strength of mind to fight without rations. To be a feared and respected leader, his men must see him model strength and endurance. His was brutal with his body. He showed himself no quarter. King Radolf learned to quell the rage inside him that always boiled just below the surface, like a volcano preparing to erupt from its earthly crust.

His warrior tutors had been scouted from across the realms. Each had a reputation that could strike terror in the hearts of even the most courageous knight. They were swift, ruthless and deadly.

At night in secret chambers, he would hold a private war council with these killers, away from the meddling of the Bishop. Each man was masked. Shrouded in secrecy, the hidden identities of his private council reduced the risk of spies revealing the players in his game. Bishops had eyes that reached out like tentacled sea monsters.

After his morning training, the King retreated in solitude to steady his mind and be alone in his own counsel. Today his troubled mind fought to embrace the peacefulness of the morning.

Although his guards were close, they remain hidden, behind the dense trees. Only this small clearing, created for the King's falcon hunt, was open and uncovered by the impenetrable canopy of leaves. The clearing was a sun-drenched haven in the autumn light that renewed his strength. Those who dared to appear here un-summoned by the King, invited death. Justice was served with the swift release of a crossbow, leaving the perpetrators' bones to be cleaned by scavengers.

The King in armour had his crossbow and poll axe within easy reach. Always prepared for enemies, his quiet solitude belied his lethal cunning.

His fingers were numbed by the frigid morning air as he caressed the cold razor-sharp metal axe. He imagined the weapon doing his bidding, and smiled a little inside his mind.

The poll axe was a weapon of such deadly precision, that all who saw it, knew that its bearer was a powerful killer without mercy. Its heavy metal top was decorated with four weapons of destruction merged into a symphony of death. When a man saw the King thundering towards him, with a weapon of this power, he knew to give up his final prayers before the tip drove through him.

The hammer on one side could crush a man's skull on impact. As it danced through the air. the razor shape axe could cleave a limb neatly, right through even the strongest armour. The opposing partner in this dance of death would stare, transfixed at the King. Then silently as if in waltz he would turn to stare at the life draining out of him. The inevitable slump would come as the victim fell silently to the welcoming earth, his lifeless body transforming him into a messenger of hopelessness for the remaining opposition.

Should the bearer of the poll axe wish to take a prisoner, the knob could render a man unconscious with a single blow. This is not an easy weapon to use. But the King was well practiced. The mere sight of him riding towards a target would strike fear into the hearts of all of those who dared to face him.

Now the King sat under one of the trees, picking at the fallen leaves. The dew of the morning was, with each advancing day, surrendering to the frosty heralds of winter.

King Radolf reorganised his thoughts about current events. His mind, a chess machine, surveyed the enemy and engineered moves to his advantage. The Bishop was ever watchful and close to the King, closer than the Knights. But he had no Queen to stand in the Bishop's way. This weakness must be eliminated. And soon.

According to his original plan, the hatchling should have been ready for training. The silent man cost him dearly, as he waited. While there was no shortage of coin, the King saw no purpose in paying a man for an absence of results. Yet, he could not turn the silent man away, for he might wait decades to find another trainer.

But the hatchling had arrived in a weakened state because that fool, Nabal, had failed to care for it in the first hours of life. Now, its life-force had to be rekindled. Although Galdolf was fit for the task, Nabal's incompetence had cost the King precious time. It would be months before the creature's growth would make it strong enough for flight. Flight was also a problem. The absence of sky, so critical for life-force, would further stunt the creature.

How he longed to have the creature in his stronghold free to show its true might. But the timing was not right. He needed to conceal this prize while the Bishop remained close. He thought of the ancient texts in the Christian Bible. The Leviathan in the book of Job. What a creature. A dragon-like serpent of the seas. No one could strip or penetrate its outer coat. Its scales were joined fast together, clinging so that no man could part them. An armour that any warrior would crave.

The warlords of old had tried to harness these creatures' strength and power. But now King Radolf had within his stronghold a dragon. The firebrands from its mouth would be his to command. He imagined the strength of its neck as he rode. Like the Leviathan, his dragon would strike dismay into the hearts of all that would cross him. When he rose, all his enemies would be filled with terror.

He could see it in his mind. The dragon was King of all that are proud. And King Radolf would be King of the Dragons. Just as he had trained this falcon, so too would he be master of the dragon.

Yet there was another whom he would need to conquer to execute his plan completely. Radolf shook his head - that was a thought for another day.

Φ

The Cardinals' timing in their recent appointment of a new Pope had created an uproar amongst the nobles. Popes were required to be appointed from the nobility. But Pope Paul's breath had scarcely left his body when the Cardinals elected the new Pope – Viktor. He was sworn in the following day. Another first.

This move had interrupted his plans. Yet, King Radolf took smug satisfaction at the chaos that followed. He had to admire the Cardinal's stealth. But the fact remained that he was in uncertain waters.

Not even the King's spies had foreseen these events. The new

Pope, Viktor, had risen through the ranks to become a Cardinal and had ascended to King Maker status. A Pope who had no known allegiance to any Noble family was hard to read.

What game were they playing? Why break with centuries of tradition? Was the Pope a pawn that the Cardinals thought they could manipulate? Or did they want a Pope who could not be manipulated by the nobles? The lack of clear information infuriated the King. He was locked in a dance with a partner who, although knowing the steps, danced to a different rhythm.

He saw each player in his mind. A chess piece in the ultimate game of Kings.

This latest bout of illness had left Pope Victor weak. King Radolf wondered if this meant the end of his short reign.

The abrupt invasion of a horn alert jolted the King from his musings. That sound meant the arrival of news of grave importance. Signaling to the bird, King Radolf mounted his horse and galloped out to meet the approaching guard.

"My Lord King, there is news of Pope Viktor," announced the guard. Digging his heels into the horse, the King rode with haste back to the castle.

He rode on a hidden side path for a little way until he came to a large stone. The guards rolled the stone back to reveal a secret tunnel that lead to the King's private stronghold. Lamps burned brightly against the smooth cold walls of the tunnel.

Mute, by another of the King's brutal commands, servants watched cautiously as King Radolf's fierce strides echoed through the passage. The servants were never allowed to leave. The entrance and exit were locked down. The servants were always well fed and had comfortable quarters but remained imprisoned for the Kings bidding.

The King raced up the stone stairs, his lanky frame vaulting over three of them at a time. At the top, he steadied himself and reached for the lever that would open his private entrance. He looked for disturbances within the curtain of spider webs that would notify him of an intruder. His eyes darted left and right waiting for the grinding sound. He counted to ten, then fell to his knees. A blade, released from one side, sliced through the air above his head. He moved to the side, his body flattened out on the rock wall, avoiding another blade rolling past his torso with millimeters to spare. No matter how many times he used this private entrance, his chest always heaved when he faced the obstacles that protected the tunnels. He got to his knees and crept over three steps to reach the next lever. His forehead glistened with sweat as an axe on a pendulum swung overhead. With the axe still swinging, he pulled the final lever at the end of the Shaft of Peril and stepped towards the curtained opening to his own private chambers. He stood quietly and listened for a moment. Hearing no sound, he stepped into his chambers.

He had no need for the fussing of servants now. He changed swiftly into a richly embroidered green velvet outer garment with embellishments all the way up to the collar. He selected a dagger to suit his mood. It was encrusted with small emeralds, their deep green twinkle enhanced by the voluptuous velvet. The blade was razor-sharp, most effective for piercing. He would break the fast using this dagger as a utensil. He smiled, thinking of the Bishop's watery blue eyes.

The room was lit with heavy chandeliers dripping with melted wax. The long hours of war council were evident. A fireplace, carved with battle scenes, rearing horses and flying dragons, depicted the history of the Dragon Wars.

The stone table was already burdened with the meal and not surprisingly, the Bishop's fingers were already busying themselves. In the summer months, the King had once seen the tell-tail bruises on the Bishop's legs, as he had lifted his robes to avoid a muddy puddle. The Bishop had honey sickness.

King Radolf himself despised sweet things. They made a man a slave to pleasures that fogged the mind and weakened the body. But for the Bishop's visits, his cook was always given free rein to prepare as many of the sweets as her craft could design. This morning she had made lavishly sweetened custard tarts infused with saffron. The suckling pig was drenched in honey and large bowls of salty crackled pig fat lay before the Bishop.

With any luck, the Bishop's gluttony would quicken his demise. No assassins would be required. No rumours would implicate the King. Although when the Bishop had first been appointed, it was King Radolf himself who had recommended both a cook and a physician.

King Radolf had personally poached a cook from another kitchen. She had a delectable reputation for what other Lords had called "the most tempting pastries in all the Kingdom." The King had paid for her spices and she always had enough cinnamon, sugar and honey to ensure that her pastries remained richly sweetened. At each winter he had also sent her (and her brood of brats) new winter furs and boots.

The Bishop's physician was also of the Kings choosing. He was very well provided for and, in the name of "medicine," the King had provided the physician with an apprentice who was one of the King's spies, to provide news on the Bishop's well-being.

King Radolf preferred the plainer meals of peasants. His mind felt clearer after eating the salmon so freely available in the river. But today, because of the frosty weather, he ate some of the aromatic venison pie that his cook had added to the repast.

"Bishop, tell me news of our new Pope," King Radolf coaxed.

"Viktor has been attacked by a band of masked thugs during the Procession of Honour," replied the Bishop, holding out his hands for a servant to wash.

"It appears the attackers were the late Paul's supporters. Rumour has it that Pope Paul's own nephew conspired with high ranking military officials and nobility to plan the attack. The group attempted to gouge out the new Pope's eyes and cut off his tongue," mumbled the Bishop between mouthfuls of chicken stuffed with grapes.

Resting his face in his hand, King Radolf pondered the repercussions of this attack.

"Why the mutilation?" asked the King, although he had already guessed the answer.

"A blind and dumb Pope would immediately be disqualified, and another Pope would have to be voted in. One deemed to be more worthy. There would also be accusations of misconduct brought against him," announced the Bishop.

"Where is Pope Viktor now?" demanded King Radolf.

"He was dragged into the church. It is said that he was smuggled to the Cathedral of Eternity. But that has not been confirmed," replied the Bishop.

The Paul supporters were the type of Nobles that King Radolf despised. They had an entitlement mentality. They believed that they deserved to lead or have special privileges by birthright. Birthright did not provide strength. It merely rested on the shoulders of other greater men in history. Men who had proven their power. Pope Paul's nephew had assumed that upon his uncle's death one of his family would be named successor.

"So, no one really knows where the Pope Viktor now is?" asked the King.

"That would be correct," replied the Bishop.

Bishop Rawlin eyed the King nervously. The King was not submissive to the Church. Nor was he free with his tongue. Even the confessional produced little evidence to use against him.

The King was generous in ways that other Kings were not. He made Bishop Rawlin uneasy. The Bishop recalled the temptation of Christ in the wilderness. Having not eaten for days, Satan tempted him to use his power to create bread. Bishop Rawlin rubbed his aching leg and eyed the remaining pastries on the table. He had a sinking feeling that he was trapped on a web of sticky silken threads, with a predator lying in wait.

And that predator was the King, lying in wait for the moment when the timing would be perfect.

TWENTY-FIVE

Yakhal and Galdolf

The Master of the Prison leaned his long frame back in his chair as his fair blue eyes glanced over the prisoners in the stronghold. This center tower of the castle, in previous generations, had been the dwelling of the nobles, as it was the easiest to defend. But in later generations, the nobles had moved to the outer chambers to be more comfortable and live in more luxury than the stronghold could provide.

Now the stronghold was used exclusively to house important prisoners that no one wanted to escape. Galdolf was from a long line of Prison Masters, and their wisdom and knowledge had been passed down through generations by the telling of stories. But this wisdom did little to comfort him when he looked at the little baby dragon. A Prison Master was at the mercy of the King's orders. But Galdolf instinctively knew that these set instructions would bring the ultimate destruction of the entire kingdom.

The prison was a harsh environment. The King would sometimes command that a prisoner be beaten. Galdolf would often choose to do the beatings himself. He hated the beatings, but knew he was the only one who could measure the strikes - so while there was evidence of a beating, he did not cause the debilitating injuries that others would have inflicted.

When a prisoner was to be executed, he would sneak herbs into their final meal to help dull their senses, and to protect them from the pain that would often come from the King's cruel methods. The prisoners learned to respect him, but not to fear him.

Family dinners at a Prison Master's home would often include some of the biggest horror stories for the day, and in this way many lessons on how to be an effective Prison Master had been passed down from father to son.

Although it was common to put people into solitary confinement, it produced the worst kinds of mental illness. Prisoners who were in solitary confinement for lengthy periods suffered from such a violent form of madness, that it would be nearly impossible to deal with them, and they could become even more dangerous with extended periods of time. On release this madness could cause the death of more than a few people, before the prisoner could be finally subdued.

But this time, his prisoner was not a mere human. It was a

dragon, that once mature, would have the ability to breathe fire. Galdolf remembered his grandfather's stories of the great dragons from the Dragon Wars and how the intense heat of the fire had caused solid walls to crumble to ashes. Yet his arrogant and cruel King thought that he could somehow control this dragon, by separating it from its mother.

A dragon, kept from its mother in the early years, might well grow to be a powerful tool of destruction and might be able to be controlled for a while, by its captors. But given time, it would exact its vengeance. If the dragon learned to hate humans from its early years, not even the greatest of Dragon Whisperers could subdue it.

It was for this reason that Galdolf deliberately went against the King's orders. After the naming ceremony had been completed, Galdolf had two duties. The first was to strengthen the bond between them, but in a positive way. The second was to build up the young dragon's strength. Once a week, he received an order from the local fishermen, which his son would collect from the Prison gate. He increased his order by two extra fish a week. Two days a week, on the same day and at the same time, he would enter the dragon's cage.

The cage was an enormous steel structure, with thick bars and wire mesh, built to accommodate an adult dragon. It had a small gate with a large lock that allowed one adult human in at a time. Galdolf only entered the cage when the other guards were on their meal break. He insisted that his guards took their meals outside of the Prison, as a way of keeping their lives as normal as possible. Many a guard had succumbed to madness, while constantly working with prisoners, and he wanted calm and reasonable men working with him. During these breaks, the time that he spent with the dragon would not be noticed.

Entering the cage, he lifted Yakhal with his great big hands. The young dragon was now the size of a large cat, and he placed it onto his lap as he sat cross legged on the ground. Although not as bulky in size as many of the guards, Galdolf had a lean sinewy sort of power. This made him agile and his quick wits had made him an intelligent soldier who could keep the stronghold safe in an attempted invasion.

He broke off pieces of fish and held out his calloused hand: the little dragon greedily gulped down the pieces. Galdolf always felt that perhaps he had a better calling, to work in the stables or some other place where he could work with animals. But as many families would pass down their professions to their children, there were not a great many choices available. He chuckled to himself as he watched the voracious eagerness of the dragon and thought that he was not much different from any growing human boy.

"Ah yes, Yakhal one day, you too will soar through the skies. While I do not know the joy of flight, I have felt the wind on my face, when I have ridden the swiftest of horses. It is a joy mixed with power. When I look up to the skies, with my arms outstretched, I see the blue-sky racing by. The trees seem to blend together. I feel so free that I could do anything I want to do. You too will fly one day. You will feel that joy," he kept his voice hopeful, "when you finally escape from this pit of humanity." There was an edge of sadness in his voice.

The little dragon curled its silvery tail around Galdolf's forearm and began to make a sort of purring noise. Unbeknownst to Galdolf, the dragon had the same slanted blue eyes as its mother and would grow into a Silver Wing dragon with enormous power. Once the fish was finished, Galdolf would rub his big fingers down between the dragon's ears in a backward and forward motion, massaging the head of the baby. The dragon would reward him by rubbing its face against his beard.

Occasionally the little dragon's vigorous affection would catch Galdolf's beard in the silver barbs on its head, leaving a small bald spot on the human's chin when they tried to disentangle.

He dared not do more than two of these visits a week because of the concern of being discovered. But he had taken time to develop a few clicks and murmurs, which he used exclusively to communicate with the baby dragon. For the guards and prisoners, they were just strange murmurings that made no sense. But for the baby dragon, they were signs that someone cared for it.

He wished that there was a way to show Yakhal the open sky. That he could see the possibilities of soaring, as he was created to do. But that would be far too dangerous for him. He stuck to his plan, praying that one day there would come a time when the dragon would be free. For now, perhaps his stories could create a bond strong enough for the dragon to discover that not all humans were a threat. In this way, he might save humanity from the destruction that the King's plan would surely bring.

TWENTY-SIX

The King's Counsel

No King stands alone. Power is always maintained by those who care for what the king cares for.

King Radolf's masked spies sat in quiet ceremony at the stone table. Only the King knew their identities. The sound of their voices. In this way, no one would ever know when a spy was close at hand to exercise the King's vengeance.

"We have placed one of our kind close to Pope Viktor in his hiding place. We will know of the Holy battle plan as it emerges. The Pope seeks to flee to one of his allies. He will harness the power of his allies to solidify his power." A masked Lord Teebald unrolled the scroll sent by the spies.

"Between him and his allies lies Ruin Mountain. He will have to cross it to get to there." Lord Teebald used his dagger to plot out the route on the map.

"But Ruin Mountain lies just south of our domain and not beyond Holly Hill Cave," replied the King.

"Not so my Lord King. The Dragon Wars destroyed vast sections of the mountain. Many of the Lords have built their lands on the former mountain plains. But they rise again beyond Holly Hill Cave. And again here...." He silently drew the line where Princess Christine's lands were. No one ever named those lands. The humiliation of the missing Princess outraged the King, who still had found no queen.

"The Copper Fire Dragons are said to have a blast so great; they are able to melt mountains. It was the Copper Fire Dragons who helped forge the tunnels," continued Lord Teebald.

"Why is it then that I have a Silver Wing in my stronghold?" King Radolf demanded.

"Do not underestimate the Silver Wings, my Lord King. They are the swiftest of all the species. What they lack in brute size, they make up for with their intelligence and strategy.

Silver Wings can also cloak themselves in the night sky, their bodies merging with the stars.

When Megadeus, the last of the Silver Wings fell, it was as an act of sacrifice for his mate. Up to that point, he was undefeated," continued Lord Teebald.

"Undefeated" spat the King. "Then why was he the last of their kind? So much for their intelligence."

"The warlords of old tricked some of the Dragon Whisperers to poison the water source of the caves where the Silver Wings held their naming ceremonies. At the time there were many hatchlings.

They would have had whole nurseries of hatchlings and their naming ceremonies would be held with an audience.

The Dragon Whisperers would add fragrant flowers to the water. They washed the hatchlings faces and then the dragons drank from it to grow their life force.

The Warlords located the traders who supplied the flowers. They suffused the blossoms with a toxin. It did not take long for the poison to leech into the water source. The Dragon Whisperers never knew that they were indeed poisoning the hatchlings.

It was a time of great mourning for the Silver Wings."

The King glanced at the Iron-masked man. A silent nod confirmed the story.

"And what of the Bishop?" asked the King.

With a low bow, Lord Teebald withdrew to his seat.

The apprentice rose. His face was masked by a simple linen mask with embroidered eye slits. With fewer possessions, he often thought that the masked council was overly paranoid. But he owed his new home, horse and medicinal herb garden to the King. Soon he would have enough coin to afford a wife. So, he would remain masked during the council.

"He grows weaker each day. His breathing is laboured. The Honey Sickness is very advanced. I suspect that within a few weeks we may have to call the barber-surgeon to amputate his leg. I have instructed him to eat fewer sweet things and to walk the grounds. But he struggles to move even with a cane. I am unable to improve his circulation even with repeated massages. His morning urine is sweeter than ever," came the report.

"How long?" asked the King.

"For the amputation, days, perhaps weeks at the most." replied the apprentice. "But if he does not change his diet, I suspect he may fall into the sleeping death before the amputation."

"Thank you," replied the King. "I expect your report to be compiled and presented with the physician's seal. It will be dispatched to the Cardinals." He dismissed the apprentice with a flick of his fingers and turned back to the table.

"And what of our succession plan?"

Lord Teebald rose again.

"Our forgers have completed the patents of nobility and the historical records. Our priest has completed his studies under our own tutor. Masons have already completed the work on the church."

"We found a village completely devoid of life. A gift from the sickness," he continued.

"We have established a congregation, a mayor and even a Lord. For weeks our treasurer has compiled the tax records. Our Priest is ready to be presented to the Cardinals upon the death of the Bishop. If all goes according to plan, our Priest will be nominated as Bishop for the Northern Kingdom. We require only one assignation of a Cardinal who has visited our Kingdom. But I have a man working on that plan, as we speak."

Our Priest will speak with great fondness of his time as a boy in the Northern Kingdom. If he plays his part well, he should shortly be appointed the new Bishop, upon Bishops Rawlin's greatly mourned passing."

"Very good," responded the King.

Soon, very soon, he would be free to run his Kingdom the way he saw fit.

"What of the hatchling?" asked the King.

The Iron-masked man presented his scroll to Lord Teebald.

"The hatchling has grown to primary pre-hunt status. It scans the cage for rodents. Its interest is piqued, but it has not yet initiated a kill. Galdolf has completed the naming ceremony. The bond now lies with him. This has weakened the bond with the mother. The absence of sky is stunting the growth. But with the appointment of the new Bishop, we will be able to take the hatchling to the open field and have it hunt with the falcon.

While we have need of Galdolf now to grow the hatchling, when the time is right, we must break the bond with Galdolf.

When it witnesses Galdolf's death, the void that we need will open. This is when the darkening will happen. My training will commence at that time." Bowing, the iron-masked man withdrew to his seat.

Finally came the request that every man feared.

"And the Queen?" demanded the King.

Lord Teebald had drawn the shortest straw that morning. It was true that the King did not kill every man who gave the report. But there were an alarming number of forced 'silent oaths' that emerged from the war council room after a Lord had not exercised caution in selecting his words. A forced oath was the term that men only whispered about. The King would have the tongues of those who displeased him with their words or who revealed the King's secrets.

"My Lord King. The Ladies of the bordering lands grow weak. Too much pampering, I fear."

He hesitated for a moment. He dared not say that the King's nocturnal habits had flown on whispers of pillow talk throughout the Northern Kingdom's nobility. Even power-hungry Lords would be reluctant to offer their daughters to a man known for such brutality with women.

"It is my belief that we need to widen our search. As we have created a Bishop's successor, perhaps we can create a Queen. Perhaps from one of the Warrior Nations? We can train her in the ways of the Bishop's religion and place our own Queen of steel instead of one of the ladies that currently feed the Queen pool."

"There are ladies who allow their Lord King's nocturnal passions to extend beyond their chambers, allowing him to satisfy the need for an heir and as well as their other appetites," he concluded, swallowing slowly. He rather liked having the use of his tongue.

The King narrowed his eyes.

The plan danced before his darkened heart. A warrior queen, who shared his passion for power. And his other passions … the idea had merits.

TWENTY-SEVEN

Left Behind

Captain Julian's demons returned at night to haunt his dreams. Ghastly sunken faces of starving prisoners and the cruelest torture methods would weave their hideous strands through his mind. Like many men who had seen the horrors of war and suffering, Captain Julian appeared to have a normal life, but relived his torments at night. Nighttime was the mind's time to sort through memories and store them, the way the great monasteries had stored and sorted scrolls.

Each night he would thrash with unseen assailants and awaken in sheets wet with the sweat of his battles. In his dreams, he had heard the agonizing screams of a young woman. There was something tangible about this dream. While most dreams were in muted tones, this one was vivid, painted in crimson - the colour of blood. Like a sign painted on wood for all to see.

The dream felt significant, but his mind was still a fog. What was the dream? Why was this one different from before?

He splashed icy water on his face to help clear his head. Then he drank some of the milk from the pail. He smiled at the foolishness of a grown man drinking a child's drink. Up to the age of 5 children only drank milk. From the ages of 5 to 14 they could drink watered wine. This is because the water in the rivers was often contaminated by the remnants of dysentery, making it unsafe to drink.

He had also discovered that the stronger wine, reserved for men, intensified his dreams. A healer had taught him to have milk in his quarters at night to soothe him when woke from his night terrors. He sat staring blankly at the wall, with no thoughts.

Then the first tendril of the memory began to enter his conscious mind. Suddenly the whole memory assaulted him, and he was filled with dread for Nadine. In a stark second of clarity, he knew it was the cat that was the cause of torment. He had to warn her.

He entered the outer court. Lady Christine was already awake and organising the kitchen staff with instructions for provisions for the journey.

She came out of the kitchens, her dress covered with freshly ground flour, and gasped at the unexpected sight of Captain Julian, sitting alone at the table.

"You startled me, Captain Julian," she said, finding one of her soft smiles to greet him with.

"Forgive me Lady Christine," he replied with some formality. I did not think that you would be here.

"There is something that ails you, Captain Julian?" Lady Christine asked.

He smiled wearily at her. "As observant as always, I see."

He hesitated.

"It is the girl's cat," he replied. "Do you know the history of the time the Bishops began their first campaign to have King Radolf's father removed from the throne? They tried everything they could to prove that the King and his family were heretics."

"I am sorry, I do not know this story. My time in the courts was brief and I was not allowed any companions except those vetted by the King himself." A pained expression came over her face.

Captain Julian was filled with regret. "I am sorry Lady Christine. I do not wish to cause you pain. But this must be said. King Radolf's mother was known to be truly kind and, much like you, cared for all those within her environment. From the highest to the lowest. She even took time to leave fresh meat out for the cats that lived in the area. Cats are considered working animals, helping to free the villages from rats, so they are not kept as companions. But because the Queen was in the habit of caring for these creatures, the cats would approach her directly, arching their backs as they nuzzled her hem. At the time when the campaign against her was at its highest, there were sly little rumours spread that she had a 'familiar'. People believe that witches have small animals with them which are helpers from the devil."

"I see now where you are going with this," Lady Christine felt the beginning of understanding. "Because of his mother's suffering,

King Radolf passed a decree that no one in the Kingdom could keep a cat as a companion. I have personally witnessed the torture of a young woman, who was accused of having a familiar. I know that it is superstitious nonsense that a cat is an embodiment of an evil spirit, but the decree is in place and if Nadine is found with a cat, I shudder to think what would become of her, let alone the cat. And think about what could become of our entire party if she is travelling with us."

"I thank you for this warning. I will speak to her myself," said Lady Christine.

Φ

Lady Christine's polite knock on the door did little to rouse Nadine. Lady Christine entered the room to find her sprawled out on the bed, with the cat curled up at her feet. She pulled the bedcover over Nadine, so to provide the girl some modesty before waking her. A lady should never have her nightdress shown to anyone unless she is fully awake. She lightly touched Nadine's shoulder, but the girl did not rouse. Startled, she called out Nadine's name. Nadine moaned and covered her head.

An exasperated Lady Christine went to the window and pulled back the heavy curtains, allowing bright light to stream into the room. "Lady Nadine! It is time to rise." Nadine sat up, ready to protest, when she remembered where she was. Her mother would want her to remember her manners.

A few moments later a servant arrived with a tray of breakfast. While Lady Christine knew that she could not stop Nadine or those she cared for from going, it troubled her terribly that her family could fall prey to yet another one of the Northern Kings murderous plans.

As Nadine ate, Lady Christine delicately broached the subject. "Lady Nadine," perhaps it is wise that you leave your cat with us during your campaign." Nadine threw a defiant look at Lady Christine.

"No! Never!" she said with hardened eyes. For a moment Lady Christine did not know how to answer. A lady's answers should always be diplomatic, and battles won through a logical set of reasons.

But being a spirited woman herself, Lady Christine pressed on. "It would be far better for her to remain here. I promise that I will personally care for her."

"I said NO!" retorted Nadine, turning her head away. There was no way that Lady Christine could know that Nadine had never gone to sleep without her little cat in her arms or that the cat gave her a sense of purpose and soothed her nerves.

"Nadine!" Lady Christine grabbed onto Nadine's shoulder, trying to further press the matter. With that, Nadine jumped up, and still in her nightdress, raced out of the door. As Nadine came thundering down the stairs, a startled Captain Julian and Lord Logan stared in disbelief as the young woman, dressed only in a nightdress, came bolting through the inner court. Captain Julian sensed the reason for this behavior and followed the girl.

By now Nadine had climbed the nearest tree that she could find and was sitting on a branch clutching her knees with her back pressed against the truck. Captain Julian, looking up at the tree, was amazed that the girl could climb with such fleetness up a tree that many of his soldiers would never dare attempt.

He realized that to call her down would be a waste of breath. So, calling for a throwing hook, he tossed it over a nearby branch and worked his way up the tree. Then easing up next to her, he spoke with great sadness of some of the things that he had witnessed while living in the Northern Kingdom. While he did not want to terrify the girl, he wanted to save her from suffering.

Nadine's eyes filled with tears.

"Nadine. You shall return to the cat. I know that Lady Christine is true to her word. Think about your family. If you are taken, what would become of them?" He gently put his arm around her shoulders. She was the same age as his own child would have been, if he had been blessed with a child in his younger years. Removing his cloak, he draped it around her shoulders and helped her down from the tree.

TWENTY-EIGHT

Death Comes to Us All

The ache in Bishop Rawlin's leg was intolerable. His heart thundered. His body was desperately fighting infection.

The prayer beads dropped from his grasp. He sought to reach them. But the Bishop had not stretched to the ground in six months. His muscles heaved under the burden of his flesh, and he drew laboured breaths. He would have to pray without them.

Bishop Rawlin had repented repeatedly. He had tried to refrain from the pastries he so loved. He had struggled. But each morning, their sweet seduction re-appeared.

Of the seven cardinal sins, his main transgression was Gluttony.

To his dishonour, he knew that he had spent his life in self-gratification, his lavish surroundings, a testimony to greed.

For years he had preached about the evils of drinking. Not the occasional ale or mead in the tavern, but the indulgence that weakened the senses and caused husbands to lash out at their women, or the drunken stupor that stopped men and women from working.

He ignored the whole text: "Do not join those who consume too much wine or gorge themselves on meat, for drunkards and gluttons become poor, and drowsiness clothes them in rags."

He had focused so on the brew that he had neglected to examine the threat of food. Not the simple pleasures of good eating. The insatiable desire for more and more.

He knew the judgment in their eyes. The Bishop with no self-control.

Had he not urged for a change in the fare on his table? The apprentice assured him he had. Fever shook him at night. Dark dreams were his continual guide.

The stink of the room overpowered him. It had been days since the physician's apprentice had massaged his legs. No one had washed him.

Or had they? The chamber pot was empty. Someone must have come.

There was fresh honeyed ale on the table next to him. But

sweetness clung to his palate and a film of white thick mucus coated his tongue.

Another wave of paranoia swept over him. The king's dagger danced in his dreams. He heard whispers that wove a tapestry in his mind. There was something forbidden lurking within the castle, a secret that the King's gold silenced the urge to discover. The voices outside were endless. Whispered plans and plots. Why would they not leave him alone?

He strained to overhear. Was he mistaken? Was that the King's physician's voice? More than once he imagined that he heard one of the court's spies right there in his chamber.

A rush of clean air followed the physician into the chamber. "Bishop Rawlin…." Silence caught the remaining words as he stared in disbelief at the ale on the side stand. Where was his apprentice? Death was sneering at the Bishop and still, he ate. "Bishop Rawlin, I have returned with the surgeon."

"No," grunted the Bishop.

"But sir. The wound. It is infected. When the poison reaches your heart, you will die," complained the physician.

"To delay is madness."

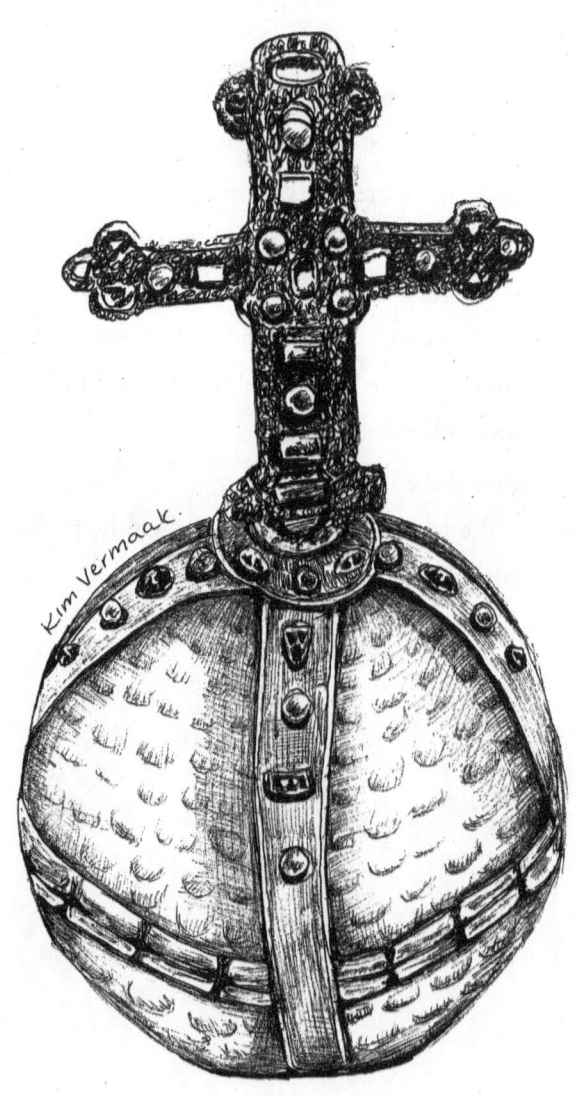

Kim Vermaak.

TWENTY-NINE

The Confession

Bishop Rawlin knew what had to be done. "Summon the travelling Friar," he told his messenger. Not the one that stays near the castle. I seek Friar Watt from the healing district. I wish to confess. Be certain he brings with him, the scribe."

"But a Friar… surely you do not prefer someone of such low rank. Not to receive your confession."

"Bring me the Friar and do not disappoint me," said the Bishop with more spirit than he had demonstrated in weeks.

Φ

Friar Watt looked at the summons. "Are you sure he asked for me? A Friar does not hear a bishop's confession. Especially not ... Bishop Rawlin."

"He asked for you and your scribe. Now get moving, the Bishop is unwell," responded the messenger.

The smell assaulted Friar Watt as he entered the room. Was this a bishop's chamber? It smelled like the workshop of a tanner.

The physician apprentice hovered; his eyes guarded.

"Oh, Lord in heaven. Who is responsible for this?" Friar Watt's accusing eyes fell on the apprentice.

"Get me hot water and rags. I will not accept a confession like this. Not from a man bathed in his own filth. And bring a chambermaid in here. Now!"

The Friar picked up the fallen prayer beads and pressed them into the bishop's clammy palms. The dying man deserved some decency.

"Bishop Rawlin. Can you hear me?" The Friar's hand calmed the Bishops brow.

"If you permit me… I will bathe you myself," he spoke as if to a child. But anger boiled below his soothing tone.

A once great man now lay in ruin.

The Bishop nodded.

Foul smelling bed sores oozed, and some had dried into crusty scabs on the Bishop's flesh. It took hours before the Bishop began to feel human again. The chambermaid busied herself with pails of water. By mid-afternoon, the chamber was ready for a proper confessional.

Gratitude filled the bishop's troubled mind.

Holding the Bishop's head, Friar Watt helped him sip the clear river water he had brought with him. He scraped the Bishop's tongue until a pink hue emerged amongst the sores.

Friar Watt cleaned the wounds, breathing through his mouth to help prevent the nauseating stench of infection from invading his senses. Burning salt eased off the infection. He massaged the Bishop himself. And the Bishop closed his eyes in shame.

For so long he had been condescending towards Friar Watt. Yet here he was showing the compassion that Christ had shown.

"I must leave you for just a few moments to talk to your cook," said Friar Watt.

Friar Watt watched the cook from the doorway. No greens or meat crossed her hands. The kitchen seemed devoid of any decent nutrition. In the corner lay the salmon he ordered.

He could no longer curb his anger. Slamming the fish on the block, the Friar raged.

"Woman, this kitchen of yours… it is from the devil. Clear away these pastries."

"I have done nothing wrong," she cried. "It is the Bishop who cannot curb his appetites."

"Do you not know what befalls those who tempt the children of the Lord?" challenged the Friar. "Even a simpleton can recognize that the Bishop has honey sickness. You are poisoning him with these, cakes," he spat.

"I do not tell him what to do. Every morning the apprentice tells me that the Bishop desires more pastries and honeyed ale," she protested.

"I will have your keys for the spices." Seeing her hesitation, the

Friar narrowed his eyes.

"Now!"

She handed over the keys.

Fair Watt fingered the keys. The King's steel. A Bishop would not have a key like this. Throwing open the door, he saw the stock of sugar, honey and saffron. Saffron was a year's wages. The Bishop's home was full of hints and signs of the King's gifts. The pantry and the fine fur-lined boots of the cook painted a clear picture in the Friar's mind.

While he marveled at the ingenuity of the idea, dread filled his heart. The King had woven his plan masterfully. Not even a King Maker could prove that a King could assassinate a Bishop with delicacies.

If the plan became known, would anybody believe such an accusation? What was King Radolf's plan? Why destroy the Bishop?

"My scribe will supervise this meal. Do not disappoint me. I will not hesitate to accuse you of witchcraft. The vile pus in the bishop's body will be the evidence of my claim," he warned.

"You can't do that," she sobbed, as the blood drained from her face, leaving her as pale as her unbaked pastry.

"They will burn me."

"You fret about your body burning. What of the Bishop who burns with fever in this very house?"

"You will prepare the meal I have asked for. It will free his mind and ease the quiver in his body. I will restore his dignity. Then he can start his confession. I prefer no fevered rantings of a tormented spirit."

"When I am done, you will confess."

Calling to the chambermaid, he ordered "You! Burn these. There! In that fire." He indicated the sweet delicacies cooling on the table, and all the luxuries of the pantry.

"What!" cried the exclaimed the cook. "These belong to the Bishop."

"I am certain he did not buy any of them. But you need not trouble yourself. The Bishop will have no further desire for them. This will be his final meal."

"No matter what his weakness, he once served the community well. Before he became sullied by this vile Kingdom. I will clean his body, so he may have a burial worthy of a Bishop."

Tears of humiliation streamed down the cook's face as the Friar stormed out.

The Bishop held more colour. It pleased Friar Watt that he could offer such comfort.

"I have asked my scribe to oversee the kitchen for your meal. We will have fresh salmon and vegetable broth to help build your strength."

"Thank you for coming," croaked the bishop. His eyes brimmed. "I have much to confess before I leave behind this world," he whispered. "But your scribe must be here when I confess. He must record my words. He must get my confession to the Cardinals."

The confessional called for several refills of the writing quill. A web of danger formed on the pages. The Bishop laboured under the weight of the confessional. The Friar understood, then, why he was called. Who else had the courage to deliver the truth?

Did the truth set them free? Or would it remain hidden within the eyes of a dead man on a spike outside the castle walls?

Too many people saw them enter. How could he bring word to the Cardinals?

The candle flickered and smoked as it reached its end. The flame died. The Bishop slumped. But he was calmer than he had been in days. Friar Watt reached over and whispered the final prayers. At last the Bishop's laboured heart carried his soul into eternity.

THIRTY

Discovered

Was a King's command worth a man's immortal soul? The apprentice felt the burn of the Friar's eyes. And in his head, he presented his excuses. He had done nothing wrong. The Bishop condemned himself. It was the Bishop's lust for food that caused the honey sickness. They could blame no one for that. He just bore witness to it. The cook made the pastries. His job was to report the Bishop's progress to the King.

But he could not shake the scorn of the Friar.

"You are not worthy of this station," rang the memory of the Friar's voice. Even the scribe seemed cold and accusing.

The feel of the soft leather of his new boots reminded him who he served. He was a messenger. Nothing more. The King would find out that the Bishop was dead. Of that he was sure.

Should he tell of the Friar's visit? What were the contents of that confessional? He had tried to overhear.

But the ill temper of the cook after the Friar's lashings had brought crashing sounds from the kitchen, and he could not silence her without leaving his eavesdropping post.

"What did the Bishop confess to?" he asked himself again.

What thoughts did the Friar plant in his mind?

Panic rose in him.

The rows of heads on the spikes grew longer every day. He touched his neck. The empty eye sockets of the heads danced in his imagination.

He knew that he had not served his profession. A man lay dying in the room because he did not have the courage to stop the honey sickness. His thoughts became a knot of plans, excuses, reasons and imaginings.

But he would repent.

After he went to the King, he would flee this place.

He could take up another commission somewhere else, free from the King's clutches.

He would serve the people better next time.

Or perhaps the King might reward him for his loyalty?

But maybe the King would wish to eliminate witnesses. He shuddered.

He would never be free of the King's clutches.

Friar Watt's threats rang in his ears. Would he see the cook in hell? Would they forever be locked in torment at the wrongs that had been committed against the Bishop?

If an eternity in hell was to be his place, what difference would it make to tell the king?

When he watched how the Friar had taken care of the Bishop, the contrast did not go unnoticed. The King's wrath was unrelenting. If he had any compassion none saw it.

But the Friar had a righteous anger. He cared for the weak. He heard the confessions of the humble. There was little tolerance for those who corrupted others.

If he reported to the King, would he condemn this innocent man?

THIRTY-ONE

Into the Northern Kingdom

Lady Christine entered Nadine's bedchamber. The room had fresh flowers in it, as was the custom for visiting ladies. She carefully placed her parcels on the bed and began to arrange them.

She had been to the local armour merchant and purchased a sturdy outer garment like those the pages in warring parties would wear, with woven leather providing protection as basic armour. She had seen to it that this one was fashioned for comfort on a more feminine form.

There was a distinct chill in the air in the mornings. For this reason, Lady Christine had also provided Nadine with more sturdy fur-lined boots, gloves and a warm fur-lined cloak.

Nadine entered the room to find Lady Christine preparing the new clothing. Her face lit up when she saw the armour. As a child, she had pleaded with her father to teach her some of the skills that he had learned as a knight. Having been on many a campaign and seen how men would roughly take women as their right to plunder, he had trained both of his girls in techniques to help them defend themselves.

Finally, Lady Christine took out a beautifully crafted dagger.

"This, Nadine, was a gift from my mother to me. She gave it to me to keep me safe. It has passed down from mother to daughter. Captain Julian took it from the Northern King's display and returned it to me. I now give it to you. Return it with yourself and my champion once you have rescued your family. I wish to see this dagger again, in your hands at this court. Promise me that you will return."

Nadine nodded silently and she took the dagger from Lady Christine's hands. With this Lady Christine abruptly left the room and hurried to her own chambers.

The memory of King Radolf's face when he had entered her chambers after imprisoning her parents flashed before her. She had heard the women's cries when he called for the servants. As they were not yet officially wed, she knew that her betrothed had no place in her chambers. She had grabbed her mother's dagger in defense of her own honour, for there were no champions or chaperones for her in this loathsome place. Holding it before her, she had pleaded with him to let her be, at least until after the wedding. But he only saw her pleading as weakness.

He had wrestled the knife from her hand. "Why it is as pretty as you are," he had sneered. He had begun to beat her, trying to force her into submission. Sobbing, she had cried for God to rescue her. And he did. At that moment, the King's Captain of the Guard had called out.

"My Lord King, there is trouble at the gates!" Knowing that the Captain of the Guard would never dare interrupt his nightly pursuits unless it was of utmost importance, he let the bleeding princess drop to the ground.

It was on that night that Captain Julian had come for her. She shuddered to think what would have happened if he had not arrived. She prayed that Nadine would have the Lord's same protection. She decided to pray and fast until they returned.

Lady Christine had left a lady in waiting with Nadine to help her dress. A lady of a warrior Lord's wife, she was accustomed to preparing women for battle. She had found her way to them after the great sickness. Being the sole survivor of her party, she needed new employment and a place of shelter.

Lady Christine had taken pity on her and welcomed her into their court. It was only after some time, that she had learned the secret craft that the woman practiced. Because of Lady Christine's experience with the Northern King, she now had need of those skills to help keep Nadine safe.

The Lady in waiting carried with her a bag of special small hooks, sharpened to vicious points. Brutal men would often grab a maiden by the wrist. She sewed several lines of hooks into the lining of the wrists of Nadine's garments. They were so cleverly concealed, that the naked eye could not see them. But should a man grab onto her wrist, there were sharp enough to slice open his hand. She cleverly sewed these into all Nadine's garments. She had carefully observed the way that women sat and walked and ate, so Nadine would not accidentally hurt herself. She worked swiftly so that the waiting men would not bemoan the amount of time that Nadine was in the chamber.

Nathan, Lord Logan and Caption Julian where discussing plans for the trip. Nadine entered the room, wearing her armour and secret weaponry. Nadine knew that no matter what, she must never let Lord Logan know of the history between Captain Julian and Lady Christine and the Northern King. Even if Captain Julian had knowledge of the territory, she was to act as if she thought the knowledge had merely come from his previous campaigns.

Nadine opened her pouch and took out some folded parchment.

"I think this may help," she said holding up the hand-drawn map of the terrain that the Dragon Whisperer had described. He had drawn it from his sight through the eyes of a dragon. It was a sketch of the Northern King's Castle and surrounding strongholds. The relief on Captain Julian's face was enormous. Nadine, having provided this map, would ease the risk of exposure. His secret would be safe.

"I thank you," he said bowing before her. Nadine stifled a little giggle at this gallant gesture.

The plan was to ride long and hard until they were on the outskirts of the Northern King's Territory. They would take with them enough men to fight off any opposition, but a small enough party that would not easily capture the attention of the King's patrols. Each man wore limited concealed armour. To the outside world, they were travelling merchants. They had with them a cart filled with furs and other lightweight items that could be traded. But the real reason for the cart was to carry out the baby dragon if need be.

The King's road was fraught with danger, so close to the Kingdom. They remained close and alert. Justice was a fluid term in these parts.

Lord Logan was loved by his people. He was fair and just. His people thrived. His imperfections made him more loved, a lord that normal people could identify with.

A leader like King Radolf modelled only cruelty and fear. The landscape of humanity here was littered with examples of this cruelty that bled into the hearts of those who served him.

Ahead a woman's screams pierced the sky.

Captain Julian rode out ahead to investigate.

"No! Don't take her!" came the cry.

"Mami, Mami!" The call distressed Nadine. She pulled away from Nathan and ran to the trees.

In front of a small thatched cottage, soldiers were dragging a girl away from her parents. A soldier yanked the rope that bound the small girl's hands. Her dirt darkened face stared back, the shadows only broken by enormous pools of blue, rimmed in scarlet from weeping. Though she was no more than five or six years old, her face was a picture of human suffering.

The mother lunged forward, gripping the little girl's arm. The soldier lashed out at her. "Begone woman!" he bellowed, "lest you suffer what your husband did."

To one side, crumpled to his knees, was the girl's father. Blood streamed from his head. It dripped onto his hands. His defeated eyes glowed with impotent tears. Torn clothes and a crumpled body bore witness to the beatings he had suffered in trying to protect his daughter.

Nadine recoiled in horror. But then lunged forward.

Captain Julian pulled her back. "No, Nadine" he cried. "There are too many!"

Nadine glanced at the soldiers. A wail of rage boiled up from inside her. Captain Julian roughly clamped his hand over her mouth. "You will give our position away," he whispered fiercely.

Guilt flooded through Nadine. She was powerless to free the girl, and she felt helpless.

"We did nothing," she cried, her defeated eyes reliving the scene.

"Nadine," said Captain Julian, gently wiping away the tears from her face. "These are the Northern King's men. Your heart is honourable and you have great courage. But you have yet to learn strategy. We cannot defeat them. Not now."

Staring at the ground, Nadine's heart filled with venom.

"You speak of strategy when there is so much suffering!" she spat. "That girl is now an indentured servant. She will work to pay for her parent's taxes."

"While we can do nothing for her now, we can still help your family. If you were to be taken by the King's men, who vastly outnumber us, what would happen to your family and the other villagers? Would our vainly spilt blood avenge them?" he asked.

Captain Julian knew all too well, what a prize a beauty like Nadine would be. With her exquisite blue-green eyes and in the flush of early womanhood, she would be presented to the King.

A quiver of revulsion rose in him. He had seen what the King did to girls who fought him. The submissive ones would live even though they would be empty shells of despair. But the fighting girls...

He forced the memories from his mind.

Nadine turned her tear-streaked face towards him.

She nodded silently.

Holding her head, he softly kissed her on top of her head and smoothed her hair away from her face. It reminded her of her father's soothing hand and her heart ached for him now.

On his shoulders, she would laugh at the wind. She could be brave, and she could win every battle. When she had him back, they would drink warm milk at night watching the flames dance in the moonlight and tell stories of brave knights and fearsome battles, when good always prevailed and no-one was ever left behind.

Her father had once served as a knight. But he had chosen a simpler life. She wondered if he too had grown tired of the suffering. Tired of the senseless brutality of mankind. Did the Christ they knew really die for all these people? She stared blankly at Captain Julian.

He gently led her back to the group. The lost girls still haunted him. But he had saved the Lady Christine and he would give his life to save this girl.

His worried thoughts brought many questions. Would the suffering she had endured in her journey break her or would she rise in strength and become the warrior he saw buried in her?

Not for the first time on this journey, his mind played out his role. He had a history with the Northern Kingdom. He prayed that none of the King's guards would recognise him.

Nadine longed to hold Tiber. To feel the comforting vibration of the little cat's purr. The softness of her fur.

Captain Julian led her back to Nathan. Having seen Nadine fight for what she cared for; Nathan knew what turning back had cost her. He wrapped his arms around her in a fierce hug that sheltered her from the world.

Nathan rearranged the furs on the cart. He gently led Nadine to lie on the fur and covered her. She did not resist. Depression filled her mind drop by drop until the sea of despair was so heavy that all she could do to block it out was to succumb to sleep.

Lord Logan patted Nathan on the back and sighed. Not every battle could be fought.

He had done everything in his power to eradicate these things from his lands. But now he was in sight of the Northern Castle. He had no power here.

They rode in silence. The cart noisily rattled along. The rhythmic sound a cocoon around their troubled thoughts.

What lay in wait at the castle?

They arrived shortly before midday. As the travelers lined up, two guards began to question and search people, to see if they were true merchants, and confiscated any weapons that they found. No one was permitted to carry weapons into the courtyard, to prevent the risks of fights and of course, to protect the King.

When it was their turn, the guards sifted through the furs and skins on the cart. The guards eyed the only girl in the group suspiciously.

"This is my daughter. I am teaching her the skills of a tanner, as I have no sons," said Lord Logan.

Captain Julian had added a false bottom to the cart to conceal their weapons. He had raised an eyebrow when he saw the dagger that Nadine had placed on the pile of weaponry. But he understood the gesture of Lady Christine and said nothing.

They had kept some tanner's knives in open view. He knew that the guards would confiscate these, but that this would minimize the possibility of additional searches.

"You should have come earlier," said the guard. "There is only one stand left, and it is near the stronghold. You would not want this pretty little thing to be frightened by the prisoners screaming," sneered the guard.

"That is quite all right," said Lord Logan, taking Nadine by the hand and leading her to his other side. "I am sure that the position will serve us well." He was so tempted to strike this insolent guard for his dishonorable attitude toward a lady but knew that he could do little without giving up their cover.

Reminding Nadine to keep close to them and not wander off, Lord Logan and Captain Julian quickly surveyed the area and set up their mobile stall as close as possible to the stronghold gates. They draped the furs over the cart so that the underside was well concealed.

During the next few hours, they traded with the locals and took turns to visit other stalls, speak to people and explore the courtyards. They enquired if any of the merchants ever did business with the prison. They heard that once a week a fish merchant would meet up with Galdolf and after that Galdolf's son would collect the fish order and take it home.

Nathan discovered that he had a gift for trading. He thoroughly enjoyed the bartering and haggling over prices. He even managed to get the nearby fish merchant to roast some delicious herbed fish for their lunch. There was a busy hum of movement and chatter in the market. With dozens of customers stopping at their cart, Nathan was filled with a giddy form of happiness that he had not felt in ages. Lord Julian was amused by the change that he saw in a normally timid Nathan.

"I do believe, lad, that your fortune lies not with horses, but as a merchant," he remarked.

Every now and then, the tavern door would fly open and a roar of laughter would erupt. Sometimes there would be shout and some poor drunken soul would be flung out onto the courtyard.

Captain Julian had decided to spend part of the afternoon in the tavern. Wine was known to loosen the tongue, so it was the easiest place to learn the current secrets of the locals. Shortly after noon one of the guards from the stronghold entered the tavern. Captain Julian ordered a large vessel of strong wine and two jacks. A jack was a leather vessel for drinking that was sealed with pine tar. He shared a table with the guard and, more importantly, shared his wine.

"Hello, friend," he said, pouring two jacks of wine. "How strange to see a stronghold guard outside of his post. I presume you have just finished your shift. Would you like some wine?"

The Guard, still reeling from his recent gambling losses, was delighted at the thought of free wine.

"Thank you, I won't say no. I am just taking a break. This Galdolf is quite different from the Prison Masters from many of the other Kingdoms. He insists that we take our meals outside of the stronghold. He says that a break away from the madness of the prisoners is good for our mental health."

Captain Julian, who was careful to drink only when the guard looked directly at him, continued to top up the guard's jack. Now, well lubricated with wine, the guard lurched forward and smiled in a most conspiring way. "And you know what else, he confided in his new best friend, "Galdolf has in his care a baby dragon."

"I don't know how to explain it. But those two have some sort of bond. When Galdolf is off duty, the dragon paces the cage, and when it does sleep, it is just for a few minutes and then it wakes up with a start and seems to be searching around. It also sleeps at the furthermost side of the cage when Galdolf is not around. When Galdolf is on duty, the baby dragon sleeps for longer and seems calmer, and often we see it gazing at Galdolf for long periods of time."

"How fascinating," said Captain Julian, learning in close to help keep the man's voice low.

"I cannot explain why," the guard continued, "as no one has ever seen Galdolf go near the cage, let alone touch the dragon." With that, there was a clanging from the courtyard and the guard reluctantly drew up his bulky frame and thanked Captain Julian with a wide sweep of his arm, knocking the remaining wine flying. He staggered off back to his post without apologizing.

Captain Julian, reeking of alcohol from the spilled wine, returned to the group. Lord Logan sniffed the air suspiciously and asked, "Did you have a good lunch?" Captain Julian simply smiled and began to share his findings with the group.

Close to sunset, the travelling merchants began to pack up their wares and prepare to leave for the night, or book rooms in the lodgings that the castle had to offer. For the sake of privacy, Lord Logan decided they would camp elsewhere. They met with the guards of the main gate to collect their tanner's tools.

It had been a busy and productive day and Nathan was delighted that Lord Logan had given him a part of the profit. Nadine thought that he did indeed walk a bit taller than he had when he walked in. He was sporting a grand new dagger holster made of fine leather – another indication of his success in negotiating.

They now had to find a suitable place to set up camp for the night.

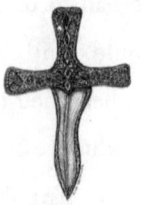

THIRTY-TWO

The Seal

The apprentice's hand flew to his neck as he eyed the spikes outside the castle, his breath heavy in his chest. The embroidered tunic he wore was drenched with sweat as he struggled to quell the wave of panic.

He was never a brave man. Even in his studies, there had been bullies, boys of greater physical power than his own. He had learned to avoid them. His father had died years before, in the war. There had never been a man to teach him. He did not know that he needed to stand up to a bully. But to all men comes a time of reckoning. A time of choices. Once a boy let the fear of a bully master him, he was lost. The apprentice had fallen into this trap. Now all his choices were dominated by fear.

These past few months he had enjoyed the gifts of the King. He felt that he had the King's protection. But now he had to report to the King and inform him of the Bishop's death.

The guard ushered him into the secret war chamber.

He was left alone, and in the silence, his conscience howled out to him. He was a man of healing. The idea of an innocent's blood on his hands did not rest easy with him. He fingered the sealed scroll nervously. The wait for the King seemed to drag on and on. Not even the blazing fire in the grate could remove the chill he felt creeping up his spine.

The apprentice felt King Radolf before he saw him. A heavy darkness descended when the King arrived.

"You have news?" enquired the monarch.

"Bishop Rawlin is dead, my Lord King," replied the apprentice.

"When?" demanded the King.

"This very evening, Sire."

"I thank you for letting me know." The King rose to leave.

The apprentice hesitated for a moment. His choice weighed heavily.

"My Lord King, there is more," he stammered.

Pausing, the King inclined his head.

"Continue," he eyed the apprentice suspiciously.

"Bishop Rawlin had a visitor. He gave a confession. And he requested that it be written down……. and sent to the Cardinals." The final words came out as whisper.

Instantly, he knew that he had made a mistake. There could be no wife. No far away practice.

......unless he could find a way out.

"I intercepted the scroll," he blurted out.

"How so?" asked the King.

"The Friar's scribe sealed the scroll with the Bishop's seal. They placed it in a basket. But when they were preparing the body, I swapped it with a blank scroll," elaborated the apprentice.

"And the Bishop's seal?" asked the King.

"They removed the Bishop's ring while they cleaned the corpse. I only needed it for a few minutes. I sealed the blank scroll and I returned it afterwards," he explained, talking very quickly.

A hint of respect flickered in the King's eyes. This apprentice may well prove useful. He called for the scroll.

"Tell me," the King asked while the apprentice fumbled for the scroll. "To whom did the Bishop give his confession?"

"Friar Watt. From the healing district. He brought with him a scribe, who works in the area." replied the apprentice with growing confidence.

"Is that so?" the King's voice trailed off as he opened the scroll. "Perhaps you would like to read part of the Bishop's confession," the King said with a smile. "You may approach," he encouraged.

The apprentice stepped forward gingerly and peered at the scroll. Coming to the King had indeed been a mistake. He had underestimated the Friar. There was nothing on the scroll at all. The apprentice's eyes never left its blankness, as the King's dagger struck his remorseful heart.

But there would be no spike on the wall for this apprentice. Silent servants whisked his body away. No warning would be shown to alert the Friar and his scribe.

THIRTY-THREE

False Prophets

The simple scenes of the procession of Christ were beautifully crafted in Father Stephen's church. The masons had layered the stones according to the pattern he designed. Although the furnishings were simple, there was enough beauty to create an air of reverence.

Father Stephen was a strikingly handsome man. Now that he had abandoned the practice of shaving the top of his head, his features were more pronounced. He had the regal presence of a man of importance. The oversized ill-shaped robes had long ago been burned. He now wore finely cut simple robes that revealed his chiseled masculinity as he strode through the village.

He had overseen the finances of the monastery before he was disgraced. Now he would use that knowledge to help grow this village. Once he was appointed Bishop, he would be awarded a cathedral. In time he would grow his own empire with the King's gold.

Monastery life was about self-discipline. Early morning mass, hours before sunrise. Eight sets of mass in total. Hours of spine numbing work on manuscripts. For some, grueling labour in the fields.

It had been the pilgrims that turned him. Their gratitude at being received meant gifts of thanks. Some simple. Sometimes lavish. A monastery was not without treasure for those who knew how to manage it.

He used the discipline to his own advantage now. He spent hours of study into the workings of the church hierarchy. Studies on his new role and lineage. The forgeries lay beside a well-worn candle.

He would be true in his presentation of the sermons. His natural charm had always easily drawn both men and women. Little touches, such as a fireplace within the church, would warm villagers. It would be a welcome place to come on Sundays. They would willingly give up their gifts.

"Good morning, Blacksmith," he smiled. "Is the new workshop to your liking?"

"Why yes, Father Stephen. Soon my tithing will increase. The new colt is a fine one indeed. The furnace burns hot. With the King's gift of iron and steel, soon my wares will be the envy of all tradesmen. I have just this morning added the King's Craftsman sign outside my door. I have had good fortune indeed"

"This pleases me, my son. I know that you suffered greatly in the illness. This village lost its Blacksmith. But now you can begin to rebuild your life. Blessings to you."

"Father Stephen," called the Blacksmith.

"Yes, my son?"

"A gift for you. Please accept it."

It was an eating dagger. Made from the finest steel with the Priest's name carved into the blade. The handle was inlaid with a row of semi-precious stones. It was indeed a beautifully crafted dagger.

"Thank you, my son. You have been blessed in your calling as a blacksmith. I shall cherish this gift and use it often," he affirmed.

Father Stephen was in a fine mood when he arrived at the home of the widowed seamstress. He heard the scuttle of children inside before he knocked on the door.

"Father Stephen, welcome," blushed the widow as she and her three children bowed before him.

The youngest brought a plate of freshly baked cookies and some honeyed ale to the table for the priest, then quickly retreated with the other children into the back room.

"How is your health my child?" he asked, his eyes never leaving the woman's face.

She blushed under his gaze. "Much better, now, thank you."

"This is pleasing. Has the new commission for the Lord's wife been completed?" he asked

"Why yes. I know that modesty is the best way, but I am pleased with the result," she said shyly as she presented the garment.

"This is true, but we are called to use our talents. And I see that you have no shortage of those," he said touching her hand.

She hesitated in her instinct to pull her hand away. Surely, it was not wrong to have a man of the cloth touch her hand.

"I have heard that you have to travel to visit the Cardinals soon," she said.

Her fidgeting amused him.

"Indeed, I must leave my beloved villagers for a time," he replied sadly.

"People say it is because you are to become a bishop," she pried.

"Yes, some do say that. But only time will tell. Tell me, are you happy here?" he said, taking in the room.

"Why yes. The cottage is quite lovely. And the children are so enjoying the illustrated scrolls that you gifted them. It keeps them busy when I work." She hesitated. "I have made something for you," she said, holding out a fine-looking new robe for the priest.

He could see that she must have worked for many hours on the discreet embroidery at the cuffs and collar. The thread was only slightly lighter than the garment. Enough that the wearer and those close to him could see the detail. But not so bold as to attract attention.

"Why it is a masterpiece," he exclaimed, his fingertips teased the fabric. "I shall wear it on my journey to the Cardinals."

He dragged his eyes away from the garment and turned back to her.

"I too have a gift for you. I have seen how hard it is for our widows to manage their children with no husband to ease the burden. So many of them lose the luster of beauty they have been gifted with. I have found this ivory comb and I thought that you, being the hardest working of all the widows, should have it," he said

The gift puzzled her. "Is this not vanity?" she asked with a frown.

"Vanity? No, dear child. Your customers will be of noble birth. You will be received in their courts. You cannot embarrass yourself or them. You can still be modest. But care for your body as a temple of the Lord." he said pushing the comb closer.

"I am sorry. Forgive me. I am a simple woman," she said through lowered lashes.

"Please, will you use it now. I wish to see if I can recommend the craftsman to others. Do not be shy, you are safe with me."

The widow removed the covering from her hair, and let it cascade down her shoulders. Under his guidance, she brushed it until it gleamed in auburn brilliance.

The priest sighed. Being the King's Bishop was going to be a very pleasurable station.

"I must get back to the church. There are several preparations to be made before the festival tomorrow and I must leave immediately afterwards," he suddenly announced.

The widow quickly covered her hair and carefully packed the robe for him. She felt strangely ashamed at the abruptness of his departure.

Father Stephen hurried back to the church, his heart racing. It was too soon to let his passions loose. The King had little tolerance for weakness. He needed to be more careful.

In his private chambers, he checked that the maid had packed his travel garments correctly and replaced one of them with the new robe.

As he stepped into the church, he saw a kneeling man, and made a small sound of annoyance. He was not in the mood for a confession right now. But something about the man's form intrigued him.

It was a Friar.

"Brother, you are welcome here," he spoke with humility although his heart quickened.

Friar Watt lifted his eyes, gauging whether Father Stephen had recognized him.

Friar Watt was a careful man. Although he serviced the healing quarters, he was not a timid man. Nor was he a fool. He liked the saying: keep your friends close and your enemies closer. It had been rather a bold move coming here. But now he saw that the priest did not know who he was, he planned to keep it that way.

"I am Friar Walter." It was not a lie. His name was Walter. But since boyhood, his friend had called him Watt and the name had stuck.

"I have heard that you will be travelling to the Cardinals. I too must travel that way. I have some scrolls that must be swapped for the annual monastery borrowings. I have come to ask if I may travel with you. Although I am a man of faith, I have heard that there are kidnappers and bandits along the way. I believe that two are greater than one when travelling," said the Friar.

"But of course. This makes sense. I would very much like to see some of the scrolls if I may. But first, you must dine with me. I am afraid I will not be much of a host for this evening though. Tomorrow is a festival and I have last minute preparations. A room shall be made ready for you immediately. Please rest yourself, while I alert the servants," said the Priest.

Friar Watt swallowed hard. Was this what King David felt like when he dined with King Saul? Two men, both anointed by Samuel, but only one remaining true. Friar Watt recited 'The Lord is my Shepherd' over and over in his head. He prayed for the peace of the Lord and that his enemy would not sense his anxiety.

It was imperative that he made his way to the Cardinals.

The meal was simple but flavourful. Pottage of leeks, peas and shredded pork. The pig had been slaughtered just that week and rows of bacon hung in the parish kitchen, as the cook busied herself with her winter stores.

The two clerics stepped carefully around the typical nostalgic musings of two brothers in Christ. They did not speak of their histories. They spoke of the daily things, like the preparations for winter, the challenge of pagan beliefs and the loss of lives to illness.

The manuscripts were the only risky topic, but they had to be addressed.

"Why is it that you are leaving so close to winter?" asked Father Stephen.

"A valid question," replied the Friar.

"One of the monks has been gravely ill. He was their best craftsman. He did the illuminations. There was a backlog in the manuscripts…months of work."

"But why not wait until the winter is over, before undertaking the journey?" asked Father Stephen. "Surely the Cardinals will understand."

"I am sure that is true. But the word is spreading that the current Pope is not popular with the nobles. If a simple thing like managing the transcript of God's word cannot be managed, then what will that say of his leadership?" answered the Friar, carefully choosing his words.

"Are you a supporter of the new pope?" asked his host.

"I am a supporter of the authority that God has placed over us. If that leader has failings I cannot say. But I can pray for our leaders. That they may have wisdom. That if they transgress, they can find repentance." he explained.

"Wise words…"

"I must say that these manuscripts are truly magnificent. The craftsmanship is to be commended. I will send for my messenger to get us extra protection against the frost so that they remain in perfect condition." He folded his napkin, wiping his fingertips lightly.

"I have enjoyed our evening together. You will be a welcome addition to our trip. Tell me, are you a chess player?"

"I am indeed," admitted the Friar.

"Very good. One of the carvers in the village made me this travel set. It has all the pieces, as well as a board that is divided into quarters. It is all placed in this leather bag. Simple and effective for journeys. I simply attached the board and a game is set. Sadly, I have not yet a worthy opponent. But I sense in you, I may have found one," said Father Stephen.

"It would be an honour to play with you." the Friar bowed his head in submission.

"Excellent."

"Now I must bid you good night."

Glancing over his shoulder, he added: "Did you know that King Radolf, too, is a great student of the game?"

THIRTY-FOUR

The Quest

Friar Watt and Father Stephen left before sunrise. The cook had packed provisions that would last them for the trip.

The journey towards the far borders of the Northern Kingdom would take them over Ruin Mountain, past the Ancient Ruins and towards the South.

It would take several days to reach the crossing where they would ferry to the Monastery of Fortitude. The Pope's army had secured the borders. Once within the borders, they would travel via horseback to the Mountain Top Sanctuary where the Cardinals held their votes and deliberated important matters.

They planned to travel light to avoid detection.

Father Stephen pulled his cloak a little tighter around himself. "The weather has turned. The cold winds will soon be upon us," he shuddered. There was a chill in the air. In a little while the snow would cap the peaks of Ruin Mountain. But that was meant to be weeks away, according to the calendar.

"I have to agree," said the Friar. He was grateful that he had accepted Father Stephen's offer of the fur-lined cloak. Travelling without a cloak in this weather was a sure invitation to a fever.

"Through the mountains, there is a crossing that the human traders sometimes travel," suggested Father Stephen. "It may be in our best interests to choose that pass."

"The pass comes out directly at the Ancient Ruins," replied Friar Watt. "There is a well-known group of outlaws there."

"I am aware." responded Father Stephen. "But we have limited choices. It is either going back, proceeding through the pass or traveling around. We won't make around it in this weather. At least the pass offers some refuge along the way. There are caves in which to spend the night."

Friar Watt pondered the choices for a while.

"I have heard that the bandits are more prone to kidnapping wealthy travellers. As simple clergy, I suppose it is worth the risk. But we must proceed with caution. I would not want these manuscripts to end up in the wrong hands."

"Indeed," answered Father Stephen.

By the time they reached the pass, the gale had picked up. Far from being a shelter, the pass channelled the frosty air through the mountain. Their shins ached with the cold. Blasts of frigid air burned their cheeks. They needed to find a cave. The two men bent forwards, pushing against the icy wind. Friar Watt could not feel his fingers.

"The cave!" yelled Father Stephen, giving a sudden shout.

In the diminishing light, they had almost missed it.

"Can't... see... my hand," coughed out the Friar.

He fumbled for his tinderbox. Then he lit some kindling. The light brought hope against the bitter cold. The Priest shuddered as silky strands of rock spider's web clung to his face.

"Wolves..." Friar Watt exclaimed as he kicked away a cluster of animal droppings and bones. He pulled some twigs from his pack and built a fire for them a little deeper into the cave. They huddled close together. The tension in their bodies eased.

"Let us give thanks for this shelter," said Friar Watt.

The Priest nodded. He stared at the flames, unable to speak.

"Father Stephen are you alright?" asked Friar Watt.

"Mm, what?" asked his companion.

"Are you ill?" pressed the Friar.

"No. No. I am sorry my brother. I was lost in my own world for a moment. I fear my brain is still frozen. We must eat. My cook packed us some softened bread. And for a night like this, let us have some wine," said the priest.

The men ate in silence, each pondering the path ahead of them. Friar Watt had placed the bag with the manuscripts close to his sleeping mat. He slipped the handle over his wrist as he settled down for the night.

The simple security measure did not go unnoticed by Father Stephen. He admired his companion's dedication. Friar Watt was a man of honour. He was a man who would be hard to betray.

In the distance, wolves howled. He hoped the fire would keep the beasts away. Sleep came easily to the two exhausted men.

The Friar woke early in the morning. He checked his manuscripts. All were there. He prepared a simple meal.

"Father Stephen. It is morning." He shook the Priest's shoulder.

A groan greeted the Friar. Friar Watt smiled. He was accustomed to travelling. But the large monastery clergy rarely ventured too far. If they did, local villagers always housed them in relative comfort. The travelling Friars were hardier.

"May God be merciful to us, with today's weather," said the bleary-eyed Priest. "I ache all over."

"It will be a sunny day today. I am sure the walk and the sun will ease off that ache," said the Friar, presenting a hot brew.

"What is this?" asked the priest. The Friar laughed. "A special strengthening tea. I got the water from the dripping walls in the cave. I use this for villagers recovering from long illnesses."

The warmth of the tea forged through the Priest's body. He sighed with pleasure. "You must give this recipe to my cook," said the Priest happily.

"Time to go!" interrupted Friar Watt.

Father Stephen felt like a rebellious child. The cave was no inn. But he was battle weary from the previous night's war with the weather. They stepped out into the blinding light of day.

It was as the Friar promised, a better day. Soon they had left the cave far behind them. From this point, they could see the forests that surrounded the Ancient Ruins.

Father Stephen watched the Friar as he moved through the

rocks. It was good to have an intelligent travel companion.

He had a definite presence. A man comfortable with who he was. He was steadfast in his purpose. It was easy to see how both men and women could trust him. A good man was hard to find these days in the Northern Kingdom.

They needed one more night in the mountains before they ventured into the forest at the Ancient Ruins.

"We have covered good ground today," observed the Friar. I think we can set up camp early tonight.

"I agree. Then we will have enough light for that game of chess," replied the Priest.

"Do you ever wonder why in this game; the bishops move diagonally?" asked Father Stephen as he lost his bishop to the Friar.

"Perhaps…" pondered the Friar, "It is because Bishops are meant to think differently to Kings. To be the spiritual guide of a Monarch means to set aside selfish gain and to present the heart of God."

"And a monarch is meant to serve the people. To create a kingdom where the people can be blessed by God's favour."

"Indeed," replied Father Stephen.

THIRTY-FIVE

Tiber

Lady Christine sat staring at the timid creature. Tiber's green eyes had not been settled since Nadine had left. There had never been a cat in the court before.

At least not an invited one. Nadine had left detailed instructions, which she tried to execute. But Tiber was restless. She could not be held. Lady Christine had tried to comfort her. But it was no use. All the methods that her own healers could come up with had failed.

Fearful that Tiber would run away, she had taken to locking Tiber into Nadine's chambers. Fresh food and water were freely available, and they kept a wooden tray with soil for her to relieve herself in.

"Call for my messenger," she told her lady.

Nadine had rescued Lord Logan at great personal cost. She should not have her little companion suffer.

Tiber paced around the room. She settled on a tunic that Nadine had left behind. Pawing the garment, she sniffed it and lay with tucked paws, staring back at Lady Christine.

The lady quickly slipped out of the room, careful to not let the door open too wide. The previous day had been spent chasing Tiber to stop her from escaping.

Moments later the messenger peeked cautiously into the room. Behind him, a group of guards stood nervously, waiting for the cat to dart out once again.

While Lady Christine could appreciate the gentle beauty of the timid creature, the guards were still steeped in the superstitious warnings of their ancestors.

"You called for me, Lady Christine?"

"Yes, Reginald. Come and sit here with me."

Steeling his spine, the messenger stared tentatively at Tiber. All his instincts were to get as far away as possible from this cursed creature.

"My lady?" he coughed nervously.

"Do you know the route to the Medicine Woman that Nathan and Nadine visited?" her eyes darting back towards Tiber.

"I do," he replied.

"I need you to travel to that place and by any means bring the Medicine Woman to me," she said.

"Are you unwell?" he asked.

"Not I, but this creature vexes me. I think that if I do not find a way to settle Tiber, my nerves may well shatter," she chewed the inside of her cheek as she stared at Tiber's unyielding eyes.

"I see," said the messenger. He remembered only too well, Lady Christine's anguish at Lord Logan's capture. The servants still muttered about her outbursts in that time.

"I will take care of it myself, my lady," he said rising.

"Is there anything else," he asked before he left.

"No. Only, how long will it take?" she asked fretfully.

"If we travel by river, one day my Lady," came the reply.

"One day," she signed. "Very well. Please call for my scribe. I must record a withdrawal from the treasury. I will have the payment ready for you within the hour. By the time you have gathered the provisions, you will have the coin. Here is a letter in my own hand."

Rising she pressed his hand into hers. "Thank you," she said looking deep in his eyes. Lady Christine saw people in the way that many ladies did not. "God speed."

Her gentle smile could melt even the most hardened heart in Lord Logan's lands. The messenger returned her smile with a tenderness that made her eyes shine.

If caring for this creature would make the Lady happy, he would travel to the ends of the earth to find the Medicine Woman.

True to Lady Christine's word, within the hour, Reginald secured the pouch to his belt. But there was also a sheath of coins pressed in a long flat shaft that lined his boots.

Ever cautious, Lady Christine told Reginald, that should he be confronted by bandits, he must not hesitate to relinquish the coin pouch to the bandits. No life was worth losing to save mere coin. The concealed coin in his boots would be enough to persuade the Medicine Woman.

Upon her request, he dressed simply, without a hint of the lady he served. Riders took the messenger and his companion as far as the crossing. There they stepped onto the raft and pushed deeper into the river with the poles.

By midday, they had reached the second crossing. Using some of the coin, they secured fresh horses and entered the clearing close to the cottage before sunset.

Elizabeth glanced up from her bench. Soft candlelight greeted the approaching travellers.

Sliding the small panel from the top of her door she stared out at the two strangers on her doorstep. Patients seldom arrived at this hour.

"Can I help you?" she cautiously enquired.

"Are you the Medicine Woman, known as Elizabeth?" Reginald enquired.

"I am," she replied.

"My lady," he bowed. Presenting the letter through the slot, he respectful stepped away from the door awaiting her response.

The panel slid closed. But the door did not open.

Reginald glanced nervously at his companion.

Perplexed, Paul asked. "What do we do now, Reginald?"

"I know not," shrugged Reginald.

Suddenly the door swung open. Elizabeth stood before them. Her skirts abandoned for riding breeches.

She hung a sign that said "On a quest. Come back in two weeks!" Below were a few illegible symbols intended for the Dragon Whisperer, who would be returning for his ointment. She was sure he would know where to find the remedy she had hidden for him.

"Well, who do I ride with?" she asked the stunned men.

"Ah, with me, my lady" announced Reginald, taking her bundles.

"Well don't just stand there. Let's get going."

"Yes, my lady," he replied.

Pausing for a moment, she said. "I suspect you may be hungry. I have packed provisions for us." She gave each of them a hunk of her special softened bread, which they tore at gratefully while riding towards the cross over.

Although there was no rest, Paul and Reginald savoured the delicious cheese, bread and dipping sauce that she had packed. The honeyed ale was the best they had ever had.

They took turns in pushing the raft and eating. Elizabeth had even supplied night furs for the journey and by the time the morning sun greeted them, they were well filled and eager to see Lady Christine.

At the crossing, two guards waited with fresh horses and more food and wine.

Elizabeth was happy to listen to the tales of Lady Christine. Reginald shared the frustrating attempts to calm Nadine's cat and how his superstitious fear clawed at him every time he had to enter the room.

"She is more afraid of you than you of her," she told him.

"But she makes the most terrifying hisses."

She laughed. "It is her way of asking you to stay away. My dear Reginald, you are perhaps twenty times her size. She seeks only to let you know that despite your size, she will protect herself."

As her laughter rang out, the gates came into view.

The gates swung heavily open and revealed Lady Christine's relieved countenance waiting to greet them.

Reginald helped Elizabeth to dismount.

The two women fell into each other's arms like long lost sisters.

Reginald smiled softly and Paul blushed at the sight of the two women's unceremonious and extremely emotional greeting.

Shaking his head, Reginald took his leave and sought the

comfort of his bed and his wife. In working for Lady Christine, he had found not only a caring employer but also a friend whose tender voice and deep wisdom had helped him to better understand the fairer sex. His wife had noticed a distinct but welcome change in his love for her.

"Come Elizabeth," Lady Christine linked her arm through Elizabeth's. "Do you mind seeing Tiber first?"

"Of course," smiled Elizabeth.

Tiber's eyes flew open as the sound of the door. She had sensed the footsteps and cocked her ears but was not fully alert until creaking roused her.

She nervously awaited the humans.

Two sets of eyes peeked around the door, scanning the room. Tiber still lay on Nadine's tunic at the top of the bed.

"Tiber," called Elizabeth gently.

She carried with her some honeyed milk. Tossing the contents of the water bowl into a chamber pot, she poured the honeyed milk and set it before Tiber.

Tiber eyed Elizabeth, sniffing it cautiously. She remembered her from before. But where was Nadine?

Elizabeth stretched out her hand, her palm facing upward. In it lay a few strips of dried meat.

Slowly Tiber closed her eyes. She sat very quietly, keeping her eyes closed. A sign of trust.

Lady Christine followed her lead and she too closed her eyes, although she could not resist peeking every now and then.

Tiber stretched and moved her small sleek body towards Elizabeth. She sniffed at Elizabeth's hand. Grabbing the slither of meat, Tiber retreated and ate it keeping a suspicious eye on the two women.

The Medicine Woman remained still. Again, Tiber came for the meat and backed away. At the third sliver, Tiber stayed, and nibbled directly from Elizabeth's hand. She licked at the healer's fingers and sat quietly next to her on the bed.

Finally, Elizabeth spoke. "I miss her too," she gently told the cat. Slowly Elizabeth moved to kneel beside the bed.

Tiber gently placed her delicate white paw on Elizabeth's face. They held each other's gaze. "Nadine will return," Elizabeth softly told the cat. Slowly her finger reached for Tiber and carefully stroked the cat's satiny fur. Tiber purred in appreciation.

The only mother Tiber had known was far away in a dangerous land.

"I will stay until Nadine returns," said Elizabeth.

"Thank you," replied Lady Christine. "You can comfort both of us."

"It is your fear for Lord Logan, that is driving her away," told Elizabeth. Cats sense human emotions. "Your anxiety adds to her fear that Nadine may never return. For her to come to you, she must see that you are confident in their safe return. Have faith Lady Christine. I will pray with you every day for their success. You are not alone."

Elizabeth lifted Tiber and gently kissed the kitten on her forehead. "Little one, I must bathe now. But I will return to you and then we will sit in the sun and chase butterflies together."

Tiber closed her eyes and settled back onto Nadine's tunic. Her face a peaceful mask.

Lady Christine ordered a deliciously hot bath with lashings of lavender oil to soothe Elizabeth after her night's journey. A lady gently massaged Elizabeth's shoulders Another had already returned with an emerald dress that would draw out the emerald specs in

Elizabeth's eyes. It was embroidered in delicate gold thread around a scooping neckline Another of Lady Christine's ladies brushed the fiery curls of Elizabeth's hair until it shone like a polished mirror.

The cook had prepared a selection from the simple recipes and instructions Elizabeth had sent back with Nathan. Outside in the garden, a table was laid for the women to enjoy the midmorning sunshine.

Elizabeth looked splendid in the green dress, and Tiber was quite happy to be carried out to join them. She thought she look rather fine against the velvet, too.

The guards looked hesitant. One of them rubbed the scratch that burned across his cheek from his attempts to return the frightened creature the previous day.

Sensing their mood, Elizabeth said, "She will not run."

Asking for privacy, Lady Christine erupted in a flood of tears. Her sobbing so engulfed her that she could not speak of her terrors. Elizabeth discerned the unravelling of a secret that Lady Christine had been containing for a great time.

THIRTY-SIX

The Manuscript

The sight of the forest filled both clerics with dread. But the cause differed for each. Being a mole for the King's war council was one thing. But betraying a good man was a different matter altogether.

"Friar Watt. I have a bad feeling. Perhaps we should turn back," said Father Stephen.

The Friar stared at his fellow man of the cloth. He saw the panic in the priest's face.

"These woods, they are not safe," the priest pressed. His eyes fixed at a spot in the trees.

"Stop!" yelled Father Stephen.

The Friar spun around as the arrow flew.

It hissed as it sliced the air past his ear. The two men raced towards the trees as a volley of arrows descended upon them.

An arrow grazed Father Stephen's cheek. His hand flew up to the wound. The arrow had not succeeded in penetrating his face, but it would leave a scar.

The Friar lay on the ground. An arrow lay buried in his thigh and another in his arm. Father Stephen inspected the wound. "Dangerous but not fatal," he muttered.

He pulled the bag of manuscripts from the Friar's hand. Then rubbing his hand in the Friar's seeping blood, he smeared it across the Friar's face and neck.

"Be still my brother," he whispered, and stepped out of the trees.

"The Friar is dead."

The Captain of the Guard stepped in the direction of the Friar. Two arrows protruded from his body. Another lay impaled in the ground near the Friar's neck. From the blood, the guard imagined that it had cleared through the neck. "You retrieved the manuscripts?" asked the guard.

"I did," replied Father Stephen as he climbed onto his horse. "Just look at my face," cried the priest. "I am a man of the Church. Not a warrior."

"Oh, stop sniveling. Just look at mine," sneered the guard, showing off the ragged scar around his jawline. "I got that from a Contron," he winked. "The ladies love a good war story."

"I am a..."

The guard cut him off. "Yes, yes, you are a man of the cloth. You need not pretend with me. I've heard all about you, Father Stephen."

"We will clean your wound when there is enough distance between us and this place," said the guard. "We don't want you bringing down wrath upon us."

Φ

The Bandit King waited until he no longer heard the group. He slid down from the treetop lookout. Another rescue. He sighed. What a life he led.

He pushed the Friar over. The man groaned.

"Be still my friend. They may hear you. Here bite down on this," he said, pushing some cloth into the Friar's mouth. He snapped the first arrow in two, and slid it clean through the wound. It had missed the main artery. The other wound was similar, and he could remove the arrow without too much extra damage.

"Well, someone up there must love you," he said, tying off the blood flow. "Here. Drink this, it will dull the pain."

Friar Watt gulped down the wine. He recognised the herbs.

"Thank you," he gasped, between pants of pain.

"Let's get you to the ruins. I fear another storm is on its way and you need a safe place to heal," said the Bandit King.

When Friar arrived at the Ruins, no amount of meditation could banish the pain. Along with the missing bag of manuscripts were his precious healing herbs. Friar Watt had treated many wounds in his lifetime. He knew that without his herbs, infection would set in and he would be dead in days.

The bandits carried him as gently as they could. They knew the Bandit King had little tolerance for roughness with his rescues. "You are in good hands," said one of them to the Friar. "We are all rescues of the Bandit King."

He brought with him fresh bandages for the wound set down a small carved chest. Friar Watt pushed himself against the wall. "You have a healer's chest," he remarked.

"Yes. My wife was a healer. She taught me how to care for my men, when in battle. If it was not for her teachings, none of these men would be here today," he spoke as if in a trance.

"She died?" asked the Friar.

"Yes," replied the Bandit King, his jaw set.

"I am sorry. I see you must have loved her a great deal." Both men fell silent.

"So, these are the notorious Ancient Ruins," said the Friar "The home of the Bandit King."

"Just until the end of winter." said the Bandit King.

"Why until then?" asked the Friar.

"We had an escape. It is just a matter of time until they raid us. But this place has served us well. Each man here has enough reward to start a new life," the Bandit King revealed.

"You were born into a different life," said the Friar. "What changed?"

The Bandit King stared at the Friar. It had been a long time since he could call a man a friend. "I was a Lord in King Frederick's Kingdom. I had land, a title, a family," said the Bandit King staring at the wall.

"King Frederick. The missing Princess's father?" asked the Friar.

"Yes. King Frederick and his Queen left to attend the wedding feast. Meanwhile, the Northern King sent his thug army to destroy our army and slaughter the Lords. I was in a meeting of the tribes of the Horse People when they came. King Radolf is a master at planting spies. He must have had one in my household."

"He knew that I was unwavering in my loyalty to King Frederick. So, he cut down my family first. I was riding home when I heard the screams. I tried to get to them. But they were trapped in the stronghold. The flames were an impenetrable wall that burned up all who tried to approach. I got these scars from trying to reach them. Then the men came for me. I know not why I lived or how I got away."

Previously hidden rage surged in the Bandit King's eyes.

"And each rescue you do is an atonement for not being able to rescue your family," added the Friar.

"Nothing can replace them," said the Bandit King. "But each of these men can get a new chance. Each of them was cut down by the Northern King. But each of them now has enough treasure to start afresh.

"Now enough of the past. Let's see you live to another winter."

The Bandit King tugged at the Friar's robe near the leg. "I have brought you fresh clothes. But still, you wear this bloodied robe."

"I am sentimental." replied the Friar Watt.

"That Priest. He took your bag. The King's men would have killed you for it. But I think…." the Bandit King touched the robe again. He felt something within the lining.

"…. that you protected something of great value."

"You are a man of discernment," said the Friar.

"And you Friar, are a man of great cunning," smiled the Bandit King. "To go to these lengths, you must have known that the Priest would betray you. Now I wonder, what secret is worth risking your life for?"

"What does the King not want people to know?"

THIRTY-SEVEN

Friar Watt and the Bandit King

The shadow of death toyed with Friar Watt outside the Ruins. Dirt on the arrow. It had travelled straight through the leg. Now it lay buried inside the wound and had brought infection. Despite the Bandit King's best attempts, fever raged through the Friar's body. The Bandit King did not leave the Friar's side. He placed cool rags on the Friar's forehead, changing them as soon as they were warm; he threw extra coverings over him when he shook with the next bout of chills and shivers; he dripped cool water between the Friar's parched lips all through the night to try and save the man.

But the Bandit King could see Friar Watt needed more help. The forest had once been rich with the healing herbs the Ancients had grown. But their enemies had destroyed the gardens and few of the herbs remained. The Bandit King's stock was low and only the healers in villages grew what he needed now. He would not find them in the forest.

He brightened a little as he recalled the woman his wife had studied with… she was sure to have them. He had heard Lord Logan speak of her. But she was a day or so ride away. It was a risk to go all that way. But the Friar's need was great. If he sent one man… but, no. He would not be able to answer the healer's questions. The wound and progression of the fever would need explanation.

The bandits had planned to stay the winter. But now that seemed impossible. He lifted the Friar.

"Come, my friend. You must drink." The Bandit King held the fresh river water to the Friar's mouth. The Friar's skin was hot to the touch. Should the fever continue, the Friar could develop brain fever.

He called the cook. "What did the hunt produce today?" he asked.

"A few pheasants," replied the man.

"Take one and boil it until the bones are softened. We must prepare a broth for the Friar. Do we have any salt left?" asked the Bandit King.

"Just enough to last us the winter," calculated the cook. "We will need to ration it."

"I am sorry, but I will need half," instructed the Bandit King.

The cook looked horrified. But he recognised that the Friar's need was greater.

The Friar was only half conscious. But the searing burn of the salt packed into the wound caused him to thrash in pain. His knuckles went white as he clenched his hands.

The Bandit King's brow furrowed. It had been years since there was a quest worth risking his life. He knew that the Friar must get to the Cardinals. But the timing would not be to the Friar's liking. This journey was impossible for the Friar at this point. Dead men do not serve any purpose.

He called for his men.

"Friends, our guest is in danger. I must leave you now to help him," he said.

"Are you mad?" asked their best archer. "You did your best. No man here would say otherwise. First, it is almost winter. And second, this man will slow you down. If someone recognises you, they will execute you."

"Yes, there is a risk. But I cannot do what I need to save him here. What I need can only be found in the village," replied the Bandit King.

"You will endanger us all," their weapon maker pleaded.

"I plan to go alone. You are welcome to stay or go to the village of your choice. There are many places that would welcome men of your talents," said the Bandit King.

"You cannot take this man alone," said the shield maker, named Dodd. "I will go with you. You need someone to hold a shield in front of that thick skull of yours." He smiled, showing his lost tooth.

"You will protect me?" laughed the Bandit King. "You did not even protect that tooth of yours." Dodd shot a vengeful glance at the cook who grinned with his arms folded.

"It was that vicious cook of yours who hit me in the face with that blasted pot," he spat.

"Well, that is what you get for telling a cook that his food tastes as if it fell out of the behind of a cow," said the cook. The men roared with laughter.

"I, too, will go with you," said the archer. You will need someone to watch your back. The Bandit King smiled at their loyalty.

"I thank you, friends. I will leave at sunrise. Those who wish to travel with us will show their intentions by being ready. No man will be thought any less of, should he not wish to come."

At sunrise, all the men stood packed and ready to travel. They made a comfortable litter for the Friar. Every man owed his life to the Bandit King. Each of them had suffered because of the Northern King. Getting the Friar to fulfil his quest filled them with hope.

The litter bumped along the path. Jolts of pain from the wound burned through the Friar. He rambled with delirious shouts at unseen demons. They travelled slowly, taking the time to let the Friar rest. If the Bandit King could just get the Friar to the Medicine Woman. He knew that she would save him.

In the morning, they came to the clearing. The road led to the Medicine Woman's cottage A group of bleary looking travellers passed in the opposite direction. Curious the Bandit King asked. "Where are you off to?"

The eldest of the group answered. "We travel to Lord Logan's lands."

"For what purpose?" asked the Bandit King.

"Our Medicine Woman is there."

The Bandit King shot a nervous look at the men. The group's elder mistook it for concern for their Friar. "It is but a short distance. I am sure your friend there will suffer if you do not take this trip with us."

The Bandit King turned. "I will take only one man. The rest of you can set up camp here or travel through to the village near the Medicine Woman's home."

"That will be me," said Dodd. The rest of the men agreed to set up camp and wait for the Bandit King's return.

The cook prepared rations for the Friar, their leader and Dodd. They once again fed the Friar broth and wiped the sweat from his face. They attached the litter to the two horses. Then the Bandit King mounted his horse. He rode to face his destiny, grateful for Dodd's company.

THIRTY-EIGHT

Lady Christine and the Bandit King

Lady Christine had set up a small dwelling for Elizabeth. She was a free spirit. The Medicine Woman was welcome in Lady Christine's home. But the castle walls stifled her. Tiber moved in with her and together they made a contented pair.

At night, Tiber settled in the basket. In the morning she awaited her meal on the windowsill of the cottage. She spent the day watching for Nadine.

Reginald had travelled to the Medicine Woman's cottage to retrieve her most precious herbs and those that would wilt without her care. And having heard that Elizabeth was in residence, the neighbouring villagers made their way to her in a steady stream.

But at midmorning, her doors would close for an hour. At that time, Lady Christine would visit for tea. Elizabeth's company kept Lady Christine sane while she waited for her husband's return. A supply of sleeping remedy warded off the nightmares. The cook, too, was kept under Elizabeth's ever-watchful eye. Lady Christine's anxiety over Lord Logan's journey to the Northern Kingdom had made her a nervous eater, constantly seeking comfort in food. While Elizabeth could not stop her from eating, she could direct the cook to provide healthier options.

If Lord Logan was to have an heir, Lady Christine needed to be in good health. It was Elizabeth's hope and intention to bless them with the conception of their long-awaited child.

That morning a patient had arrived with a persistent skin infection. She had taken some time to mix a complicated remedy.

"I am sorry," she said to Lady Christine. "I am not ready for our tea arrangement. The paste must be mixed from these herbs before the remedy separates. Do you mind pouring?"

"Not at all. It will be fun to be an apprentice for a while," Lady Christine smiled. A pounding on the door startled them. Elizabeth gave her new friend an exasperated look.

"Well, it looks like I will also have to answer the door," said Lady Christine. "Good day to you," she said opening the door with a flourish. Her next words froze in her throat and a stunned silence filled the room.

"Oh! Lord Jefferson!" Lady Christine gasped and crumpled to the floor in a faint.

"Princess Christine!" The Bandit King stooped to lift the fallen princess into his comforting arms. For a moment, Elizabeth just stared. Then she cleared the bench and placed a pillow on it.

"Bring her here," she instructed.

Behind them, the Shield Maker coughed. "Um, what of the Friar?"

"Yes, yes, Dodd," said Lord Jefferson. "I take it, you are the Medicine Woman, Elizabeth?"

"I am," Elizabeth responded, trying to clear space for the second patient. She looked at Christine and then at the Friar and considered where her help was most required.

"I think she may just have fainted," said Lord Jefferson. "I will watch over her, while you care for the Friar."

"Thank you. Was it an arrow?"

"Yes," replied Lord Jefferson. "Clean through."

Dodd stood at the door, clearly a little uncomfortable. Elizabeth turned her attention to him.

"You may take the horses to the stable at the end of the pathway. Tell them you are in the care of Lady Christine. Come back immediately. And ask them to send for Lady Christine's chambermaid. We may have need of you both."

Elizabeth stripped the Friar's garments.

"I see you have tried to clean this wound. You have done well. You kept him alive. But I fear that some of the fabric from his clothing may have lodged in the wound. That is what is causing the infection. We will have to reopen the wound and find the remnant."

"Will Princess Christine be all right?" asked Lord Jefferson.

"Lady … Lady Christine will be fine. She has had a difficult week."

"Where is that man of yours now?" Elizabeth questioned impatiently. Her mind was spinning – considering the title Lord Jefferson had used to address her new friend.

Soon enough Dodd and the chambermaid arrived. Lady Christine murmured.

"You, over here. Stand with the Friar," ordered Elizabeth.

"Mary, please accompany Lady Christine home. I will call on her as soon as I have finished with the patient."

Seeing Lord Jefferson again made Lady Christine feel quite woozy again. Lord Jefferson bowed.

"Forgive me, Princess Christine. I did not mean to startle you."

"It is Lady Christine, please Lord Jefferson. In this place, please address me as Lady Christine. Not Princess."

"Yes, my Lady," replied Lord Jefferson, bowing again. "And no more bowing," she said, holding up her hand. She leaned on the chambermaid and they made their way to her quarters.

Elizabeth put the flint to the fire. She placed two of the metal grasping spoons in water to boil. She looked through her collection of daggers and chose one with the thinnest of blades. She submerged it in the boiling water then placed a clean cloth on the table and laid her instruments out.

"Now, gentlemen, I would be grateful for your strength." She pressed a leather strap between the Friar's teeth. A drop of opium seed oil nestled on the Friar's tongue.

She steeled herself and cut directly and deeply into the wound. Foul smelling yellow pus erupted. Friar Watt thrashed in pain.

"Steady him," the Medicine Woman ordered with an air of authority both men did not resist. "I want him as still as possible."

Elizabeth pressed down on the sides of the wound. Gushes of pus mixed with blood spewed from the wound. When it cleared, she pushed a pincer into the wound. The Friar's jaw spasmed. She gently dug in further and located a scrap of cloth. She pulled it, sodden and foul-smelling, from the Friar's leg. She pressed the boiled clamps into the passage the arrow shaft had made as it passed through the flesh. Again, the Friar grunted in pain and bit down firmly on the leather strap. The other two men held his limbs tightly still and grimaced at the smell of the cauterising. Elizabeth packed herbs around the wound and covered it. Then she poured more of the drug into Friar Watts mouth, allowing the exhausted man to slip into unconsciousness.

Elizabeth rubbed her hand against her forehead. She stared at the chaos and mess around her. It had been years since she had worked with a wound like this. Lord Jefferson took her arm and eased her into a chair.

"You rest now," he said quietly and then set about cleaning up. He threw the soiled rags into the fire and washed down the surface. "May I take your apron?" He held out his hand. Elizabeth removed the sullied garment.

There were a few drinking vessels on the shelf, so he chose one and poured Elizabeth some tea.

"Thank you for taking care of our friend," he said.

Dodd, however, sat silent. Shocked by the whole experience, he was unable to utter a word.

No-one spoke for some time.

Their train of thought was interrupted by a gentle knock.

"I beg your pardon," curtseyed a maid. "The Lady Christine has requested you join her for dinner. She has sent two of her maids to keep watch over the Friar."

She offered a pile of freshly laundered clothing, bowing her head.

"This is for you, Lord Jefferson. There is a washroom just back there. You finish up while I watch the Friar."

It had been many years since Lord Jefferson had worn a Lord's clothing. He looked at Elizabeth.

"Is Lord Logan at home?" he asked.

"Why do you ask?" Elizabeth gave him one of her interrogating glances.

"No reason. I simply heard he was away."

"Lord Logan is on a journey to the Northern Kingdom. We expect him back soon enough," replied Elizabeth.

The set of Lord Jefferson's jaw indicated his anger. His eyes narrowed and showed a rage-filled icy blue.

"I think you should go on ahead of me," said Elizabeth. From his conduct in her rooms, she sensed he meant Lady Christine no harm. But she discerned a dark secret between the two that would need privacy to discuss. She was momentarily overcome by a longing for the quiet life of her own cottage. Simple pleasures. The sunny entrance. Her fragrant garden. This new cottage was comfortable, but nothing quite like her own home.

Dodd wanted no part of all this drama. He spent the night in the local tavern, where there was a comfortable room upstairs. He filled himself with pork pie and honeyed ale, hoping a pretty waitress would give him a smile.

Lord Jefferson found Lady Christine seated at the table chatting to one of her ladies. She glanced at him from beneath her lashes. Beatrice rose and acknowledged the Lord. She left, into the shadows.

"Please Lord Jefferson, come sit with me," she smiled. But the smile fell short of her eyes. She looked like her mother, with the same gentle, yet commanding spirit. Even the furrowed brow that lingered when faced with trouble news, carried the essence of the Queen. Lord Jefferson saw why a man such as Lord Logan would appreciate her. There was a gentleness and purity of spirit that did not wane despite danger. The royal family had always remained dignified even when faced with enemies. But now the Princess's face grew pale. Lord Jefferson had seen too many battles not to read her now. He picked up her fear like a hound chasing a fox. The moment dragged on, full of words yet unspoken.

A small cough cleared the air. "I think the winter will be arriving early this year. Do you agree?" she asked.

"Perhaps," replied Lord Jefferson.

The meal laid before them was fitting of a man of his former station. It brought back painful memories of the life he had lost. Lady Christine realised he was waiting for her to begin her meal. In the castle it would be customary for the royals to begin eating first. She reached for the wild boar which the cook had prepared with great care. It was fragrant with the spices her father had favoured.

The aroma brought back memories of the annual first hunt of the season. Lord Jefferson had never missed the first hunt with King Frederick. The last hunt he had participated in had been his son's first and last. The boy had been so excited as he rode his pony next to his father. Lord Jefferson's eyes clouded at the memory.

"May we speak plainly?" asked Lady Christine.

"Yes," came the simple reply.

"As you are alive, I must ask. Are you here to do King Radolf's work?"

Lord Jefferson's face turned dark. He held the look of a snarling wolf. "King Radolf took everything from me. My title, my lands and my family. Your father was a great man. Dare I say, Friend? I would have fought with him to death. Yet I did not protect him. I did not discern that there were spies within our kingdom. It cost me my King, and my family. So no, I am not here to do King Radolf's work."

Lady Christine laid her hand over his. She saw his torment. "Lord Jefferson, I will speak with my husband. He will grant you a haven here."

He looked down at her hand. His frown deepened. "You have your mother's heart and your father's loyalty. I thank you. But I cannot stay. Once the Friar is out of danger, I must leave. Perhaps even sooner," he said glancing over his shoulder.

"Why are you running?" asked Lady Christine. Lord Jefferson stopped and stared at her.

His head turned slowly while he measured words. "Running?" he asked

"I see it in your eyes. All your movements. Jumpy. There is something you fear. What is it?" asked Lady Christine.

"Running…" he repeated. "You know nothing of the man I now am my Lady." The words sounded strange in his ears. Here was a Princess masquerading as a Lord's wife. While her kingdom lay ransom to a cruel man.

"I may ask you the same question. Why do you hide here, in

this place?" he asked, his voice rising. "Your Kingdom is worth fighting for," he added. Lady Christine recoiled as if he had struck her.

"Forgive me. I forget my place," retracted Lord Jefferson. He rose to leave. "I thank you for your hospitality." His jaw set and his eyes hardened.

"And you... know nothing of what I have endured Lord Jefferson. I was but a girl. A bride promised to a vile and cruel man. Alone in a castle, stripped of my parents, my chaperone and my ladies. Hearing young women screaming in the corridors. Knowing that one day he would come for me. My parents starved to death just meters away from where I lay." She covered her pain with anger. But it was not anger towards him; it was anger at the Northern King. Anger that she had long ago suppressed.

"Had it not been for one of the guards who took pity on me and brought me here, it sickens me to think what could have happened to me." Her eyes dared him to press her.

"Lady Christine when I see your face, I hear the screams of my wife and child as they burned alive. A death for heretics, not innocent women and children. Not even your father would allow burning in his Kingdom. He would have avenged the innocent. He would have fought for his people. The love for his country flowed thick in his veins. Your mother had this passion as well. Yet besides the likeness of your face, I see in you none of her love for her country."

Lady Christine let out the softest of whimpers, as she heard him speak of her parents. Parents she was not even allowed to bury. Her heart ached with longing for them. She turned her face, so he could not see her fight back the tears.

He knew he had pushed too hard. But the pain that they had both suppressed for years could no longer be contained. He wished that he could comfort her. But to do so would unleash emotions that he was not yet ready to face.

He reached for her, the way an uncle would have. He longed to protect her against the storms that would come, now that the truth was bubbling to the brim. Soon it would spill out and she would be forced to speak to Lord Logan. When that time came, he needed to be away from this place. He could not stay knowing that his family had died in vain. That there was no one worthy to claim the throne. This time when he turned to leave, she did not try to stop him.

THIRTY-NINE

The Oath

The Bandit King made his way through the gardens back to Elizabeth's cottage. He searched for a pillow and gently moved her head into a comfortable position. Then he found a blanket and covered her, tucking the edges around her. He rekindled the fire, which had burned low while he was at dinner.

Now he sat staring at the Friar. For what purpose did the Lord bring this man to him, the Bandit King? He who embraced the life of an outlaw. He who made victims of wealthy men for his own gain. But here he sat, right in Lord Logan's territory. Lord Logan, the man whom he had wronged.

It was Friar Watt who risked his life to do what was right. Now perhaps was the time to take a risk himself. Sifting through his healer's chest, he removed the false bottom and took out his wife's cross. She had given it to him to carry when he went away. "Trust in the Lord always and lean not on your own understanding," she had told him.

It had been years since he prayed. His anger at the loss of his family was too great. His soul had been numb. But now, as he held the cross, an urge he could not fathom overcame him, and he got onto his knees. He held the cross tightly and he prayed. He prayed for the Friar. He prayed for the Princess. And he prayed that one day he could show honour to his friend, the king, who died at the hand of a tyrant.

The Bandit King found Elizabeth's supply of parchment. He placed two gold coins on the shelf and removed some sheets. He wrote two letters. One to the Friar and one to Princess Christine. Inside his healer's chest, his ring hid alongside his wife's cross. He had not sealed a letter with his ring since before the night King Radolf had claimed the lives of his wife and child. But now he sealed both letters using the ring and placed them on the table. He left more coins and a small note to use them for additional remedies for the Friar.

Now he would find Dodd and tell him of his plan. The Bandit King stepped out into the cold night air. He did not see the shadows move with him.

Dodd smiled in his sleep, his body relishing the warmth of the inn's bed. With a full belly and a night of merriment, he felt pleased at his good fortune. He was suddenly startled awake by the weight of a man on the end of the bed. He drew his dagger from beneath the pillow and waved it unseeing in the dark.

"Put that away before you hurt yourself," said the Bandit King.

"Man, you are lucky to be alive," said Dodd.

The Bandit King laughed. "And you are lucky I am not one of the King's men. I see you enjoyed your evening," he said glancing at the empty flagon beside the bed.

The man smiled ruefully. The Bandit King never allowed drink at the Ruins. He said it dulled a man's senses. Dodd was excellent at making shields and setting traps. But he was no knife fighter. In this state, the Bandit King would probably have to keep watch over him. That drink was sure to come out at some point in the night.

"We have to leave," said the Bandit King. "What?" cried Dodd. "This is the first bed that I have slept in years. What is the matter with you? Can't a man have at least some comforts."

"Come now. You will be able to buy an inn full of beds at the next village. But we cannot stay here tonight. We must move on," said the Bandit King.

Dodd snorted in response as he pulled on his breeches. He had half hoped to entice the waitress to have a private lunch with him the next day.

The cold night air was in sharp contrast to the warmth of the bed above. They roused the stable boy, paid and quietly made their way out of the village. Only a few minutes out of the village the Bandit King's prediction came true…. the drink decided to make its way out into the night air. The Bandit King heaved the shield maker off his horse and positioned him at a tree. The smell of it made him want to gag as well. It was no wonder that the Bible told leaders not to be drunk with wine. It made fools of them all.

The sounds of the vomiting concealed the noise of their pursuer. But the Bandit King saw the glint of a short sword just as Beatrice stepped out of the shadows.

"Good evening, Lord Jefferson. Or should I say, Bandit King?" she asked.

The Bandit King drew his sword.

"You are one of Princess Christine's ladies. What do you want?"

The shield maker swayed on his feet. "Come here, you treacherous woman and I will teach you a lesson," he slurred. Beatrice rolled her eyes. "A fine guard you have over there."

She thrust her sword into the ground. "Come, you drunken fool. I will fight you with one hand behind my back and still give you a whipping."

The Bandit King could not help smiling. He put away his sword. "How may we assist?"

"My name is Beatrice. I protect Lady Christine. Contron Warrior blood runs in my veins," she told them.

"Controns have no female warriors," said the Bandit King.

"Yes, and no," explained Beatrice. I am the daughter of a spoil of war. My father took my mother in the manner that all Contron warriors take women. By force. But with time, his heart turned. He grew to love her. When she died of the fever, he shaved my head and took me into battle with him disguised as a boy. He trained me. I learned to see signs in men. To see how they took women. How to protect myself. I vowed to teach other women these skills."

The Bandit King was intrigued. "What do you want with us? Do you mean to drag us to Lord Logan's stronghold?"

"I mean to recruit, you." she said.

"Recruit us?" This evening was getting stranger by the minute, he thought to himself.

"Lady Christine cannot remain hidden forever. Lord Logan has accompanied Nadine to rescue the dragon hatchling. If they succeed, the King will find out who is responsible. If they do not, the royal torturer will extract the truth from them. Either way, he will descend upon us. I can train her and protect her only to a point. She will need an army. I need men I can trust. Men who will join this quest."

"How do you plan to get Lord Logan to let the Bandit King fight for his wife?" he asked.

"You have presented a challenge. But Lord Logan is a good and sensible man. I feel he would understand the circumstances. You leave that to me. Only let me know where you plan to make camp, so I may find you at the given time."

"How do I know that you will not betray me and see all my men hung?" asked the Bandit King.

Beatrice pulled her dagger from her belt. Slicing her hand, she presented it. "I will make a blood oath with you now, Bandit King." A Contron blood oath was the highest honour a warrior could present.

Piercing his own hand, the Bandit King accepted.

FORTY

An Unexpected Reunion

Upon leaving the castle of the Northern Kingdom, Captain Julian saw a woman who startled him, with the familiarity of her face. It was partially covered, yet he could see the fairness of her skin and the thick raven hair that hung on her shoulders. The deep blue eyes framed by thick dark lashes, caused an awakening in him.

His mind suddenly raced back, and he could see his wife being tossed onto the cart of corpses, all dead from the sickness. When the sickness had struck, the dead were burned to prevent the spread of infection. No individuals could be buried. The bodies were tossed into large open pits, where they were burned. There were no graves to be visited and family members had to mourn the loss of their loved ones without the normal rituals that began the process of healing the broken hearted.

Captain Julian's mind raced. He tried to fight off his feelings. He realized they were normal longings that any husband who has ever lost a wife might feel if a woman with similar features passed by. But the stirring that he felt in his spirit could not be calmed. He even recognized her walk. The rhythm with which her skirts flowed as she walked stirred him. She was just a few paces away from him, but he dared not confront her while still within sight of the guards.

Then as they moved onto the main path that led to the villages, she stumbled on a stone and dropped one of her parcels. Captain Julian leapt forward and grabbed the parcel as she bent down to retrieve it. Their eyes met, as he handed her the parcel. The woman gasped. Tears welled up in her deep blue eyes. Captain Julian placed his finger on his lips, to quieten her, while still holding her gaze. She turned back and glanced at the guards and then nodded silently.

Then she walked over the man she could see must be the leader of this little group.

"Sir," she said to Lord Logan. "Your party may need shelter for the night, as I believe that there may be rain soon. Please may I be of assistance? My sister has lodgings not far away from here. There is a shed to keep your stock safely and enough room for your whole party.

For a moment, Lord Logan hesitated, then after glancing in Captain Julian's direction, and seeing him nod, he agreed.

Captain Julian helped the woman into the cart and once she

was settled, they began to make their way to the lodgings. The cart rattled along, and Nadine looked curiously at the woman.

"You know each other," said Nadine quietly. The woman wore a scarf around her head, which with the rhythm of the cart had moved slightly back from her face. Although the woman was young, there was a great sadness in her face, which was scarred with several deep marks, which were not initially visible.

"Yes," replied the woman, without offering any more information.

The party came alongside the house, whose welcome lights were of great comfort to the travelling party feeling the pinch of winter in the air. The woman suggested that they take the horses to the stables. Nathan made a move towards the horses, but Captain Julian said, "No Lad, you have worked hard today, and we are in a strange place, let me take them."

Abruptly the door opened, and a woman called out, "Sophie, is that you?"

"Yes, Sister, it is. Please take care of our guests, while I lead the horses to the stables." At the sound of her name, Captain Julian gasped, and like a man possessed almost bolted with the horses towards the stables.

Sophie followed slowly behind him. He waited for her in the stables, his mind racing with questions. When she reached the doorway, he could no longer contain himself. He grabbed her, pulling down the scarf, moving in close as if to kiss her. But she flinched and pulled away.

"Sophie, my darling wife, why do you pull away. How have you come to be here? Where have you been all these years?"

Sophie began to cry.

"Julian, I am so sorry, but you can no longer love me, for I have grown ugly." She looked up at him, allowing him to see the full extent of the scars on her face. For a woman as beautiful as Sophie once had been, the scarring must have seemed dreadful. But in truth, the scars were only one cheek and part of her forehead. Her long raven hair covered most of the scarring on her forehead and the scarf had concealed her cheeks, making her appear exotic and strange, like women he had encountered on his travels across the sea, who intentionally cover their faces. Her lovely eyes, although clouded by sadness, were still the deep pools of blue they had been when he very first saw her.

"My darling Sophie, I would have given my life just to hold you again. How can you say that I cannot love you? All these years I have lived with the loss of you and I vowed never to love again." Reproach filled her eyes.

"How can you torment, me? I know that you left the castle with Princess Christine. You may have loved me once, but you have since found comfort in another."

Captain Julian did not know whether to laugh or cry. Sophie must have been close by all these years and yet never revealed herself.

"The Lady Christine is married to Lord Logan, who is part of our party. She knew that I was still in mourning for you, but I vowed to get her to safety, as I had seen the death of her parents and knew that it was just a matter of time before the Northern King would either lock her in the tower or find a way to have her killed. To protect everyone, we never spoke of the journey and told everyone that we were brother and sister. We knew that if word got to the Northern King that his betrothed was nearby and had married another, he would surely invade whatever place she had fled to and have everyone killed."

"Sophie, you are my wife and my one true love and unless you have married again, you will once again be mine and live with me," said Captain Julian in a determined voice. Sophie did not doubt his resolve, for she had always known him to be a man of his word. But in her heart, she felt that over time she would become an embarrassment to him. He looked into her eyes and saw her fear.

To calm her, he took her tenderly in his arms and let his finger run softly down her scarred cheek.

"I have seen many wars and known much sorrow, but this I know to be true, true love knows no time, no boundaries and overcomes the weakness of body and all scars. We are the Lord's gift to one other, and no matter how that gift is wrapped, it remains a gift. We shall be together until we reach the grave."

Sophie slipped her hand quietly into his and she knew that he meant what he had said. Together they walked to the house to share their news. But Captain Julian made her promise not to reveal Lady Christine's identity, and to allow her to speak to Lord Logan herself when the time was right.

Having been gone so long, they were greeted with rather puzzled looks. The story rushed out of them with great excitement, of how Sophie had been so gravely ill that she was believed to be dead, but that she had been revived when the choking smell of the purifying fires had reached her. With clouds of smoke all around, she had easily escaped without anyone seeing her. After surviving some weeks in the forest on berries, roots and the occasional bird that she snared, she had made her way to her sister's house, who welcomed her with immense joy, as the quarantine period had long since passed.

FORTY-ONE

The Way in is Revealed

Now amongst family, Captain Julian visibly relaxed and greeted his sister-in-law with a great big hug. She smiled happily as she saw that the glow of love had returned to her sister. Sophie introduced her nephew, Trevor, to the group. The household seemed devoid of a husband and father, yet the house was not overly feminine. It was Nadine who asked if Trevor had a father.

"Oh yes, replied Trevor, I do. It is just that his work keeps him away from home for strange hours. But I see him at least once a week when I collect the fish order from him at the Prison."

"At the Prison?" asked Nadine giving him a curious look. "Why yes, replied Trevor, my father is Galdolf."

"Is that so?" asked Captain Julian. "Why, what excellent circumstances we find ourselves in."

"How long can you stay awake for?" Trevor asked Nadine, with a mischievous smile.

"As long as it takes," replied Nadine, winking at Nathan and shaking her little pouch of 'stay awake herbs' which she had saved from her visit to the Medicine Woman.

"Can you stay awake the whole night?" asked Trevor with a twinkle in his eyes.

"Yes," replied Nadine and Nathan at the same time.

Nadine was never one to shy away from a dare, so she and Nathan prepared their brews and settled to a grand night of proving to Trevor that they could indeed do it.

Nadine began to prepare an ointment for Sophie. Elizabeth had taught her a remedy for the reduction of scars. She was just beginning to mix the paste when a low rasping sound came from the floor beneath her.

Trevor quickly pulled away from the table, moved a rug and opened a trap door to reveal his father, Galdolf, standing in a tunnel directly below the house. Galdolf was indeed startled to find these strangers in his home peering down at him, at this hour of the night.

After all the introductions and realising that his sister-in-law's husband was once again reunited with her, Galdolf felt a joy that he had not felt in a long time. In a prison, there are no family reunions and little chance of happiness.

While he dared not stay for too long, Galdolf was eager to help with the plan.

"How is it?" asked Captain Julian, that I never found out about the tunnels, when I was a guard at the prison?" Lord Logan shot a look at him and he realized that he had spoken too soon. Nadine closed her eyes, willing away the confrontation she knew must come.

But they remained silent as Galdolf continued.

"These tunnels were carved out centuries ago by the Dragon Whisperers and their dragons. Prison Masters were appointed custodians of the entrances by the Dragon Whisperers. It was their solemn oath to protect the locations of these tunnels. It is an oath handed down from generation to generation. While no one has seen or heard of the Dragon Whisperers for decades, I am still honour bound to conceal the tunnels. I do allow myself one small privilege. That is to visit my family. I use The Prison Master's secret entrance which is concealed within the prison."

"I have seen a Dragon Whisperer," Nadine revealed to Galdolf. "You have!" exclaimed Galdolf. "What was he like? My grandfather used to share the stories with me when I was a boy. But I have never met one."

"He is incredibly old. He seemed almost as old as time itself. And very stern. I was rather terrified when I first met him. He has a great copper coloured dragon with enormous talons. And Nathan and I rode on it," Nadine shared her story with Galdolf.

"Now tell us of the hatchling," pleaded Nadine.

"He is a fine little fellow. With crystal blue eyes and an elegant, yet sturdy body. But he came in a very weakened state. Whoever stole him, did not even take time to care for him and I thought he would surely die. If it were not for the stories of my grandfather, I think that I would not have succeeded in reviving him," said Galdolf.

"I feel as if you have found a special friend," said Nadine.

"Indeed, I have. I had to perform the naming ceremony. I named him Yakhal," revealed Galdolf.

"What is the significance of a naming ceremony?" asked Lord Logan.

Galdolf explained it in this way, "When a dragon hatches, its life force uses a burst of energy that weakens the hatchling. The mother must hunt and bring back live prey, or at least prey that has not yet reached the final stages of death. The live prey ignites the hatchling's hunting instinct. This serves to add more life force to it. The first sight of the mother will form the first stages of the bond. The hatchling's eyes remain closed until the mother brings the first food. That is why this hatchling did not open its eyes until I formed the bond. The closing of the eyes prevents the hatchling from bonding with other creatures. If the thief had fed it, the hatchling would have bonded with the thief. But the thief's ignorance or cruelty, I cannot say which, delayed that process. I had to force feed the hatchling because it was so weak that it did not stir when it first tasted the prey."

"But when he finally opened his eyes, I was the first creature he saw. By not naming the hatchling, the next stage of life force is stripped away, and the hatchling will die. But naming a dragon when its mother still lives, causes physical and psychological changes in the mother. Her life force flows in rhythm with her hatchling. If she does not name it, the bond is ruptured. While she will still feel the life force inside her, throughout her life she will feel the disharmony in her body. And she will feel the pull of the hatchling towards the other source of the bond. She will also be unable to telepathically trace him. She is completely at the mercy of those who have taken him, always yearning for her hatchling, but being unable to find him. By saving the hatchling, I was harming the mother," Galdolf explained.

Nadine now understood why the Dragon Whisperer had told her that the mother had suffered a great trauma. It was not just the removal of the hatchling. It was a rupture in her very being. One that not even a reunion could ever truly mend.

She thought of the women in the village, who had stillborn babies, or lost their babies to sickness or who had their children taken as indentured servants. She now knew why her mother would pray for these women, why she sought to comfort them.

A silence fell on the group as they absorbed the severity of the situation.

At last Nadine spoke. "If the hatchling has indeed bonded with you. How can I hope to safely remove him from your care?"

"I will need to hand him to you myself. And I will need to leave this place so that I can be travelling close to you. The best way would be for me to travel through the tunnels with you.

But, when the King learns that the dragon has been taken, he will hold me responsible. And if he finds me gone, he will come for my family."

"Lord Logan, I have to ask if you can take my family with you." Having heard of the Northern King's reputation Lord Logan agreed without hesitation and Captain Julian let out a small sigh of relief.

He rose and plotted out the route and details for them and together they crafted a plan for the escape.

"Now I must return to my post. I have already been gone far too long." With that, he lowered himself back into the tunnel and was gone.

FORTY-TWO

The Dragon Rescue

Sofie stepped out into the crisp morning air to find her husband and Lord Logan loading the furs onto the cart. "Leaving so soon," she smiled sadly.

The golden yellow and sandy pinks streamed into the dark sky, and the dawn bid the early morning stars farewell. She drew her shawl close and wondered if they would ever see this sight together again.

Lord Logon had seen many farewells. "Make this moment count," he said, his eyes full of compassion. He moved to the rest of the group, granting Captain Julian precious private moments.

Sofie touched Captain Julian's face. "Take care. After all this time, I could not bear to lose you again." Her eyes brimmed with tears.

Pulling her close, Captain Julian buried his face in her hair and inhaled the scent of peach kernels. With closed eyes, he murmured, "You will be in my arms again soon enough."

The taste of their farewell kiss lingered as he turned towards the King's road.

"Turn away, boy," Lord Logan said, slapping Nathan's shoulder. "You will get your turn soon enough," he grinned, glancing at Nadine. Nadine's blush was buried in the furs that suddenly seemed to require rearranging.

His face beaming, Captain Julian's voice reached up to the trees.

"There is a pretty girl I know.
Whose heart is as pure as snow
But when she is seated on my knee.
My heart sings to set her love free."

"Come on. You lovesick rogue, let's go show the Northern King what we are made of and get us all home to our loved ones," called Lord Logan.

"Do you think I should retire and become a tavern singer?" jested Captain Julian.

"Which tavern owner has wronged you, that you wish to deplete their profits?" retorted Lord Logan.

Nadine shook her head and grinned at their boyish games.

Lord Logan wondered how the preparations at the inn were

going. Galdolf had told him that his plan would endanger his family. Once the King had discovered the young dragon had been taken, he would turn to the Prison Master. Galdolf had to protect his family. They had to get away but could not raise suspicion from the King's men.

In the distance, a small travelling party left the inn moving away from the Kingdom. Once out of sight of the King's Tower Guards, one man doubled back. He secured his horse in a tree close to the inn and awaited the signal.

The grey walls of the castle grimly welcomed Captain Julian back to a place built on bloodshed and tears. His earlier mood evaporated through the heavy metal gates. At the inspection process, he dutifully handed over the tanner's tools for weapon confiscation. Once inside, the bustle of the market lifted some of the heaviness that he felt.

People flowed through the stalls. The air thick with busy chatter and heavy with the exotic scent of spices from faraway lands. Lovers strolled hand in hand, while cooks' apprentices raced from stall to stall to gather ingredients for the week's feasts. Caged chickens, squealing pigs and the smell of droppings merged with the whiff of rotting fruit, fresh produce and sweaty bakers carrying huge baskets filled with freshly baked round loaves of bread. Delicious aroma burst from the tavern door, as patrons entered or left.

Ladies with sizzling sausages and flatbread on large trays moved around enticing hungry shoppers to buy a quick bite to eat. Noticing Nadine's eyes follow the trays, Lord Logan bought them each a portion before they set up the stall.

Despite their position so close to the prison, they gained a stronger following than the day before. Several ladies eyed their stand through lowered lashes and faces covered by fans. Lord Logan knew who the object of their attention was.

Seeing Nathan's lure for the fairer sex, Lord Logan allocated himself the task of handling the coin and left the trade to the two younger members of their group.

Their cart displayed the fine red and gold fox furs in the front with the larger fuller bear furs at the back. Nathan placed iron and silver carved cloak pins on some of the more delicate furs. He had bartered some furs with the local silversmith for the pins. His handsome young face quickly enticed many of the ladies of the court.

Nadine would hold up a highly polished mirror, while he positioned the furs and pins on the ladies' shoulders.

"See how the colour brings out the hazel in your eyes," he would remark. "The black of this exotic wolf makes your eyes look like the eternal beauty of faraway seas. Full of mystery."

His eyes sparkled when he told them how lovely they looked. Delighted with the lavish attention, the ladies quickly parted with their coins. Some of them even coyly pressed a few extra coins into his hand, while they lingered longer at the stall.

Nadine was equally talented at luring in nobles who were looking for a gift for a sweetheart. Her talent was to get them to buy the accessories she had acquired the previous days: Little sprigs of lavender to scent the new furs, or intricately woven combs to make a woman's crowning glory shine.

"You will be the envy of all the Lords when your sweetheart's hair gleams like the moonlight," she said, adopting Nathan's flattering techniques. She had a way of running her hand delicately through the furs that transformed hardened warriors into staring drooling fools. While flattery did not come as easily to Nadine as to Nathan, her blue-green eyes were a call that could not be ignored.

With the cart set up and Nathan captivating his customers, Captain Julian announced, "Well, I am off to the tavern."

"Practicing for your new career?" teased Lord Logan. "Please do leave some customers in the tavern. We don't want too many witnesses to our games today."

"I will have you know that before I married, there were many maidens enthralled by my singing," Captain Julian declared with mock indignation.

Grabbing Captain Julian's bicep, Lord Logan said, "I think the ladies were more enthralled with these than your singing."

"Well since these are already pledged to another, I will just have to stick to singing today," he said turning towards the tavern. "Let's see if I can find better admirers from the Tavern Jesters."

"Be quick, before these two finish all the stock," Lord Logan called after him, winking at Nadine.

A burst of laughter erupted from the open tavern door, as Captain Julian entered. The ebony paneling in the tavern was illuminated by a roaring red fire and dripping candle chandeliers. Steaming platters of wild boar, seasoned with wine and wild spices, burdened the heavy wood tables in front of nobles, seated in a more private section of the tavern. This section had individual carved chairs and was adorned with tapestries of battles and charging horses.

Closer to the doors, rows of heavy tables with long wooden

benches, designed to seat twenty men on each side, were filled with groups of tipsy men singing. Their fare was simpler, with pies, warm bread, dipping sauce and row upon row of frothy ale. The waitresses in wide skirts, tight bodices and large messy aprons, weaved their way through the crowd.

The chaos was interrupted by a loud slap, indicating to the crowd that some drunken fool had tried to get more than a meal from a waitress. This was greeted with roars of delight and a sheepishly looking perpetrator whose red face became buried a little more deeply in a mug of yet more ale.

Once or twice a side door would open, and guards would hurl a repeat offender out into the adjacent pig pen. The tavern was a writhing mass of humanity in different states of merriment. Spit pots near the tables, that occasionally reeked of more than spit and were quickly removed by servants struggling to keep the tavern in some sort of order.

Captain Julian bought a large vessel of wine and two leather drinking cups. For a while he stood, trying to scan the tavern for an open seat next to a jester. Seeing several jesters, he chose the one who was dressed the leanest. A heaving customer, who had run out of coin, stumbled past leaving a vacant seat next to his target. Noticing a few more desperate new patrons Captain Julian hastily claimed the seat.

"Hello friend," he said. "How are your takings for the day?"

"Slim pickings indeed," replied the jester a bit too gruffly for his profession.

"Why is that?" asked Captain Julian.

"Well, the King announced a special tax for the Pope's army.

The proclamation is hanging near the gates. This means that there are fewer coins to spend on jesters. But I also must pay taxes. So, what do I do now?"

Captain Julian offered the jester some wine. "I have had some good fortune here with my furs. Come share some of my wine." The jester would not say no to free wine. Soon, filled to merriment, he began to tell jokes and boast of his talents.

Glancing at the tools that lay on the bench next to him. Captain Julian realized with a gladdened heart that he may have found the perfect man for the job. "I have heard that some jesters can perform a fire breathing act. Is this true?" asked Captain Julian.

Well lubricated with wine, the jester boasted. "I am a skilled fire performer, fire juggler and fire eater."

"If that is true, then I may have some more coin for you," said Captain Julian fingering a single silver coin. The jester stared drunkenly at the silver coin and licked his lips.

"What do you have in mind?" he asked.

"Well, as I have said, I have found good fortune at this market. But I notice that some of the wealthiest nobles are reluctant to come to the side of the market near the prison gates. You see we arrived rather late yesterday and could only find a spot near the prison."

"Now if a man of your talents were to put on a show near our stand, we may well attract some wealthier nobles to our side. I think a nice strong breath of fire facing towards our stall would really help. But I also don't want our furs to burn up, so maybe do the blast aiming at the prison gates, so that we have the show, but I do not lose all my wares. Do you agree?"

"What would be my wages?" asked the Jester.

"I will pay you three silver coins now. And three silver coins once your act starts." This was an arrangement that the jester could not refuse.

Realising that a drunk jester could not perform a fire act, very well, the jester declined another helping of wine.

"I hear that the pork pie in this place is legendary," Captain Julian said signaling the waitress. "We will have two pork pies, bread with dipping sauce, two rounds of cheese and two custard tarts," he ordered.

The jester grinned at the sound of the order, his mouth already watering at the thought of the meal. Pulling back the hardened upper crust of the pie released a hot burst of flavour. The pork was drenched in rich thick gravy, folded into the pasty with smoky fat and glistening bacon. The rich aroma brought glances from neighbouring tables, as diners reached over to discover the origins of the tempting smells.

The jester ate with a frenzy of man who had not seen a solid meal for many days. He even dipped bits of the hardened crust designed only to seal in the gravy. With globs of rich gravy pooling around his chin, he used his hand to scoop it back into his mouth. Realizing that he could not eat another bite, he carefully put the cheese into his pack.

To ensure that his act did not disappear without completing his performance, Captain Julian remained with the Jester until the allotted time arrived.

After a period of trading, Nadine began to cough. Great big hacking coughs, and she spat out the green herbs that she had pounded into a paste, on the ground in front of the guards.

The guard leaned over to inspect the ground. A thick glob of mucus tinged with green, glistened on the stone courtyard. Recoiling in horror, the guard screamed, "Get out! Get out now!" Covering his face with his cloak, he backed away from her.

"You! Go get the girl's companions," he roared at a lower ranking guard. "Get them out of here now!"

"Where are they?" asked the dumbfounded guard.

"You idiot, they are the fur traders. Were you sleeping when they arrived? Just go. I want those people out of the market now!" he spat.

Nadine ran out of the gates, with a great show of sobbing. Once she had reached a tree suitably out of range, she quickly changed into Trevor's well-known winter cloak. She arrived back at the castle just as the fish merchant was leaving.

She watched as Captain Julian came out of the tavern followed by the jester. The jester moved to the area of the market close to the prison gates and began a greatly complicated juggling act, which had the crowd in awe.

It was then that what appeared to be Galdolf's son arrived for the fish order. Being slightly late, he was greeted by the guards, who were heading out for their break. Captivated by the juggling act, they never noticed the disguised Nadine enter the prison.

Nadine hastily painted some of the fire powder near the doorway and got Galdolf to drop some at the gate, as he closed the great doors. They quickly made their way to the cage. With small quantities of sleeping potions that Nadine had given to him the night before, Galdolf had lulled the prisoners to sleep for a short while, so that there would be no witnesses to the first part of the escape.

He had secretly and silently unlocked the cells, to give the prisoners a fighting chance to get away.

Descending the stairs, he removed a stone from the wall and pulled the lever to open the secret passage. Racing back up, he surveyed the prisoners. All seemed to be going according to plan. The prisoners were all asleep. They had measured just enough potion to put the prisoners to sleep, but not enough to drug them through a huge commotion. Galdolf knew that they would be tortured to reveal what had happened to the dragon, should they remain in the prison and be found.

He entered the dragon cage and reached down to pick up the young dragon. He touched his forehead to the dragon. The Yakhal tilted his neck and gave a curious look at Nadine. Then he looked back at Galdolf. The Prison Master handed Nadine a large woven sack, with a strap that went from one shoulder to her hip and placed the young dragon gently inside.

"In this way, your arms will be free to use, should you have trouble. Do you have your dagger girl?"

"Yes," she replied. "I am grateful for your help," she said, knowing the risk he was facing.

He gently touched his forehead to Yakhal once more and bid them farewell. Then he closed the secret passageway and went up again.

But one of the prisoners was not asleep. He had not taken the potion and had kept to the shadows at the side of the cell, alert and unnoticed. While Nadine and Galdolf gathered the young dragon and prepared to leave, the prisoner had snuck out of his cell and made his way to the secret passageway that Galdolf had inadvertently revealed.

Galdolf arrived back at the gates shortly before the guards returned. He readied himself to open the gates, as the jester changed his act from juggling to fire eating. The jester sent out a blast of fire from his mouth directly towards the prison gates, exactly as Captain Julian had instructed.

The black fire-powder ignited into a fireball, which billowed out towards the courtyard. The explosion reverberated through the stronghold and echoed around the courtyard. New explosions erupted as the flames engulfed some of the stalls. Great columns of fire rose to the sky as men and women ran choking and gagging from the scene

Humiliation had fueled the guard to push Nathan and Lord Logan ruthlessly out of their market stall. The sooner he had them out of his sight, the better.

"Get out, get out now, you scum. We don't want your disease breading type around here," he snarled.

Lord Logan and Nathan almost laughed at their good fortune. They were already far away from the stall when the fire began to rage.

Galdolf himself was thrown back by the explosion and fell, hitting his head. No one noticed the concealed padding in his helmet which cushioned the fall. Nadine had given him a pouch with oxblood, which he squeezed onto his arm and forehead. Groaning, he crawled to the entrance, where he slumped as if overcome by his injuries.

The prison guards rushed from the tavern to where their soot-covered colleague was trying to move Galdolf away from the flames. Members of the King's Guard scurried forward to secure the area.

Near the inn, the man waiting in the tree fired a burning arrow to Galdolf's house, aimed at the thatch. The house quickly began to burn. Seeing the flames in the distance, the Captain of the Guard cried, we are under attack. "My family, my family," bellowed Galdolf.

As the prison began to burn to the ground, the prisoners, grateful to have found their cells unlocked, found their way through the choking flames to the entrance, some of them even managing to sneak away completely undetected.

Galdolf saddled a horse and slumped over it, letting the arm with the oxblood hang loosely to the side, and holding the reins clumsily with the other hand. No one tried to stop him; they thought he would soon succumb to his wounds anyway. Galdolf hung on for what seemed like an eternity and then as he reached the travelling merchants with a cart full of furs, he pulled himself upright and said, "Does this party need an ex Prison Master?" with a smile. There were shouts of laughter all around. The party began to make their way to Lord Logan's lands, full of plans and ideas for the preparations they would make for the great celebration when Nadine's family arrived.

But Galdolf veered away from the group to travel more closely to the route of the tunnels. He knew that the dragon would be able to feel his life force and that it would comfort him. Once the dragon was safely back with its mother, he would make his way to his family.

FORTY-THREE

Into the Tunnels

Nadine stepped into the tunnels, with Yakhal securely in the sack. Reaching up, she grabbed the torch that the Prison Master had lit for her. Turning around, she looked straight into the eyes of the dragon thief.

"Hello pretty! Going somewhere?"

Nadine gasped with fright. She suddenly realized that she had seen this man before. He was one of the travelers who had been lodging in the village inn for a few weeks before the hatchling was stolen. Besides recognizing him from the village, there was something oddly familiar about him that she could not place.

A dagger appeared from nowhere and its blade glistened menacingly in front of her face. Nadine suddenly ducked and with the element of surprise rammed her head into his stomach. Reeling and winded, the thief fell to the ground, but was quick to rebound onto his feet.

Nadine reached for the dagger Lady Christine had given her, to defend herself. But close dagger fighting was not a skill that her father had taught her. Instead of a low belly thrust, she had come in high to attempt a downward stabbing. The thief reached up to block her. The dagger went flying and clattered noisily in the dark. The thief then grabbed hold of Nadine's wrist to try and subdue her. But that is when her secret weapons revealed themselves. The tiny sharpened barbs sliced into his hand.

Screaming with pain, the thief clutched at his hand. The girl was far more powerful than he had imagined, and the hidden barbs were razor sharp. He reached for her again, trying to grab her ankles with his good hand. But again, was met with yet more barbs. Nadine kicked out and knowing that he would not reach out for her, kicked him in the secret place as her father had taught her.

"Aaargh," he screamed once more. "You witch," he spat out at her. "I will find you. The King will find you and then I will see you burned."

Far away Muquin felt a surge of fear in the young dragon. It had hissed at the thief, but without flight, it could not yet fight. Only Nadine stood between it and captivity. Galdolf also felt a wave of panic go through his body when Nadine had fought with the thief. He instinctively turned the horse closer to the invisible line along which the tunnels ran.

Nadine ran for as long as she could, checking that the young dragon was still secured in the pouch. When she could run no longer, she paused for a short rest to get her breath back. The fish order was in the outer pocket of the bag, so she fed the baby dragon, and ate some of the dried meat in the other pocket.

With her heart still racing, she began to walk, looking out for the markings Galdolf had told her about. She felt confident that the thief would not easily follow. But his threat was very real. She would not underestimate the King's wrath. And she had lost the dagger. There was no time to go back for it. But she knew what its discovery would mean for Lady Christine. Her secret would no longer be safe. Lady Christine would no longer be safe. Her only hope was that the thief would not know all the secrets of the tunnels.

Finally, she found the faded carving of a dragon flying overhead of a man. She slid her hand along the carving until she found the small hole that she could slide her finger into. She felt for the clip, which she pulled back. A passageway opened, with stairs.

Nadine reached for Yakhal and touched his forehead, trying to reassure the hatchling. She climbed down the stairs, being careful to light the torch that was positioned at the opening of the new tunnel. She closed the upper passageway so that it was concealed once more.

She knew to count out the 100 steps as she had been instructed. The distance was in fact just 50 paces, but as Nadine was so much shorter than an adult man, Galdolf had doubled the number to make up for her size.

Looking up at the count of 99, she found the horn hanging from a hook on the wall. Following Gadolf's instructions, she blew four short blasts on the horn. She waited and faintly heard four blasts in response. Holding onto her precious cargo, Nadine raced to the end of the tunnel. She looked around for another carving of a dragon flying overhead of a man. She quickly found the hole for her finger and pulled. This time there were stairs leading upwards. Nadine made sure once again to close the passageway. She moved to the side of the tunnel, against the rock wall and waited.

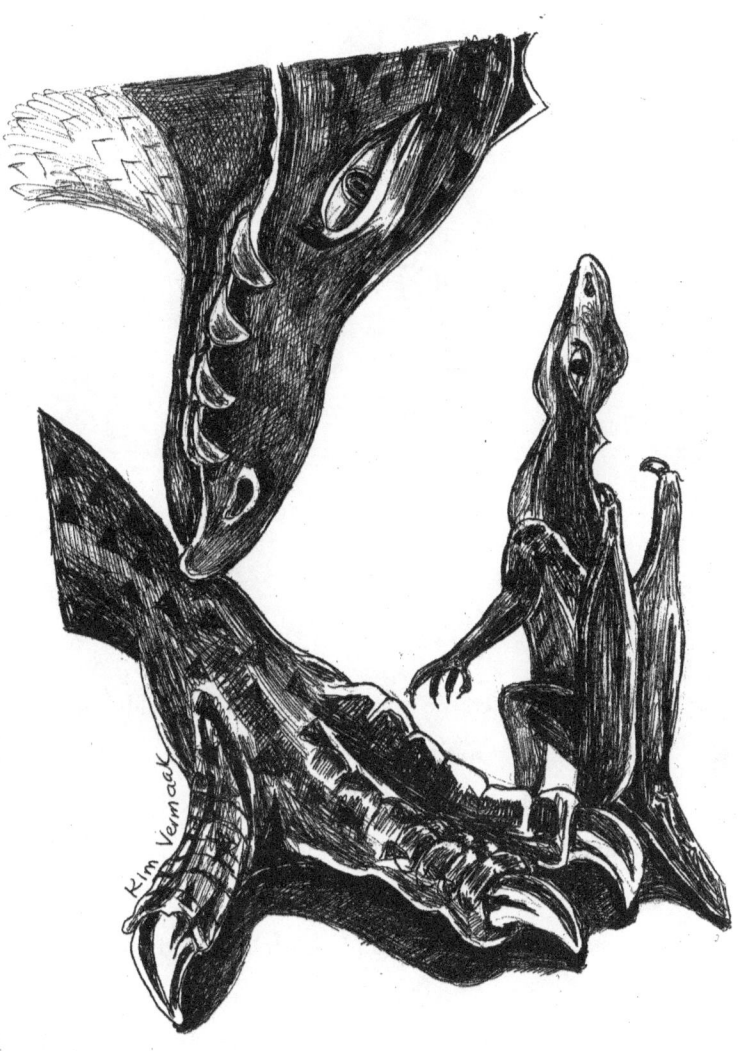

FORTY-FOUR

Reunions

Galdolf pushed the horse to the edge of its endurance. He desperately needed to get to Yakhal. Stress had drained the young dragon's life force. Yakhal had never been out of the confines of the prison. The stimulus was too great.

Muquin could not sense where her offspring was. But she could feel the life force of the man her hatchling had bonded with. He was moving fast. Blood rushed through his veins. His panic consumed her. She had to follow his essence. It was the key to finding her young one.

Nadine's lungs screamed for air. The tunnels were devoid of

ventilation. The burn in her muscles was paralyzing. But the life of her family, of this hatchling, depended on her.

"Help will come!" the voices she had heard before, called again. Could she trust them?

Cramps tore at her. Nadine's legs would not obey her urging. She could not carry on.

Nadine clutched the little creature.

"I have failed you," she whispered, as she crumpled into a ball of misery on the cold stone. Air would not come. Nadine slipped into darkness.

"Please! Lord! Air," Nadine's last thoughts flowed from her mind.

Yakhal chirped. Something was wrong. And his caregiver was not here. He felt Galdolf's fear, just as Galdolf felt his. The dragon nudged Nadine again and again. Yet, she remained still.

The girl suffered. Just as he had suffered when the thief had taken him. He was alone with no way of reviving the girl. Would no one come? He climbed onto Nadine. Yakhal rocked backwards and forwards in his misery. Galdolf had rocked him when he was in the cage in the prison. It had comforted him. Perhaps it would stir Nadine. But still, Nadine did not move.

In the dark Yakhal felt the trickle of dirt on his face. He looked up in the dark tunnel but saw nothing. He blinked away the dirt. It began to tickle faster. Yakhal spread his wing over Nadine to protect her face from the dirt. He could not move the human from the source of danger. But he could try and protect her. Bits of rock fell onto his small wings. Yakhal flinched in pain.

Above the surface, the Zairdenth and the Dragon Whisperer

tore at the roots that blocked the passageway. "Can we blast it open?" asked the Dragon Whisperer.

"No, the intense heat may cause the rock to cave in. If Nadine is anywhere close, the rock would crush her," replied the Copper Fire Dragon.

"We are running out of time. If she closed the last passage, the air will run out," shouted the Dragon Whisperer. Zairdenth found the largest root that bonded the network of finer roots together. He slashed at it with his claws. The root was thick and gnarled. He slashed again and again. The Dragon Whisperer grabbed at the twisted web of roots. Great clumps of them came away, opening the gap for the ledge. His muscles bunched and heaved with the effort. Finally, the ledge looked clear enough for them to try again. The Dragon Whisperer pulled at the lever again.

Yakhal stayed at his post, protecting Nadine as more sand fell into the tunnels. But this time came light. The sweet mercy of air rushed through Nadine's body.

She gave a soft moan. Slowly she opened her eyes. Nadine blinked into the light.

Her first sight was the nostrils of the enormous nose of the Dragon Whisperer. His eyes twinkled with pleasure at seeing her and the young dragon.

"Nadine! I heard the call from the Dragon Tunnels. We came as quickly as we could. How did you know how to summon me?"

"Galdolf," gasped Nadine. "His grandfather trained him. He instructed me."

"Ah yes," acknowledged the Dragon Whisperer. "The Prison Masters were once strong allies of the Dragon Whisperers. Now we must find this little dragon's mother. From your description of the location of your village, I believe that Zaidenth will know the way."

The Dragon Whisperer lifted Nadine to safety. She lay down next to the oak, the sun warming and strengthening her.

A thunder of hooves raced towards the enormous oak tree. The rider leapt off the stallion before it even came to a halt. Kneeling beside Nadine, Galdolf removed the young dragon from the pouch. He rubbed his forehead against the hatchling. Yakhal nuzzled his protector. Galdolf took a deep breath and sighed with relief.

Muquin slowed her speed. She sensed a calming. She would greet her hatchling with confidence.

Φ

"Come, girl," called the Dragon Whisperer. "It is time." Galdolf bid the young dragon farewell for the last time, his purpose fulfilled. He helped Nadine up onto the Copper Fire Dragon's back. Yakhal would have his first experience of flight. Galdolf wondered if the young dragon would remember his stories or if this flight would remind him of them. He had tried his best to prepare his charge for this moment.

As Zairdenth rose into the skies, Nadine felt the familiar joy return to her heart. Yakhal felt it too. His vision adjusted to the skies, and with the exhilaration of flight, his life force surge burst forth.

Muquin and Galdolf both felt the surge. The power burst into the sky in a stream of silver light that pierced the heavens.

Galdolf guided the horse to the shade of the tree. He sat down to rest for a while. The anguish of the bond overwhelmed him. Would he ever see Yakhal again?

Zairdenth glided through the trees. He sensed Muquin. The Copper Fire Dragon had buried his mate long ago and with her all thoughts of a hatchling. Now he carried the last of a new line of dragon species. Perhaps there was hope for the dragon line after all.

He slowed. It was time. Muquin saw the Copper Fire Dragon. She slowed her flight and landed a few meters away from them. Despite her suffering, Muquin stood tall and proud with her scales saturated with the reflection of Yakhal's life force light.

The Dragon Whisperer closed his eyes. Through his mind he spoke to Muquin. He showed her Nadine and the rescue of the hatchling and asked her for the return of Nadine's family.

Muquin had suffered so with the loss of her hatchling. She understood what this girl had been through. Her fear misguided her wrath against the humans. The King and his hatchling thief were the true villains. She revealed to the Dragon Whisperer where the villagers were.

"Forgive me, Nadine," Muquin pleaded, as she bowed her head. "Megadeus was right. There is good in mankind."

Nadine heard Muquin's plea. Her gift blossomed. She rubbed her forehead against Yakhal's and placed him on the ground. She laid the remaining fish at his feet and slowly backed away.

Then Muquin walked towards her hatchling. She lowered her head as he greeted him. Her first touch held a bitter-sweet agony. They had been apart for so long. Now the hatchling was bonded with another. Would he love her? Yakhal's soft purring noise welcomed Muquin. She was his life source. He knew her.

Silvery tears ran down Muquin's face. Her hatchling was home.

Muquin looked at Nadine and the Dragon Whisperer. Gratitude was only a word. It could never reveal the fulfillment of a yearning that only a mother could know. No words could ever reveal the yearning of a heart so filled with the sorrow of a love lost, that life itself seemed meaningless.

Now she knew what Megadeus had fought for. She would teach Yakhal of his Father's faith, strength and love. Of his sacrifice.

The Dragon Whisperer nodded. He knew her heart. As she would find the courage to pass on Megadesus' legacy, he would find the strength to teach Nadine.

Muquin rose up. Yakhal spread his silvery wings for the first time and flew after his mother. The pair of Silver Wings glistened in the sunlight as the horizon welcomed them to their destiny.

FORTY-FIVE

The Meaning of Family

Dorothea woke with Mikael's starving body leaning on her chest. She touched his hand. His once chubby little fingers felt bony and dry. She pulled herself up, still cradling him in her one arm. Dorothea pressed her cheek to his and listened. She could hear him breathing, but he had not woken that day. Was she going to watch her son die in this place?

Dorothea closed her eyes and again recited the words. "Yeah though I walk through the shadow of the valley of death, I will fear no evil, for thou art my staff and my rod."

She thought of the battle-wearied King David, who had written these words. He had been pursued by King Saul and had hidden in a cave.

For so long Dorothea had tried to keep her family focused on gratitude. Her husband's careful planning and management of this small group had kept them going, but now she felt that the shadow of death was staring them in the face. Nicolous seemed like a skeleton next to her. The heavy dark circles around his eyes sagged and his wound stank. For so long he had been their rock, but now he seemed like one of the fragile crumbling carvings in some deserted ruins. Maireid lay close to the young mother and her baby. Dorothea at least had her family close, but the village fire had widowed the young mother. Her heart swelled with pride as she watched Maireid's arm drape over the young woman. "She was such a good girl. Always caring for others." Thought Dorothea

She glanced at the pile of bodies at the far side of the cave. Judas was the first to die. But others had succumbed to wounds, hunger and thirst. Was perishing in the tunnels to be their punishment for not having shared enough water when they harvested it? Nicolous had assured her that there would never have been enough for everyone. He had tried to comfort her by telling her they had done their best to care for the villagers with what they had available to them.

Dorothea imagined Nadine was close. Could she dare to believe her feelings? She felt that their faith had protected them, but now she wondered if she had been a fool, making her family cling to false hope. So many days had passed. Surely Nadine would have found a way by now. She reminded herself that her beautiful and stubborn daughter had always found a way when everyone else thought things were impossible. But there were many dangers out there for a girl alone. Maybe she had expected too much from Nadine.

Φ

"Now Nadine, let's go and get your family" said the Dragon Master. Nadine and the Dragon Whisperer mounted the great copper dragon and flew towards Forever Gone Lake. The Dragon Whisperer knew the dangers of dehydration. He carried with him provisions. Water, food and healing herbs that the Medicine Woman had sent. She had taken care to send herbs for burns, and fever, as Nadine had told her of her father's injuries.

A short distance from the lake, the Dragon descended near an enormous oak tree. The dragon Whisperer jumped from the dragon's back and went to the tree. He slid his hand into an opening in the tree and pulled back the lever and a stone staircase opened beneath the tree

They descended the staircase and lit the torch. Nadine virtually ran the first 100 steps to the next level.

The stone ledge moved, and she dropped into an opening, carrying with her two large drinking pouches of water. With their lit torches they moved down the tunnel. The glow from the two torches formed an angelic arch of light. Maireid was the first to see the light coming towards her. After weeks in the darkened tunnels, her eyes stung with the force of the glare. Had the Lord come to take her home? "Maimi", she called. Dorothea had fallen asleep in her prayers for her family. In her exhausted and drained state, she could not work out what she was seeing. "Nicolous". she said, shaking him weakly by the arm. "It is Nadine!". "Our little girl has come at last!".

Nicolous looked up at the light. Nadine was back. Nicolous felt the burden of the past weeks lift. At last, he could allow himself to feel. He turned his head to look at the crumpled heap of humanity around them. The blacksmith lay with his dead son still clutched in his arms. The tanner lay with his arm around his wife's shoulders. He saw that the wine merchant had not survived. Relief flooded through him. But it was mingled with regret as he counted the dead children in the cave.

Nadine threw herself into her parents' arms, sobbing. "Nadine, your brother, he needs help," said Dorothea lifting the boy towards Nadine.

Nadine pulled the pouch of water from her sack. She lifted her brother's head. Smearing water on his lips, she said "Mikael, little brother I am here." Tears welled up in Nadine's eyes as she pressed open her brother's mouth to drip water into it.

The Dragon Whisperer moved around handing out small pouches of water and food to the remaining survivors. He searched through the group to see who had gone, and who was just asleep. The villagers began to move around, caring for their injured. The tanner reached over and kissed his wife tenderly on her dry lips.

Maireid pushed herself up from the ground and lifted the baby from its sleeping mother's arms. She shuffled over to where her parents and Nadine were. Maireid bent down and kissed Nadine on her head as she watched her sister trying to revive Mikael. She placed the widow's baby in Dorothea's arms for her to care for it and went to gently wake the mother, offering food, and water. Dorothea dripped a little water into the baby's mouth. In time, the mother could nurse her baby again, but for now, she needed to build her strength.

Nadine looked across at Maireid, blinking away her tears. She opened her pouch and Maireid saw there was a jar of honey. Pulling out the stopper, Nadine dipped her finger in it and pushed it into Mikael's mouth. Nadine prayed that the sweetness would revive the boy. As they watched, she passed the jar to her mother, who also pressed some honey into the baby's mouth.

"Mikael..." wailed Nadine Maireid, tried to pull him from Nadine's arms "Mikael Wake up now!"

Dorothea got up and placed the widow's baby back in her eldest daughter's arms. "Go care for the baby and his mother," she instructed. Dorothea touched Nadine's arm. and lifted Mikael's body into her own arms. She cradled him as she did when he was an infant. She began to sing to him. Nicolous put out his arm for Nadine to steady him and stood up. Nadine stumbled under his weight. But she clung to her father, sobbing. After everything she had been through...was Mikael going die?

"Please Lord," she cried burying her head into her father's shoulder. She saw a slight movement out of the side of her vision, she turned... Mikael's eyes fluttered open.

Through split and bleeding lips, he croaked: "Mami, I am hungry."

Nadine laughed as relief flooded through her and tears welled up in her eyes again. They all laughed. Trust these to be the first words that Mikael would utter.

The Dragon Whisperer guided the villagers towards the opening, so they could return to the village to rebuild their lives. But the young mother lingered. Without a husband to care for her and the baby, she would struggle. Dorothea looked Nicolous. He nodded in agreement to her silent plea. She wrapped her arm around the mother and her baby. "You will come with us now," she said.

The Dragon Whisperer returned. "It is time to go."

Nadine looked at them with a grin, and said "Well, what are you all sitting around for? We have a party to go to!"

Do you want to have a sneak peek at book 2?

Read on through the lessons section to get to chapter 1 of Book 2.

Stories create wisdom.

In the lessons section you can find the secret hidden tools for navigating the greatest adventure of all, your own life.

Lessons Learned from The Last of the Silver Wings

Stories carry wisdom in them. However, over time, we have reduced stories to have entertainment value only. In this book, we hope to help create examples of how you can glean wisdom from the stories that you discover in life.

We live our lives through a series of filters based on our own life experiences. This affects how we process lessons. It is why I asked some people who journeyed with me in the writing of this book, to give me their lessons learned from this story so that you may learn from others.

I give special thanks to Colin Vermaak, Margaret Keel and Judy Ward for sharing their insights and lessons learned. A special thank you to Barry Mitchell, for his gift of teaching that helped form a way of thinking for me to uncover these lessons.

SECTION 1
General Principles

There are some key principles that you will discover in this book. They are timeless truths that you can apply in all areas of your life, regardless of your age, gender or community dynamics. I encourage you to come back to this section when you are feeling low to realign yourself to your purpose.

1.   Have a Vision

When you have a clear idea of what you want to achieve, every small step in the right direction allows your vision to grow.

When you have a vision, you can build a team to mobilise that vision and together you can impact a community, a nation, perhaps even the world.

Think about the iconic speech by Martin Luther King; "I have a dream" [1]

His leadership created enormous changes in American society. But his dream started when he first noticed an injustice. His dream grew from a small initial awareness into something bigger that affected a nation and had an impact on the world.

1.   What small decisions or actions can you take today that could have an impact?

2. Serve First

When you serve first, you can grow your sphere of influence.

Nadine was on a mission to save her family. But along the way, she stopped and helped Nathan. She could have passed by; she could have escaped through the trees; but she didn't.

By stopping to help Nathan, she gained access to a team of people who would help her enter the Northern Kingdom.

1.   **How can you best serve others within your circle of influence?**

3. Connect with a Higher Purpose

When you align yourself to a higher purpose, it takes the focus off yourself and helps you to navigate life.

Faith is a key theme in this book. Nadine's parents used their faith to keep themselves from losing hope in the tunnels. Through their faith and actions, many more of the villagers survived.

The Friar held onto his faith and was an influencer for good.

We are all created with a purpose and when we remain grounded in faith, we are better able to fulfil that purpose.

1. **What do you believe in? How does this help you to live according to a purpose?**

4. Test the Motives of Others

When you invite new people into your space, test their motives before you align yourself with them.

Lady Christine was betrothed to King Radolf. It was a political alliance set up by her parents. However, Radolf's motives were dishonourable. Not finding out more about this King before setting up the alliance cost Christine's parents their lives, their kingdom and endangered their daughter.

While you cannot achieve significance in isolation, create a set of guidelines to see if your team is aligned in your vision. In a society where anyone can create a fake social media account, testing motives and guarding ourselves and our loved ones plays a bigger role than ever before.

1.   **Who is in your circle of friends and influencers? Will they help you or harm you in living out your purpose?**

5. Embrace Your Challenges

Challenges are not problems; they are opportunities to learn and grow.

With every obstacle you face, you can find something to learn, even if the outcome is not favourable.

While Nadine had a certain number of skills, she only started to hone those when she faced trials. When the eagle attacked her kitten in the boat, she had an opportunity to discover that she could overcome the eagle. While countless people had drowned in the lake, Nadine was able to cut her way free from the plants.

These challenges gave her the confidence to face even bigger challenges later in her journey.

1. **What challenges do you face today? How can you learn from them?**

6. You are never too old or too young to have an impact

There is no magical age required for making an impact.

Sometimes we are tempted to believe that when we are older or have faced many disappointments, that we no longer have anything to offer to society. Yet older people carry inside them so much wisdom, that if they apply it, can make a significant difference for themselves and others.

Other times we cannot appreciate that a young person can add anything of real value to a complex problem. This is not true.

Youth can bring a fresh perspective and enthusiasm to a problem. You are never too young to impact your community, whether it is your school, your church, your family or a larger community. Nadine impacted her family's life and that of the entire village. She searched for help when she needed it but did not shrink back because of her youth.

The Dragon Whisperer, in his advanced age, was living as a recluse. Yet, he was the very person needed in the time of crisis to help equip Nadine with skills she needed to return the hatchling.

1. **What problem in your community lies in your heart?**
2. **What would happen if you did not let your age prevent you from acting?**
3. **If you partnered with someone of a different age, what impact could you have on your community?**

7. It is Never Too Late to Make a Change

In this book, there are biblical references woven delicately into the chapters. The Bible is a wonderful place to learn about historical heroes who had to face many of the challenges we face today.

What always tugs at my heart is those who had the courage to change direction and in doing so changed the course of history.

Sometimes we feel that we have made too many mistakes to reclaim our lost identity. We let our fear of judgment stop us from stepping into a new life.

I have compiled a list of three people from the Bible who were willing to make changes.

David

I love the story of David [2], a simple shepherd boy. He was the least of all the sons in his family. But when the time came to face a giant, David used just what he had available to him, his courage, his memory of his victories as a shepherd, his sling and a few pebbles. With these he slayed his "Giant". Despite some troubling lapses in judgment, David became one of the most memorable kings. Our heroine Nadine is like David, who used what she knew and took on simple things that brought about bigger changes.

Deborah

She was a prophetess, not a warrior. However, Barak was too afraid to go into battle without her. Deborah [3] had a vision for what they could achieve, so she stepped out in faith. The result was a decisive victory against their enemies. Elizabeth is like Deborah.

She was a woman of learning and a healer, not a warrior. But she had the courage and ability to deal with the fearsome Dragon Whisperer. And she was also able to equip Nadine to continue her journey.

Rahab

In biblical times, this woman had an awful reputation. Rahab [4] was a woman who others probably gossiped about, leaving her with few friends. Yet, when spies entered her land, she saw a way of making a new life, out of the one she was sold into as a slave. By helping them, she and her family escaped destruction, and she earned a place in the genealogy of Christ [5].

In this book, Beatrice represents a woman who lives in the shadows. She was the daughter of a Contron; a child born of rape.

Yet Beatrice uses her background to help equip women to face danger. By sewing barbs into Nadine's clothing, she helped her defeat Nabal and return the hatchling to Muquin.

1. What areas of your past make you feel weak or ashamed?
2. How can you repackage your life, so you can claim your purpose?
3. Who can you teach to forgive and love themselves again?

SECTION 2

Focus on Character Learnings

In this section we explore specific characters. We encourage you to look at other characters that you may identify with and unpack what lessons you can learn from them.

1. Nadine

Do the right thing when faced with the decisions you have daily.

Nadine did not wake up one day and decide to change a nation. She wanted to help her family. She saw the crying dragon and helped her get the hatchling back. These decisions lead to saving Lord Logan, freedom for political prisoners, reunited families, the saving of a village and she prevented the destruction of a nation by avoiding a dragon war.

1.   **What decisions do you have facing you today?**
2.   **Is there a way to do good in those decisions?**

2. Friar Watt

You can show kindness even to those who others see as unworthy.

Friar Watt lived out his purpose. Even though the Bishop was greedy and corrupt, the Friar showed kindness and respect to the Bishop. He cared for the Bishop in his final hours and gave him the gift of dying with dignity. This man of God had a clear focus, and he was determined in his purpose. But it was his ability to draw alongside people that drew others to his vision. Even Father Stephen who became corrupt, saved Friar Watt by protecting him from the King's men.

The Bandit King risked capture to get the Friar the medical care he needed. Friar Watt helped men to reconnect with a higher purpose.

1.   **Who in your life can you help to live at a higher level?**

2.   **What kindness can you show?**

3. Galdolf, the Prison Master

Do not let current circumstances bind you.

No matter what family you are born into, no matter how many generations you feel you are trapped by, you can break free and make a difference.

Galdolf's family was born into being Prison Masters. Many would allow their hearts to be hardened by the suffering and injustice of the system in which Galdolf was trapped. But he used this place to bring justice and healing. We see this in the way he treated the prisoners. Even at the end, Galdolf unlocked the cells to allow the prisoners the opportunity to escape the fire. Galdolf's guards were also treated with respect. While Galdolf could not fight every battle, he took small daily actions that improved the lives of those in his care.

1. **How can you be the light to others in your circumstances?**

4. King Radolf

Let your pain in life produce character in you, so that you may be a beacon of light to others.

Society can tempt us to paint all villains with a one-dimensional view. But they are multifaceted. We can learn lessons from their struggles and actions.

An injustice stirred King Radolf's heart, when his mother was killed. He hoped to prevent people from being manipulated. This is a noble desire. But he moved from seeking justice to seeking revenge and lost the opportunity to do good.

King Radolf had a way of finding many avenues to exercise his plan. Whatever obstacles came his way, he found an alternative solution.

Imagine if people with good intentions also had King Radolf's perseverance. Imagine what good they could achieve.

1. **Which person in your life, can you learn something good from?**

5. Lord Logan

You can help empower people to face their responsibilities.

Lord Logan saw lack differently to other nobles. Other Lords were quick to take children as indentured servants. He did not take advantage of those who were at a lower station than him. His approach to debt, was to help people to overcome debt in a way that provided dignity to both the borrower and the lender. His people did not have to hide from their creditors, as he did not allow creditors to bully the villagers. Lord Logan provided a system that allowed people in debt to gradually work off the debt which was fair to both parties.

1. **How can you help people to face difficult challenges?**
2. **What steps can you take today to make positive changes in your life and the lives of others?**

6. Muquin

Even in suffering, be open to people, it will help you to go further.

Muquin's despair at the loss of her mate caused her to live in isolation. Her anger was so great that she burned the scent that would have allowed her to trace her stolen hatchling. Her rage did nothing to serve her. It was in her vulnerability that Nadine was able to recognise Muquin's need and connect with her plight. None of what Muquin did in isolation helped her to find her hatchling; it merely prolonged her suffering and caused others around her to suffer.

1. What areas of your life are you pushing others away in?

2. How can you be open to learning and growing with others?

7. Bishop Rawlin

Self-discipline can help you to keep true to your purpose.

At some point Bishop Rawlin lived his life according to a purpose. The Friar acknowledged this to the cook. However, it was the Bishop's indulgences that made him ill. These life choices lead to what we now know as diabetes. It sapped him of energy and his life's purpose. Ultimately King Radolf did not even have to have the Bishop assassinated, he simply fuelled the Bishops existing desires to cause his own death.

1. **What areas of your life do you lack self-discipline in?**
2. **What are you losing in life because of this?**
3. **What is one small daily action that you can take to improve your self-discipline?**

List of other characters that you can evaluate

- Beatrice
- Captain Julian
- Dorothea (Nadine's Mother)
- Elizabeth (The Medicine Woman)
- Father Stephen
- Friar Watt
- Galdolf (Prison Master)
- Judas (The Tax Collector)
- Maireid (Nadine's Older Sister)
- Megadeaus
- Nabal (The Dragon Thief)
- Nathan
- Nicolous (Nadine's Father)
- The Bandit King
- The Dragon Whisperer
- The Physician's Apprentice
- Yakhal

Questions to Ask

- What do I admire about this character?
- What do I dislike about this character?
- What can I learn from this character?
- What areas of my life can I apply this lesson to?

Author Lessons

For many years, I had a desire to create stories that would help people reconnect with the hero inside them. When South Africa first had load shedding, I would calm my daughter's fears by making up stories for her.

She encouraged me to write them into a book. Even my husband encouraged me to prepare short stories. But I let the fear of rejection stifle that desire. Although I have created countless stories for my children over the years, I did not take on this project until two things happened.

1. My friend Nathalie showed me how I had created a false fear in my mind. By presenting me with facts, she opened a path for me to get myself out of my way.

2. I read a section of Blair Singer's Book "Little Voice Mastery" [6], which Barry Mitchell from Uncovering Greatness introduced me to. In one section of the book, he said that within each of us we have a dream planted. One that does not go away.

3. In the book, he states that God (who or whatever you may call The Creator+) has a gift for the world. He gives this gift through people. When you deny that dream, you stop Him from reaching his children through you.

   Once I obeyed this calling, the number of people who appeared to walk alongside me was remarkable. My daughter Margaret has always encouraged me in this journey and remains the light that helps me to strive to be a better version of myself.

These two events also helped her to remember that you can follow your dreams.

Φ

Writing this book has opened my heart and my life to a group of extraordinary people.

It is my prayer that all those who read this series will find the courage to find their purpose and to act on it.

Φ

I would love for you to share your own personal learnings from the book.

You can contact me on kim@kimvermaak.com

For those who enjoy this book and want to find out more about the world of fantasy that I have created for you, the reader, you can subscribe to my mailing list and get your free download of the Dragon Whisperer's Field Guide.

You can subscribe on www.kimvermaak.com

[1] King, Martin L. "I Have a Dream." Speech presented at the March on Washington for Jobs and Freedom, Washington, D.C., August 1968.

[2] Samuel 1: 16- 2 Samuel 24: The Holy Bible, New International Version (Zondervan, Grand Rapids, Michigan, U.S.A, 2007)

[3] Judges 4 -5: The Holy Bible, New International Version

(Zondervan, Grand Rapids, Michigan, U.S.A, 2007)

[4] Joshua 2: 1- 23 6: 22 – 23: The Holy Bible, New International Version (Zondervan, Grand Rapids, Michigan, U.S.A, 2007)

[5] Matthew 1:5 The Holy Bible, New International Version (Zondervan, Grand Rapids, Michigan, U.S.A, 2007)

[6] Blair Singer, Little Voice Mastery: How to Win the War Between Your Ears in 30 Seconds or Less and Have an Extraordinary Life! (RDA Press, LLC, 2013)

EXTRACTS FROM BOOK 2

The Betrayal

"Do not call for the dragons. They cannot save her. We will send for you." the scroll read.

Gadrial slumped as he read it. He cloaked his mind. Tamyss his dragon, felt the break of the bond. "There is something wrong," he told Undor, his mate. "I cannot sense Gadrial."

"Perhaps there are some things, he does not want you to sense," she teased.

"No!" he shouted, as his tail swished in agitation.

Something about Tamyss worried Undor. They had their normal quarrels. But this outburst was uncharacteristic. There was an oppressiveness in the air.

The Concealment

"What would you have me do? Leave her to King Radolf? He murdered her parents. Allowing them to starve to death. Not a clean death, but a death of unspeakable cruelty..."

"Countless maidens suffered under his perverse and lustful appetites" he continued. "Lady Christine told me how she prayed for her rescue from the King. She all but gave up on hope. On the night he came for her, she felt as if God had completely abandoned her."

Uncovered

"Report" King Radolf instructed.

"One of our spies has infiltrated a network of opposition spies." said Lord Teebald

"From the Pope?" asked King Radolf.

"No. It is from a different source. One known as the The Trona," replied Lord Teebald.

"What do we know of this Trona?... Is that not where Lord Logan's lands are?" enquired King Radolf.

"It is indeed my Lord King," confirmed Lord Teebald.

The Confession

Father Stephen stared at the manuscript in his hands. His blood ran cold. It was blank.

How many times had the Friar concealed the true confession?

He thought by taking the manuscripts, he may keep the Friar safe. Now nothing could protect him. Such integrity under certain danger. It was admirable. Yet dangerous.

Why did he have to meddle?

The Burden

"There is something wrong," said Dorothea watching her husband...

"Nadine, the Dragon Whisperer arrived today!" said Nicolous watching her face.

She stared at him. "Why?"

"The dragon rescue was more than what it appeared. What you thought was a quest to rescue us, was just a piece of a greater plot," he said.

"I know of King Radolf's plan to use the Dragon to start another war," she said.

"But do you know that The Dragon Whisperer wishes to claim you now? …

The Bait

Sentimental women like Christine had a weakness. It was their compassion. Compassion prevented them from making logical choices. There were enough indentured slave children for him to choose from.

Just a few days ago, his guards had arrived with a scrap of a girl. He had seen her from his window. She was a pretty little thing perhaps just four or five years old. A snivelling little whelp of a girl. The girl had looked up at him as she arrived. Her eyes puffy and rimmed red. But greener than any he had ever seen. Eyes that could not easily be forgotten.

ACKNOWLEDGMENTS

To my precious parents Denzil and Belinda who were my first heroes.

You are in every page of my story.

My darling children Margaret, Nadine and Michael you were the very first hearts eager to hear my stories. You helped me to find my voice.

Mamma Margaret there is a reason the Lord granted you to me as my first born. I am a better person for having you in my life. Thank you for pushing me to write. You may never know the full reach of the influence of your love, but God does.

Nadine, special Adventure Princess you were my inspiration for this book. Own who you are for in you lies the seeds of greatness.

Michael, my special man child. What a wonderful surprise you are. Your love brings a special blend of joy, that I never thought was possible. Thank you for completing my heart.

To my other children Jonathan, Tarryn and Mathew thank you for sharing your father's love with me and for adding a new dimension to my life.

To my husband Colin, this book would not have been possible without your encouragement support and love. You are the glue that kept things together. You were prayed into my life for a reason. Those who will find joy in this book will do so because of your sacrifice.

Barry, thank you for being a reminder that purpose overrides all else and for giving me the courage to master my inner voice. Thank you for introducing me to that special blend of entrepreneurs who are the warriors of their families and communities. Each of you have touched my life in different ways. Sister Wendy and King Victor, you are a blessing. Thank you for keeping me accountable.

Nathalie, thank you for moving the boulder of fear from my path and for holding my hand through the first uncertain steps. Lisa and Karen, my beautiful friends who always love me as I am and for carving out time to chip away at my challenges. Judy (my editor), thank you for believing in me and helping my story to find wings. Judy (my friend) thank you for the generosity of your time and for being my first fan.

Ilze and Jayden, spiritual warriors and creative geniuses, thank you for your generosity.

Fairai, you make me smile every time you cast your vision over me. Thank you.

Rionette, you are the spiritual drink of water that arrives just when I need it.

Tumelo, you are the king of customer service and kindness.

Thank you for your insights.

Anni your gentle patience in digitising my hand drawn original illustrations made them come alive.

Mark and James, you don't know me, but you made me believe that I can do this.

There are various authors hacking away at their dreams who have found the time on Facebook to answer all my masses of questions. There are too many to thank, but I salute you.

Amelia and Martin. No words can ever thank you enough.

My Heavenly Father, the very first creator, thank you for the blessing of creativity.

ABOUT THE AUTHOR

Kim Vermaak always had a pen in her hand. Whether doodling, crafting poems or writing letters.

Born into an abusive family, Kim's first heroes were her adoptive parents. Through them, she learned the gift of new beginnings.

She also learned a love of reading and how she could be transported to a place where ordinary people could find the courage to rise above insurmountable odds. Through books, she found her courage.

But it was not until South Africa faced its first series of power cuts, she found her talent for storytelling. In the dark with a frightened daughter, she began to create heroes that could tap into their inner strength and win.

Through her love of reading, history and young people, Kim crafts stories that embrace the true purpose of storytelling. To impart wisdom. But in today's fast-paced society, we often reduce stories to entertainment value. This leaves little room for us to grow and forces us to relive the painful lessons of the past.

It is Kim's passion to see communities create a legacy that will empower future generations.

In her medieval fantasy series, "The Chronicles of Nadine" Kim weaves a landscape of characters all on the path their choices have carved. She welcomes readers who have learned lessons through these characters to share them with her and each other.

www.kimvermaak.com

www.ingramcontent.com/pod-product-compliance
Lightning Source LLC
Chambersburg PA
CBHW020517260626
47156CB00006B/2038